D1736417

Fred – I hope that you
enjoy this book. It was a great
pleasure for me to write it. Thank you
for your friendship these very many
years. God bless you.
Dale

Dale Hanson
3 John 1:2

# The Great Catch

## Alaskan Short Stories

DALE HANSON

*The Great Catch: Alaskan Short Stories* by Dale Hanson



Cover image artist Ernest Robertson

Cover and interior design by Jacqueline Cook

ISBN: 978-0-9981353-4-2 (Paperback)
ISBN: 978-0-9981353-5-9 (e-book)

10 9 8 7 6 5 4 3 2 1

BISAC Subject Headings:
FIC002000 FICTION / Action & Adventure
FIC029000 FICTION / Short Stories (single author)
FIC077000 FICTION / Nature & the Environment

Address all correspondence to:
Dale Hanson
P.O. Box 2870
Sitka, Alaska 99835

# Contents

# The Great Catch

## Alaskan Short Stories

DALE HANSON

*Artist Ernest Robertson*

# Up the Kuskokwim

It was his first trip up river since spring breakup and Miller Oktoyuk wanted to be the first to see what the churning ice and water revealed.

He woke early before anyone stirred in the settlement. The first fingers of dawn lifted the curtain of darkness just enough for him to dress in the room and make his way to the door without bumping anything. He gathered the things he had placed under the house the night before and walked briskly toward the riverbank, walking in the grass alongside the boardwalk so his progress would not be heard.

Near the edge of the village and close to the river a blond, long haired sled dog lifted his nose from under the shelter of his tail, saw that Miller was of no interest to him, then placed his tail over his pink nose again and went back to sleep.

Miller looked east, the direction he would be traveling, noting the speed of the water and that there was no debris floating in the current. A week before there were entire trees, root system and all, coming as a torrent. But today the great river seemed measured in its descent to

Kuskokwim Bay with the Bering Sea to the north and Bristol Bay to the south.

Miller was Eskimo. He was stocky with thick raven-black hair cut level with his brows. His very dark eyes and features were classic Eskimo but his skin was still pale with winter. He wore a dark blue parka with the hood down on his shoulder to better hear as he prepared to leave.

He retrieved the cans of gas he had hidden in the bushes near the boat and as quietly as possible he placed them on a tarp in the bottom of the Lund. He knew that any bump in the aluminum boat would sound across the village. The summer before he had painted the red and white Lund in a camouflage pattern and upgraded the motor. He untied the rope from the tree limb and slid the skiff into the water wincing when the sandy bottom grated against the metal.

He let the Lund drift downstream with the current away from the village and around the bend before he started the motor. He then motored to the far side of the bank and retraced his path up river, keeping to the outside bank, and passed the sleeping village on the other side. He saw that the red and yellow sunrise was reflected like fire in the glass windows as he passed.

Miller always explored up stream thinking that if the motor ever failed he could always drift back to the safety of his home. That and his new motor gave him a confidence he may not have otherwise had. He was pleased with the morning. With the twenty-five horse motor on the Lund, he made at least twenty miles before the sky lost it redness.

What he sought up river was dinosaur bones; in particular, mammoth bones. The prize would be a full tusk with its huge bow and graceful inward curve. Such a tusk could be more than ten feet long and weigh nearly two hundred pounds. A matched pair could be worth twenty thousand dollars.

An ivory carver from Sitka once told him that a movie producer contacted him looking for tusks to be used as banisters in the stairways between the decks of his yacht. The greatest find of all would be a full mammoth skeleton. That would be priceless to a collector. Every spring the breakup would erode and wear away the sides of the river bluffs and sometimes, just sometimes, such a treasure could be found. Miller would be the first of the season to explore the river. It would be HIS mammoth.

Rounding a bend in the river, several surprised mergansers rose from the water and flew before the boat, then veered to the side and landed in some reeds. A moose was feeding in the grass at the water's edge. It raised its head and watched the passing boat, water dripping from the grass in its mouth. As Miller continued up river its course began to enter the foothills and the riverbanks became steeper. In places the sides of the shore were cut vertically and were composed of grey clay. In other areas the bluffs were a red clay that the people called "ivasook." It is this clay the Eskimos use for the red dye of their masks. It was in these places that Miller Oktoyuk stopped and examined the riverbanks. A mammoth could be encased in the clay for centuries and preserved until the erosion of the seasons slowly revealed its presence.

At one place he was sure he could see bones protruding from the face of a bluff and he made for it. With enough speed to make it to the shore, he cut the engine and tilted the motor to save the prop, then leapt from the bow onto the gravel shore. Here and there black objects extended from the edge. They had the appearance of all the tusks that he had seen before. He retrieved his spade and shovel and worked around the protrusions being careful not to mar them. "Man!" he exclaimed in disappointment. He threw his tools into the boat and continued on. The pieces in the mud were merely driftwood that had been pickled black.

Some miles farther upstream, He found another place where a tributary river flowed into the Kuskokwim. There the waters churned grey and opaque and became a rapids at the juncture until they found a common course and settled on their journey to the ocean. Miller hesitated crossing the place. In places where the two courses met, the water seemed to violently stand upright and he considered going no farther — but the lure of a tusk bore him on.

It was at that exact place that the violence of the collision of the two waters also collided with his skiff. The vertical wave raised his bow skyward in a fury. He let go of the tiller of the motor and threw himself to the floor of the boat at the bow hoping to bring the bow down. Then the violence of the water tore his engine from the stern and it flew into the air still running. He had just enough time to dash back to the stern and jerk the running motor into the boat. Again he dashed to the bow to keep it down lest the boat sink in the fury. Then when it seemed hope was gone, the waters abated as the current took him from the anger of the water. His motor was still running with the prop slamming the aluminum bottom and dancing as though it were electrocuted. He dived back, found and hit the kill switch with his shaking fingers. For minutes he lay in the water on the bottom of the boat until he caught his breath.

Miller Oktoyuk took stock as the Lund drifted back down stream. He reattached the outboard and examined the prop. It was functional. None of his supplies were lost. He bailed the water from the Lund with a tin can and studied the crossing. "If I do not cross this now I will never dare try again," he thought. He would continue up the Kuskokwim he decided, but he would be more judicious as to the place and speed of the Lund.

He avoided the place where he nearly sank and drove slower, but kept on step to keep the bow down and quartered the waves. He refused to turn back in the turbulence and when he arrived at the far side he gasped for air. He did not know when he had breathed last and the air was clean and fresh and alive.

He was at the river junction at a precipice that he had seen before the crossing. Alders grew on either side of the bluff and there was a flat area before it with a gravel beach. Miller brought the boat to the beach and tied off. Carefully he examined the cliff sides for mammoth. He sat on a snag a distance from the cliff side and let the late morning sun leave its shadow across the surface, hoping any raised features of a buried mammoth would be seen in relief. In his mind he could see a full mammoth in the contours but he knew that it was only hope that he saw and he turned to leave.

Nearby he saw a raven. Its feathers were as black as Miller's hair and they were shiny, reflecting the sky. In the raven's beak was a large piece of meat and on the ground at its feet was another like it. The raven looked at Miller, then at the piece of meat on the ground, then back at

Miller. He thought he could read the raven's mind. The raven could fit only one piece in its beak at a time. If he flew off with the meat in its mouth Miller could get the one on the ground. But the raven wanted both. It dropped the one in its mouth and grabbed the other and the exchange occurred two or three times until the Eskimo laughed out loud.

"I think I will solve your problem," he said, and he slid his skiff into the water and continued up stream.

• • •

It was nearly noon when he found the tusk for which he longed. He had just rounded a bend and nearly dismissed the little cliff in the inside of the bend. He thought that greater turbulence would be on the outside edge of a bend of the river, and there would be greater erosion and a better chance of discovery.

He cut the engine and wondered, "Is it really worth stopping?" There had been so many stops before this one. The Lund began to drift backward when he saw an anomaly in the clay and decided to investigate.

He landed on a sandy, narrow sandbar, pulled the skiff out of the current and tied the line to a red willow branch. Slowly, he walked to the edge of the vertical bank. There were several places where he could see black protrusions from the soil. He tried to swallow his hopes.

He had seen so many things this morning that he was sure would be tusks that turned out to just be snags. He took his pickaxe from the boat and walked to the face. To his left, a black, slightly pointed object protruded about a foot from the soil. It seemed to be smooth with a purple sheen on the surface. It was very hard and dense. He picked at it with his fingernail. "It has to be," he thought with excitement mounting. "It can't be pickled wood." His hands shook as he held the head of the pickaxe with both hands at the metal end. He scraped dense soil from around the object. The end of the object was rounded and did not have lines running lengthwise. He ran to the skiff, filled his bailing can with water, ran back to the dirt and began to wash the object. It was smooth and took on a shine. "It's a tusk, I know it is!"

He tapped it with his knuckles. He wrapped his fingers around the object. The object seemed to say to Miller, "I am precious."

Whenever Miller found ancient wood snags they always spoke "wood" to him. This was altogether different. He stroked his fingers across it like Mozart would have lovingly passed his fingers over his ivory piano keys.

He continued to dig around the point exposing more and more of it. Clearly, he thought, this is ivory. It is round. It is dense. It feels like ivory.

He sat down on the gravel and looked up at his work. Then he began to smile broadly. "Yes!" he shouted. He let out a loud whoop, surprising himself and causing an unseen animal in the thicket to crash through the brush in flight. "Yes!" he shouted again.

"Hooo, hooo," he shouted! He danced. For the first time in his life he danced for joy. It was not like when the old men beat the skin drums and the ladies sang and he and the young girls of the village danced the stories with fans in their hands. This was not choreographed. This was spontaneous dancing. He shouted and hunched his shoulders, raised his eyes skyward, twitched his arms like oogarook the seal, and he tripped and fell. He fell with his feet caught in twigs and clay, and he lay on the ground and laughed and laughed.

And when the joy had subsided and "what to do" prevailed he sat on the bow of the skiff and stared at his find. And the more that he looked, the more that he saw.

That he saw the end of a mammoth tusk was certain. Then off to the right about six feet distant was a stubby end, rough and rounded, about seven inches in diameter. Was this a second tusk, the mate to the exposed one, or was it the end of the same piece? In his mind he tried to match the contours of the curved mammoth tusks he had seen before in his life with what might be in the earth before him. How deep must he go to unearth it and bring it home?

Miller began to take in the whole face of the bluff. Above and to the right of the tusk was a large rock. Behind that and above it were several curved objects protruding the surface. They were curved, black, and set in a row like limbs of a tree. But no trees grew to this size on the Kuskokwim.

He sat on the bow of his skiff and took smoked salmon and fry bread from his sack and ate as he looked. He tried to piece the picture together in his mind. He spit some fish bones from his mouth and when he did so he knew what it was that was before him. The projections that were in a row above the tusk were ribs. Of that now he was certain. Could it be a full mammoth that was before him?

Then, as he sat by the shore of the Kuskokwim whose current carried the soil from hundreds of miles away and clouded the water, he could see the whole picture. It was as if he could see through the clay. He wondered if the red-black hair would still be on the body. Would there be flesh? Would he find the points of a spear and arrows in the skeleton?

Then with a confidence he had never had before in his life he stood at the face holding his pick by the metal end and pointed at item by item as he named them to an unseen audience. "Tusk tip, butt of the tusk." He stepped to the right, "This bump in the earth is where the bones of its hip are." Above that he announced, "The ribs of course." Then as if it were the key point of his lecture he walked to the "rock."

"And this," he said tapping it with the handle, and with the sound of triumph in his voice, "is the skull of my mammoth."

He sat once again and looked at his valuable find. "What to do first," he wondered. He remembered the Yup'ik people on the coast always say when they get a whale, "Now what?"

"I must get the tusk first of all — before anyone else finds it. I will take it home and hide it and come back for the other and then I will decide what to do with the rest."

For the next hour he worked vigorously at the tusk, running the pickaxe back and forth along the sides of the tusk. He began to use the pick end like an axe to loosen and remove the hard clay but after an hour of that, only another foot of the tusk was exposed.

He sat again on the bow. He was exhausted and disappointed at how little he had gotten done. Only two feet of tusk were exposed. It was black, smooth, and shiny as if the mammoth on the other side were piercing the earth and trying to get out.

It became clear as he sat there, that he would not get the tusk in a day. Before him was his treasure and he did not want to leave it exposed as it was. He breathed deeply. He was exhausted.

Then Miller Oktoyuk saw something he did not want to see. All of his attention to this point had been fixed entirely on the bluff. For the first time he noticed something at the water line caught in the willow shrubs. That object was a blue coat just like Miller's. It was muddy and partly covered in beach sand. Most of the color was faded away and one sleeve was tangled in knots in the willow roots. In the sleeve was a hand.

Miller stared unmoving. The day had taken his strength. Dusk would soon come to his cove with its basket and take all the colors of the day. It was too much. He wanted to weep.

Slowly, finally, he stood and shuffled to the place.

The rest of the body was there too. Sand had covered most of the torso and anchored it in place from the current. A winter boot was on one foot but the other leg was tucked under the body. Whoever the person was, he had been dressed for winter.

Miller could write the chronology of events as clearly as if he had been there. The river ice was the highway of this part of Alaska in winter. All winter, the current under the ice wears away the ice underneath but it does not show on top. The person must have chanced it on his sled in late spring when the ice was thin and soft and gone through. He would have gone through somewhere upstream then he would have been carried in the current under the ice to this point.

He did not want to look inside the parka but he could see hair poking through the hood of the parka. The hair was red, mammoth red, and Miller considered the person's black hair had reddened in the sun and elements. He would not look at the face. Miller knew that it was not empty clothing at which he was looking. Someone from a village up river never made it home, but perished along the way.

He found a sturdy stick and maneuvered the body to expose the pockets and using only his fingernails pulled a wallet from a pocket. He opened it. Nothing but a name.

Miller went to his boat and sat in the stern resting with his back against the motor. Moving this body was out of the question. Only the clothing contained the body. Further, elsewhere the current would reclaim the dead man and carry him to the sea and the family would never know.

But to tell anyone would bring people, lots of people to the cove — and to his mammoth. "This is MY mammoth. I found it." Anguish and frustration filled him.

Raised a Christian, Miller did not curse. But he wanted to.

"Man!" he shouted instead. He threw his shovel at the cliff. He sat on the edge of his boat, this time with his elbows on his knees and his head on his hands. He wept in frustration.

The sun dipped behind the foothills and colors began to fade. The Eskimo had before him a mammoth and a man.

With urgency, Miller began to fill his bailing bucket with water and gathered clay from the base of the bluff and began to quickly replace what he had removed. He did his best to place moss and leaves where the tusk and ribs could be seen. His work would not survive scrutiny.

He stepped back and examined the face of earth. He put the wallet with the name into his pocket, slid his boat into the current, and departed downstream to his village.

# Bita and the Wolves

Axel Brown lived alone with his dog in a trapper cabin tucked in a stand of birch and poplar trees on the Alaska Peninsula. Had you asked, "How far is it to your closest neighbor?" he would gaze in that direction, stroke his grey beard, and then point across his lake with the handle end of whatever tool he held in his hand.

"Lars lives across this lake and those foothills yonder and beyond the next two lakes. There is a good trail to his place. He came to visit me last fall and we played cards before he left to go back. We traded books too. Come to think about it, I owe him a visit."

Axel built his cabin of peeled and seasoned cedar logs that he and his dog dragged one at a time to the site. Both dog and man wore harnesses around their chests and strained and pulled and at the end of each exhausting day collapsed and slept like the dead in a canvas tent. When the last line of tundra moss was chinked between the logs, Axel stood a distance back with his tools in his hands and appraised his work and was satisfied. The logs were well fitted and airtight, and he considered, should last the rest of his life.

His had faced his porch toward the shores of the large lake before him so he could watch the passing of migrating caribou on the edges, and Dall sheep and patrolling brown bears in the hills beyond. A short, graveled path led to the edge of the lake and the large stream that fed it. Tethered to the shore was his rowing skiff, which he believed was more stable than a canoe and could carry more.

Only yesterday it seemed as he gazed upward that the leaves above were yellow, bright orange or crimson as the sun shone through their thinness. Then, one day, they cascaded down from their branches and an Indian summer wind chased them on the ground. The leaves were brown then, and wrinkled and weightless and they moved like uncertain mice. For a few days his dog was a puppy again as she chased them and fixed them with her paws.

Thin lines of Geese flew overhead in their flocks, followed days later by the swans that had grouped after leaving the potholes of the tundra. Caribou appeared in their numbers along the shore and a dusting of snow marked the tops of the hills.

Axel got his dog from a breeder of sled dogs; she was the smallest of the litter. He was dubious and asked, "Are you sure there is sled dog in her?"

The breeder was anxious to make a sale and he replied quietly, "There's a bita' sled dog in her."

Axel wanted a companion more anything else, so he bought her for a hindquarter of moose and he named her "Bita."

It seemed the final day of fall was realized when Axel and Bita were walking along the shore near the stream. A muskrat swam in their direction. At first it was just something round moving in the water but as it neared, they could make out its round black eyes and rounded ears above the surface. The muskrat carried the grey sky in the wetness of its fur and a large clump of yellow grass in its mouth. It maneuvered into the shoreline and disappeared into the weeds of the bank where it had secreted its den. The "V" of its gentle wake seemed not to spread and disappear. Instead, Axel saw lines shoot across the surface of the lake, like cracks on a mirror. As it happened, he and his dog had arrived the very instant ice formed on the surface of the water.

Axel noticed that the tiny ripple of the muskrat's passage was frozen on the skin of ice. He turned to his dog and said, "Do you know, Bita, the wake of that muskrat will be frozen in the ice until spring. All winter long the memory that it swam by this night will be there."

Bita looked up at her master and thumped her tail on the freezing ground.

He looked down at her. "I know you don't know what I am saying but I am glad you are here to hear me just the same."

The ice remained the next day and the next and the sun barely cleared the mountains and when it did, it was obscured by thick clouds. The ice on the lake became thicker and the stream trickled into it under the surface. Then the snow fell on the lake and wind moaned in the empty branches. In the cold, puffs of steamy breath left the nostrils of the caribou as they stopped in front of his cabin and pawed the ground for food.

Deep winter claimed the valley for itself and its clutches held everything in its fist. Axel looked forward to this winter. He had many cords of wood drawn up to the cabin, and meat was smoked and stored in the cache. This year he bought a pressure cooker and canned the fruit of his garden, and he made sauce and jam with the berries he picked on the hillside. He even had a library where he could read in his slippers when the cold was severe.

The cabin smelled of cedar logs burning in the fire and bread just out of his folding oven. It was early evening. He had made French bread because it did not require milk to make and he liked the hard crusts. He made the loaves meal-size to go with his soup. He took a loaf and coffee and went to his chair by the window to begin a new book. He lit two lanterns to read by, and they cast their yellow light on his face and on the book, and the pages looked precious like ancient parchment.

Bita whined to go out and he went with her to the porch in his slippers. The air was needle cold. It pinched his nose and made his eyes water. He looked across the lake in the near darkness and a trillion stars shown like the eyes of a vast audience in a darkened auditorium waiting for the performance on the white stage of the lake.

"Amazing," he said aloud, and he recalled a Scripture that he read that day that God had a name for every one of them.

"Bita, look at that."

He listened for a moment and there was no sound anywhere. It was as if sound itself was frozen on the lake. He turned to go inside and heard a crunch of his slipper in the hoar frost on the deck and that was all.

"Bita, do your business," he said. "And come back."

He sat and lifted his book and opened it to the beginning. He read, "This is the story of Danny and of Danny's friends, and of Danny's house."

Axel stopped reading. He looked up from the yellowed book and saw himself reflected in the window, bushy grey beard and all, with thin round spectacles on his nose. He nearly said out loud, "This is Steinbeck, one of the great authors, and he begins a book this way. Not one spectacular word in it. Every word is commonplace. Wasn't he afraid a reader would be bored right off and not go on?"

"But this was John Steinbeck," he thought. "What confidence he must have had to start in such a common way.".

He picked it up and read again, "This is a story about Danny, and Danny's friends, and the house that Danny had."

"I wonder," he thought, "how many adventures begin this way?"

He set the open book down on its pages. Axel heard something. He listened. There was the soft, ever so soft, breathing of the smoke in the chimney. There was a settle of ashes between the logs in the wood stove. That was not what he heard.

He listened.

A bark, a snarl, and a yelp. But it was not from his doorway, but far out on the ice of the lake.

"Bita!"

He ran to the door and on to the deck. From far out on the lake he heard the struggle of life and death. Loud snarling and a yelp of great pain. He could hear a growl that could only come from a mouth full of blood.

"Wolves!"

"Bita!"

He dashed back inside, tossed on his wool coat, and grabbed his double barrel at the door and two shells then stumbled out the door leaving it open behind. Axel jumped off the porch and ran toward the struggle as he broke the action and tossed in two buckshot. The dim lantern light of the open door cast a faint beam across the lake.

He ran and stumbled in the deep snow. At the edge of the lake he tripped and fell face first into a drift. Snow filled one of his sleeves. His face and hair were matted in crusts of snow. He held his arm with the shotgun high above his head to keep it out of the drifts. He crawled to his feet and ran again lifting his feet high to clear the snow with each step.

He knew that he would not make it in time to save Bita the rate he was going. He began to shout. Perhaps the wolves would be afraid of a human and take flight.

"Bita! Bita!" he shouted. "Wolf, go away, go."

The struggle was at least a couple of hundred yards further out on the ice. He was out of breath.

He gasped the words, "Bita, I'm coming."

He lost the slipper of his right foot in the crusts of snow and ran barefoot.

"Bita!"

He could make out the shapes of the wolves in the snow and he could see a prostrate form in a depression that could only be his dog. The wolves separated into individual shadows and Axel aimed and fired into the mass of one and it dropped in a clump. One wolf still hung on to Bita with his teeth and Axel hit it with the butt of his weapon. There were a half dozen more wolves and they began to run and Axel fired again into the mass. He heard a yelp as he shot and there was snarling and fighting in the shadows beyond his vision.

Somewhere he had lost his other slipper and he was barefoot. His feet ached.

"Bita," he called as he fell down beside the dog. Axel was out of breath. He could not feel his feet. Bita was gasping for breath and blood streamed from her neck and body.

Axel dropped his shotgun and held his dog in his arms.

"I'll get you home girl."

With Bita in his arms he began to trudge through the snow. All strength seemed to have left his body. It took all of his strength to lift his legs out of the drifts. He stumbled and fell, landing on top of her wounded form. His arms felt limp like rubber and his legs cold hardly clear the depth of the snow.

"Here, Bita." Axel removed his coat and lay her on it. He grabbed the sleeves of the coat and dragged it over the snow.

It was more than twenty below zero and Axel could no longer feel his feet or hands. His body shivered. His jaws chattered together.

He gasped aloud with each trudging step, "Auugh, auugh, auugh."

The lantern light of the cabin seemed far away. Would he make it to the doorstep only to die there with his Bita? Axel felt himself passing out. The cabin became blurry in his sight.

His eyes no longer seemed to focus and his knees struck something solid — the edge of his porch. The dimness of the lantern light made it look farther than it was. Axel lifted his dog over the edge and stumbled into the room. He dropped to his knees and gently lowered Bita to her bed near the stove. The cabin was as cold as the winter outside and he rushed to the door and slammed it shut. He dropped to his knees again next to her.

Bita's eyes were open but fixed on nothing. She was panting.

Axel was horrified at the wounds. Her throat was ripped open and he thought her airway was torn. He heard a wheezing sound as she gasped for air. A gaping wound exposed her stomach and there were long tears on her thighs. He tried to move the matted hair and blood and discovered that he could not move his fingers.

He stood unsteadily on feet what were white and waxy.

"I can't do anything if I can't feel my fingers."

He opened the door of his stove, pulled the ashes forward and threw in another round of wood. He blew on the ashes to bring it to flame and shut the door. He rubbed his frozen feet and it brought sharp pain. He put wool socks on his feet and blew on his fingers as he held them near the flame.

"I'm coming, Bita."

His feet did not bend and he walked on his heels toward the cabinet and his aid kit. "If I am to do anything I had better do it while she is in shock and will not feel what I am doing as much."

He placed his sharpest knife in the flames to sterilize the blade. He had plenty of iodine and would use it generously.

"The worst first," he said to himself as he placed all of his lanterns near his work.

Axel cut away dead flesh first of all. "That will just rot inside when I sew her up."

Bita whimpered and Axel spoke to her soothingly. "I know it hurts, baby."

He used a suture needle but had only ordinary thread. "I hope that doesn't fester inside."

The airway was first and only took a few ties but he was unsure of folding back the mass of flesh and hide and sewing it together. "If you will just live until we can get help," he thought. "If I can get her to a vet he can undo my mistakes."

The stomach might be the worst part. There was bile and he was not sure he would get it all. He closed where the wolves had torn her intestines. He sutured the tear in the purple and placed it into the stomach cavity with plenty of iodine then finished the gap with thread.

He started on her thigh and she whimpered and kicked her leg out in pain.

"I know. I know. I'm almost finished."

• • •

He tied off the last stitch and leaned back on his heels. "I hope I did everything right, Bita." His back ached and he shivered. The fire had died down. He did not realize that he had been at his task so long. He rose to put more wood in the stove and felt the soreness in his feet. The white waxy appearance had disappeared but his feet were red and swollen. Blood had collected where the hoar frost had sliced them.

Bita no longer panted and her breathing was more restful. She seemed thirsty and Axel squeezed water from a rag into her mouth. He petted her face and said, over and over, “Hang in there. Stay alive, Bita.”

He gently placed his jacket over her form so she would smell his nearness and he stroked her head. He pulled a blanket from his bed and a pillow and lay beside her on the floor until morning.

Twice in the night he heard her whimper and he stroked her head and soothed her with his voice. Once she tried to rise but fell back on her bed. Axel thought it a good sign.

Toward morning he awoke to the soreness of his hips on the hard floor and he got up and banked the stove. He sat in a chair beside the bed where Bita lay. He thought of the day ahead and what to do. He read only a few lines of the book before he fell into a deep sleep, “This is the story of…”

• • •

Daylight peered in through the window and frost had collected in the lower corners. The light that entered was cloaked in grey with no brightness or color or hope. Axel’s thumb was still closed in his book when he awoke and his glasses had fallen from his face and rested in the blanket on his lap.

He glanced at his companion in her bed. Her breathing, shown in the rise and fall of her sides, was regular and deep and the man was pleased.

Her nose was warm and dry and her eyes opened at his touch. Her tail thumped weakly on the floor.

He squeezed water into her mouth and he placed more in a shallow dish near her head but she did not eat the food offered her.

Axel Brown stretched himself and stoked the wood stove and started the pot for coffee. There was a large crate of eggs left when the bush plane landed days before and he soft boiled several thinking Bita might eat one of them. When all was ready he bowed his head and thanked God for his provision. He had eggs with French bread, coffee, and fried potatoes, and he watched his dog thoughtfully as he ate.

“Bita, I need to get you out of here and to a vet.”

• • •

It seemed that an unwritten rule of the interior was to be aware of and respond to the welfare of each other. When bush planes traversed the land they were aware of those who lived in cabins in the wilderness. They would often just stop by for coffee and to chat. Sometimes they would drop off a newspaper or mail or an order from the trading post.

Most people like Axel had a system of telling the pilots they needed help. Most often they placed a flag out where it could be seen — like the red flag on a rural mailbox that said, "I have mail to pick up."

This morning Axel made it his first business to place out a flag where it would be seen from the air: on the ice in front of his cabin. In the past he used a white pillowcase or bed sheet but the area now was white with ice and snow. He needed something else. He dug around. He found a pair of red long johns and took a pair of slim poles and a ball of twine with him.

"Bita, you stay here and don't try to follow," he said. For he knew that she would use the last of her life to go in his steps.

With wool pants and coat and snowshoes and all that he would need in his backpack, he trudged out on the ice. He followed his route of the night before and stopped and reached into each print to find his slippers. Not far beyond the edge he retrieved the first one and he slapped the snow from it and put it in his pack.

At a distance he thrust the first pole into the snow and tamped the snow around the base with his feet. He tied his long johns to the pole by the sleeves and the underwear hung limply down, clearly too small to be seen from an airplane. He tamped down the second pole and tied the two feet of the long johns to it and it hung in the air like a red pendant.

The second slipper was found in a footprint only yards away and he paired it in the pack. His breath condensed on his beard and the ruff of his jacket and hat as he continued on to where Bita was attacked.

In the snow, another hundred yards farther out on the lake he found the place. The area was splattered with blood where she spun and her bleeding splotched the white snow. There was a wallow where she had lain as the wolves tore at her body. Tufts of hair were matted in the well.

He felt in the snow nearby and retrieved the shotgun he had left to drag his Bita.

A few dozen feet away in its own depression lay a very large black wolf. The blast of the shotgun killed it instantly and it collapsed without struggle or running. Its yellow eyes were fixed and its pink tongue hung from its mouth. It weighed about one hundred fifty pounds and Axel tied a heavy cord to its leg to drag it to the cabin.

About fifty yards farther out was a dark shape in the snow and he went to it. A second wolf lay in this depression but it had been torn into pieces and partly eaten. Axel's second shot had wounded this one and the snow told how it ran after the buckshot drew blood and splattered the snow. The others then turned on their own and killed this weakened one of the pack.

The man dragged the wolf across the frozen lake. It had frozen in the night with its legs outstretched and he dragged it on its back with the four legs thrust into the air. From time to time he stopped to catch his breath, for he was no longer a young man, and he watched the steam of his breath ascend into the air.

At the cache he hoisted the timber wolf high into the air beyond the reach of fangs and covered it with a cloth tarp.

At the porch he looked back and saw the red flag on the ice. They had only to wait for a passing airplane to notice and land and Bita would have the help that she needed.

When he entered the cabin, he went to his dog and petted her face and she seemed to wince and thrust her legs behind her like in a run.

"Fool!" he said to himself. "You have the smell of wolf on your hands."

He went to where the creek still flowed into the frozen lake and thoroughly washed, and washed and washed the memory of wolf from himself.

• • •

The air was fragrant from the thick soup he made with potatoes and lentils he had from his garden. The first of the soup he gave to his dog like a broth. He blew on the spoon the cool it and she swallowed a few spoonsful but had no appetite and the man was worried.

The man ate his soup and French bread at the table and he read the Scripture as he did so and watched his dog.

He had been reading for some time and was comfortable in his slippers and his chair. He heard his dog sigh as if for the first time she was in normal sleep. A couple of times the wood in his glass-fronted wood stove spat and sputtered from moisture in a round of wood. He heard the passage of the smoke in the chimney and he wondered why it was that he cared so much about the derelicts in Steinbeck's book.

Then from somewhere on the lake, perhaps by the half-eaten wolf, he heard a wolf howl. It was answered by another elsewhere on the lake. There was another much closer to his cabin.

Bita whined in her sleep and she tried to get up from her bed.

"It's okay, girl. You're with me. You are safe now."

But she whimpered again and her eyes were wide open, remembering the time when she was being eaten alive.

"I'm here girl."

The howling continued nearer the cabin.

Bita stiffened in her bed. Axel sat beside her and stroked her head and her back where there were no wounds.

Axel himself could not mistake it. He could hear the footsteps of wolves as they patrolled around his house. He caught himself barely breathing so he could better hear their passage.

Moments later he heard a loud sniffing on his deck at the bottom of his door. A wolf was at his doorway. He had never encountered such boldness in a wild animal.

In his slippers he padded to the door where his twelve gauge was. I one swift action he broke the action, inserted two rounds, and thrust open the door. The doorway was empty but he had heard the scramble of the wolf's escape and the scrape of its toenails in the wood before it left into the darkness. He shut the door.

"I will have to get them, Bita. They have no fear of man anymore."

• • •

By morning light, he could see that Bita wanted to move about. She would thrust her body forward to rise but she was too weak to push with her legs. And, Axel was sure, she could not appraise the full condition of her injuries. He would have preferred her to stand if only to be better able to drink water and swallow food.

"Bita, try this," and he offered her food, finely chopped with gravy to better swallow. But she did not eat.

"What do wounded dogs need. What will they eat?"

He considered what he had on hand. "I could make a fish chowder. I could make it mild for her."

"I would need to catch a couple of fish in the big stream. That should not be too hard to do. First I had better see about those wolves."

Dressed completely in wool, he went outside and walked the perimeter around his cabin. At least two wolves had circled his cabin in the night. They had spent considerable time under the cache where the dead wolf hung. A faint breeze coming off the lake lifted the hair of the dead wolf like a fur buyer testing a pelt.

"I have never seen such boldness in wolves. I will use that."

Axel hummed as he worked. He wanted his dog to know that the movement she was hearing was from him and not her attackers. He rubbed his hands in cedar boughs to remove his human smell and set two number four traps under and near the hanging wolf. He set three snares. One near his deck in the tracks of the wolves last night and two on the path they used to near his cabin. He placed limbs and twigs to steer them into his snares and traps. He looked back on his work. He was satisfied with his sets but concerned that he could not remove all of his human scent. But then those wolves seemed to be fearless and human scent had not deterred them so far.

He walked out on the lake. "What chance would there be a plane might come by? All of the hunting seasons are past. This trapper's cabin is not situated on any of the normal routes." He was not encouraged. He looked at the foothills and saw that the tops were hidden under clouds. A pilot would have to have a reason to fly through them.

He would catch a fish. The big stream was close enough that he could hear any plane coming.

At the cabin he strapped the double barrel over his shoulder. It would work well if he encountered a wolf in the thick brush. He took his fly rod and walked the trail to the stream, walking with the rod tip behind him so it would not break in the branches.

The stream was free of ice and fast moving, about forty feet across. He worked the line — ten, two, ten, two and dropped the fly into a deep pool on the far side. There was a flash of silver in the water but the trout did not strike. Three casts later his rod tip bent and he held it up and let the fish play out and tire. The trout jumped into the air to free the hook but Axel kept just enough tension to fix the hook. He worked the fish to his side of the bank, took in the slack line and lifted the trout out of the stream by its lower jaw.

Axel worked his way up stream and caught a second twelve-inch cutthroat and placed it into his creel.

There was an overhanging bank on his side of the stream where a large tree and root system cast its shadow. Axel pulled out a pile of line at his feet and began to "barrel roll cast" to the pool under the large branches. There was a large splash as another cutthroat took the fly and swam up stream away from the fisherman. He let the drag tire the fish and took care that it did not dash his way and create a slack that would let the fish escape.

There were three in the creel and Axel made his way back along the trail. There was plenty to make a chowder or fish soup — anything to get Bita to eat.

As he rounded the last bend in the trail and the edges of the frozen lake came into view, a distinct howl sounded from the west end of the lake just inside the line of leafless red willows. It was too distant for a shot even with a rifle, let alone the shotgun he carried today. It was answered by two other wolves beyond the cabin.

He spat in the snow, his spittle making a round hole in the drift like a bullet hole.

At the porch he kicked the snow off his boots and shouted, "Bita, I'm home."

He pulled off his boots and leaned over the form. He caressed her head and placed the back of his hand on her nose to feel for fever. He stroked her back and felt for warmth.

"I'm making some chowder for us girl. Mild for you and regular for me."

He squeezed water into her mouth with the rag and slid the dish closer to her to see if she would raise her head and drink.

His he made with potatoes and onion from the sack, and a few chunks of bacon. He used condensed milk and seasoned the chowder with bay leaf, thyme, salt and pepper. Later he added chunks of trout and a can of corn. Coffee perked on the stove and his French bread warmed next to the chimney.

To his great joy, his dog lapped a few bites from a shallow dish.

• • •

The man slept soundly through the night in his own bed and his hips did not ache when he awoke. Before he pulled the blankets and patchwork quilt up to his chin, he moved Bita in her bed beside his so she could sense his nearness and he could listen to her soft breathing.

No tread of paws sifted through the loose snow in the darkness of his exhausted sleep. No yellow eyes peered through the openings in the frost covered windows and looked into his own. There was no crunch of heavy wolf feet in the hoarfrost of his porch and no sniffing under the door for the wounded dog or the sepsis that marked her condition. He slept soundly and unmoving — as unmoving as his dog — until the winter dawn awoke him.

Only a few embers remained in the woodstove and he raked them forward and placed kindling over them and two birch logs on the whole and blew it into new life. Smoke breathed lustily up the chimney. When he examined his little sled dog she was listless and her sides were warm. Her pink nose was dry and her tail did not move when he spoke softly to her.

"Oh, Bita, I am so worried for you, my little dog. I do not think that you are doing well."

He looked at her again. She should have looked at him, licked his hand, flapped her tail, run to him, gone to the door. There were none of these things.

"I so need to get you to help little dog."

When he brought her food, she would not eat. He squeezed water into her mouth.

Axel dressed and walked onto the ice-covered lake. This was the only hope for his dog. The grey-haired man in the bushy beard walked on the place where he hoped the ski plane would land. To walk on the ground lent reality to what was just a concept. He walked back and forth on the place. He trudged through the snow and touched the red banner that said, "Please stop, we need help."

He trudged back toward the cabin through the edge of the birch trees and the location of his cache. He stopped mid step. He had not thought of it today. He had not even brought a weapon. A large grey bulk was hunched in the path.

Electricity shot through his body. What weapon did he have on him? As he thought he stared at the form.

The shape did not move. It was clearly a wolf hunched in the shrubs and low brush.

Axel walked toward the wolf with bold steps. Still it did not move and only then did Axel see that it was dead. Its tongue hung out its left side. Its yellow eyes with the tiny black pupils were open and facing him with lethality, even in death.

He took three steps closer and saw the snare tight around its neck. The site was not torn up like a trap-caught animal. When a wolf sensed the tightening around its neck its instinct is to charge. The snare tightens to the limit and the animal quickly dies.

He felt the dead wolf. It was nearly completely frozen but the armpits were still warm. It was nearly all grey with a few white markings.

He removed the animal from the snare and hoisted it high under the cache with the other black one and decided to check the traps nearby.

The Victor trap under the cache ladder was not sprung and he gave it a wide birth to leave no human scent. But when he trudged to the place of the second trap it was a different matter — the area was a place of chaos. The underbrush was a mass of broken brush and thick branches. Both trap and wolf were gone.

He examined the place more carefully. The frozen earth was torn and the moss and grass torn away with claw marks scored into the hard earth. Tree bark was torn from the trunks by angry teeth. The thick willow to which he had anchored the trap was chewed and broken at the base. A swath of tornado-like underbrush portrayed the route of the wolf.

Axel imagined the wolf dragging the trap and the drag through the underbrush. The wood crosspiece would catch and tangle in the brush or hang up between two trees. There the timber wolf would fight the shrubs and chew the bark from them until the wood drag would free itself and it would continue on.

The man knew the wolf would weaken each time it tangled and eventually would get to the place it could not extricate itself and there die.

"I need a weapon for this."

He chose again his double barrel but this time also took his pistol. If he found it alive he would administer the coup de grace with the latter.

• • •

He moved slowly through the swath of the wolf. He chose places where the snow would smother the progress of his feet, stopping frequently to listen for any sounds of breaking limbs, snarls or the angry growling of the canine. Should the animal hear the man in his path it would redouble its efforts to escape or worse, it would lie in wait.

A chickadee moved above; its movements sending frozen grains of old snow on his head and into his collar.

As he stood silently for a time and scanned the brush before him he could hear movement nearby. It sounded distant at first, perhaps the movement of the wolf, but then located the sound near him, a mouse moving under the crust of snow hidden from above. He also heard a soft breeze coming off the lake — the first he noticed. The breeze carried sifting snow over the crust of snow. It smelled of new snow and signaled a change in the weather.

The passage of the wolf was easy to follow apart from its footprints on the ground. From place to place it was a landscape of tornado where the drag would catch and the bark of nearby willow and poplar trees were shredded by angry teeth and claw marks dug deeply into the hard ground.

Then, the search came to an end.

The drag had finally caught inexorably between two birch trees. The paper-like skin of the trees appeared like a shredded book. From that place the chain of the black double spring trap was stretched into a straight line. It was empty of wolf save for tufts of grey hair firmly left in the jaws of the trap. The wolf had pulled free and left no trace thereafter.

Axel walked to the stream and washed thoroughly before returning to his Bita.

• • •

There was something about the breeze on his face that disturbed the old man. The grains of loose snow that blew across came across like fingers feeling its way toward his home. He could hear the grains move like crystal. A newcomer to those parts would say, "A breeze is a breeze." But Axel's mind, tutored by long experience by the lake, considered that the breeze was more a messenger.

He scanned the horizon, in particular the far side of the lake and the foothills beyond it. It was a dark grey with a redness to it. The smell was not that of bitter cold but had a moisture in it that could only mean snow — lots of it.

For Bita's sake, he hoped it would be of short duration and not like others he had experienced. One blizzard had buried his cabin to the rooftop and the chimney. Drifts banked against his cabin door and windows and could not be opened and his comfortable hut became a possible tomb. When the firewood gave out he burned first the table, then the chairs, and finally the bedframe. Floorboards would have been next but the storm left suddenly and without announcement.

He went inside and tried to get his dog to eat. She was warm, too warm, and she did not respond to his presence. He squeezed her some water and she took it.

"Bita, I am so worried for you. I hope the storm will be a short one. I must get you help." He looked at her and petted her again. "I must get us ready for this one." He brought more provisions in from the cache and he stacked one whole side of the room with birch and cedar firewood as it burned slower than poplar. He leaned the snow shovel at the door. This storm would not entomb them.

When the first hard gusts hit he was cutting more lengths of firewood with the bow saw. Each passing of the blade sounded like rapid breaths and he thought of his dog and her breathing in her bed when he left her an hour before.

• • •

The first gusts shook the cabin. None had ever caused the log walls to shiver before. The temperature dropped a few degrees but the fury of the storm manifested itself in the vast amounts of snow and the powerful wind. Snow slid under the door and he blocked it with a fur rug. Gusts howled when it passed the eaves and Bita stirred in her sleep. The chimney shuddered once and he was afraid it would collapse and there would be no draught for the stove.

Several times he shoveled the deck before the door. Twice he trudged outside in a circuit around his cabin to inspect it. In the gusts and the darkness he could not see far so he held a long stick in one hand and slid it along the wall to keep in contact with the cabin lest he wander off into the darkness. There was nothing that he could do but wait out the storm. Inside they were warm and comfortable.

He put on a stew with moose for meat and made biscuits and gave Bita the last of the trout.

Lest he sleep too long, he sat in his chair with a heavy quilt over his lap and he read. He was ending the Old Testament in his daily reading of the scriptures and read Malachi and the words were, "healing in his wings." In his mind he wondered, "healing-wings, wings-healing. I don't get the connection."

A blast of wind shuddered the cabin and blew across the chimney mouth outside and its moaning changed to a howl. The draw in the chimney brightened the embers in the fire. Snow pelted the window and sounded more like rain than snow. Axel decided not to traverse the perimeter of his cabin again as the information that he gained was no longer worth the danger. He shoveled the doorway of snow and banked the stove. When he felt Bita's nose she licked the back of his hand and he was well pleased. He took a book from the shelf by Kipling and returned to his chair to read, but against his will, closed his eyes.

• • •

His eyes opened in sudden wakefulness out of a deep sleep, like a deer that in its rest hears a distant sound and does not move until the source is discerned. The wind had stopped, stopped completely. No wind passing the mouth of the chimney caused the embers to glow in the glass of the stove. Snow pellets did not tap their fingernails on the window glass. There was no moaning of the wind in the eaves. Although the window was covered with a drift of snow, there was a brightness outside that declared the storm to be gone.

His quilt flew from his lap as he stood to his feet and strode in quick steps to the door. Only one arm had made it into the sleeve of his wool coat when he thrust open his door and stepped on to his porch. Snow had drifted over the deck and piled on the far wall, covering a line of firewood.

"I want to see the lake and my flag. I want to know that my flag is still there." He said this as he took one long step off his deck and plunged head first into a deep drift.

His face and arms were completely under the snow and he could not breathe. He pushed himself up and got to his knees and then struggled to his feet.

"What a fool," he chided himself, to forget that any snow, level with my deck, was several feet deep. Except for his eyes, he was white with snow. He shivered immediately but stayed in the drift to take stock. The sky was clear of clouds and the sun's yellow haze was just cresting the foothills. The blizzard had spent itself, but as he faced the emptiness beyond, all was white, flat and lifeless.

"I must find the flag and pray for help to come."

• • •

Dressed in wool and wearing his tallest boots, he began to trudge toward the place on the frozen lake where he thought he would find his flag. When he began, his strength was not abated with the effort and he pushed ahead, forcing himself through the depths. Each step was cruel in the effort it required. He could not lift his feet to step but rather pushed himself through with his hips and chest and dragged his legs forward. Often he stumbled. Often he fell face down into the cold. He wiped the rime from his face with his mittened hands and the crystals scraped his skin. He removed his gloves and cleared his eyes and continued on.

He looked for signs of his flag — any anomaly in the surface of the otherwise level lake. He looked for the landmarks to help locate the site. He saw none.

Axel Brown fell forward and discovered that when he did so he could made the progress of one body length. He began to lift both his arms above his head and fall forward. He would struggle to his feet, move forward, and fall again. A few dozen falls later he stood exhausted, leaning on his snow shovel, gasping for breath.

"I must be close. It has to be near."

He looked around him for any sign. "It might have blown completely away. It could be a mile away. It might be buried under feet of snow."

His breath puffed as he thought. "If I don't find it soon I will just go back and find something else to use for a flag," he decided

He looked toward the East. The winter sun, like a pale egg yolk, had just crested and cast tiny shadows across the ground. As he gazed, his weary mind only dimly noticed a thin black line to his side. The shadow nearly did not register at all, but something said, "That's the shadow of a stick poking above the snow."

He shoved toward the place with a newfound energy and thrust the handle of his shovel under the site. With the first sweep it caught on something. He dug with the shovel with a fury and found the red leg of his long johns. Soon he had unearthed his flag.

Axel reset the red flag above the snow and tamped the base in to hold it in place.

"Yes!" he shouted. "Yes!" and he thought his voice echoed back from the trapper's cabin on the shore. "Bita, you might live!"

• • •

The old man made his way back to the cabin following the tracks that he had made before. He kicked the snow from his boots and slapped the snow from his clothing and came inside.

"Bita, there is hope yet."

He hung his clothes from the rafters above the stove to dry them and listened to the fizzing as drops of snow struck the metal. As he warmed himself he stood at the window looking toward the flag on the lake. A very small breath of wind lifted the snow into the air as it were a weightless powder and it sifted down at another place. A sudden realization struck him. His mouth opened at the thought — "That snow is weightless. It will not support the weight of the ski-plane. The plane will just sink into it. The propeller will dig into it and that will be the end of it."

Axel knew with certitude what he had to do. "I will either have to dig an entire runway on the lake with my shovel or walk back and forth over it until I pack it down." Just the thought of the effort that it would take left him exhausted.

"Axel, you know what must be done. If any plane is to land today you must begin right away."

He hung his head down and looked at his stockinged feet. A single tear fell from his eyes and landed on the wool. He wanted to give up. "I am so tired."

When he trudged to the task it was with his wide-scoop snow shovel over his shoulder, skin colored chopper mittens on his hard hands, and a wool hat with ear flaps on his head. He stopped at the shore. "The strip starts here," and he thrust the shovel down at the place. "I want the plane to land as close to my dog as I can."

He started to shovel — four blade widths wide the first pass. I will point it right at the red flag to keep it a straight line.

The top layer was new snow and it was loose powder and weightless and this he threw far to the side. The next layer down was older and heavy and this he hoisted into the air, bending his back to the rear and throwing it to the side with his upper body. The snow next to the ice was compressed and supported his weight and he did not shovel it away. At the distance he gauged a skiplane needed to land, he turned for the first time and looked at his work. The light of the clear winter day cast a blue shadow in the strip he had cleared and he was confident it could be clearly seen from the air.

A painful cramp was in both of his forearms and one shoulder. He was thirsty. When he completed the next lap he would check on Bita and drink something.

"How many more swaths must I do? At least two more, maybe three."

His arms ached. He was weak with the effort. "I could just crawl into one of those drifts and go to sleep right now," he said to himself.

"I am so tired," he said to himself again. And he dared not stop so picked up his shovel and began again.

Half way down the second swath his legs gave out and he sat in the trench, his legs straight out before him. His head sagged to his chest and he was instantly asleep.

Something brought him to wakefulness. "Oh no!" he said aloud. He was afraid because he did not know how long he had been sleeping. A raven passed low overhead, its wings making a "whosh, whosh," sound.

"Thank you for the wake up."

The shovel dropped from his hands as the second pass was completed. His arms hung limply down from his stooped shoulders. Thick hoar frost clung to his beard, which he could see clearly without lifting it. His shovel felt heavy in his hands and he left it where he left off. He trudged to his cabin and stopped at the porch where he had to tell himself to lift his feet the last step.

Bita raised her head as he came into the room and flapped her tail on the floor. Her eyes were on him but she seemed hot and he feared the sepsis might be too far gone. She tried to stand but he urged her down.

He drank from the dipper and poured some in a jar to take back with him.

"I think this time I will leave a space between the next swath and the last and then go back and just tramp it down. I don't know if I could do four rows."

• • •

When Axel had completed the fourth row and tromped down the space between with his feet, it took him to the edge of the shore in front of his cabin. His throat was raw as his nose had frozen closed the lap before and he gasped for breath with his mouth open to the winter air. He had trouble focusing his eyes and he was not sure if it was the steam of his breath which blocked his view or if the outside world was out of focus. He lifted his eyes to the nearness of his home on the lake and thought he did not have the strength to walk those few remaining steps.

He smelled cedar smoke from the chimney, one of his favorite odors, and knew that warmth and comfort were but steps away, in his case very long trudging steps.

His body swayed and he found himself sitting, legs splayed out in a "V" before him. He had sweated in his efforts and his clothing was damp throughout. In moments he found himself shivering. It began at his back and it was a coldness to the bone and he began to shake without control.

It was at that time when he realized two things: He was in a mortal danger of freezing to death nearly at his very doorstep, and second, he realized that he heard the sound of an engine.

The sound was far away perhaps beyond the foothills on the other side of the lake.

Axel found an energy he did not know that he had. Perhaps it was of the reserves that God sometimes gives to his people.

Axel ran to the head of his runway. He began to shout at a tiny speck in the distant sky.

"Here! Here!"

He jumped up and down. He waved both of his arms into the sky.

"Here!"

It seemed the airplane was not heading in his direction but rather was flying parallel to the lake.

Axel screamed, "I'm over here." And he waved.

Then Axel had an idea. He ran to his flag and uprooted the stake and he waved it back and forth.

"I'm over here."

Then the plane disappeared to the west.

"No. No," he moaned. "No."

And Axel Brown dropped to the snow and wept.

• • •

Only a few minutes passed, but to the defeated man on the ice it seemed the end of everything. Then, there was a very loud roar as the bush plane on winter skis flew low over his cabin just brushing the trees, on over the lake and the prostrate figure on the ice. It made a tight one-eighty turn and landed on the blue shadow that was Axel's runway. For a few moments the prop blew up powdered snow that completely masked the airplane from view, then the pilot cut the engines and it came to a stop only yards from Axel.

"I saw your flag, Axel. I couldn't resist trying out your runway."

Axel pulled the glove from his hand as he walked forward to shake his hand.

"I'm so glad you came when you did," he said, but discovered that he was too weary to speak correctly. His own words seemed but a mumble to him.

The pilot looked at Axel in his face and realized the total weariness in the man.

"I understand, Axel."

Then Axel Brown, who was not accustomed to showing his emotions, placed both of his hands on the shoulders of his pilot friend, and wept like a child.

"It's my dog. The wolves tore her up. I need to get her to a vet."

The pilot retrieved his coat and gloves from the plane and put his arm around his friend Axel's waist. "Not to worry. We will have you there in a couple of hours. Let's get her to the plane and button up your place."

"Watch your head on the wing, Axel. The plane sits low in the snow. How do you like the new paint job? I like simplicity. Instead of a fancy logo and a high-falutin' name I just put, 'WINGS.'"

Axel just looked up and smiled. There was a weariness in his smile but it was a true smile.

"Somehow I should have known."

• • •

They were airborne in a half hour. Bita was in her bed strapped to the back seat.

"Your dog is a fighter and I am sure she will make it."

He glanced back at her. "I think you are right about that Conrad."

"Want to show you something, something I saw coming in. It's over there on the far shore. See there that line of red on the shoreline? That is all red willow and the shore there did not get as much snow as you did. See over there running along the edge in the shallow stuff?"

Axel studied the brush and could not see anything.

"Here I'm going to make a low pass and point it out." He banked sharply and began to parallel the shore, then banked gently so Axel could see an area only fifty feet below the bush plane.

"Right……there!"

And just below the window where the old man could have thrown a rock, five large timber wolves ran in file. They were in the prime of life, thick coated, and on the hunt. One of them turned its head and looked up at the airplane… and Axel Brown.

# A Day on the Tide Flats

Scott McDaniel was one of those great painters of Alaska who could do a scene and use green in the sky and it looked perfectly natural. He could do it and you knew just by looking at it what the temperature was and if there was a breeze coming off the water and even what you might expect from the day. Well, there it was before my eyes, only it was the real thing and not something on canvas. I did not see any wind in the trees nearby but I could hear the hush of the sea on the other side of them and I could imagine the waves offering themselves on the altar of the shore. Before me, the green of McDaniel's sky blended with the pale yellow of the morning sun and a few very thin red strips of cloud.

As I stood there in my rubber boots on the beach it was clear that I would have plenty of time to look at that sky because our boat was high and dry, far up on the beach with the low tide.

"You better see this," I shouted toward the tent. "I think our sockeye fishing isn't going to happen today."

I only heard a moan from the interior of the tent.

I walked over and put my head inside. "Pete, we are high and dry with the tide. We are not getting out of here any time soon."

"Huh?"

He threw off his sleeping bag, burst from the tent, and stared in disbelief at the flats. It was not enough that our skiff was there a full two hundred yards from the closest water, but the sun shone on it like a spotlight and its black shadow pointed at it like a mocking finger.

He groaned. "How did this happen? I thought you checked your tide book."

"YOUR tide book," I corrected him. "Show it to me again."

He pulled his rucksack from the tent and rummaged inside it, his moving fingers sounding in it like a mouse in a paper sack. The hands stopped and he produced the tide book, handing it to me like a limp, soggy accusation. It smelled like mildew. The page was still open to the month and day we used the night before. I folded it back to see the cover and saw what I had suspected would be printed beside the name of the sporting goods store on the front. I tapped my finger at the place and handed it to him so he could see it.

"Nice picture on the cover," I said. "But notice the date. It's three years old."

He looked at it as though his eyes would not focus.

"Man!" he shouted and threw the tide book as if it had been stuck on his fingers. He turned and stomped down to the boat in his long johns and rubber boots. He braced himself at the stern placing his shoulder under it and tried to heft it. "This was our one day to catch sockeye," he grumbled.

"You will never get that boat to the water."

He ignored me and hefted it again the veins popping in his temples. I heard gravel crunching under the keel but it did not otherwise budge.

"Look, you must have the heaviest skiff in town. A beamy cedar lifeboat and a big motor bolted to the stern." I said those words slowly and emphasized the words, "heavy and bolted."

I looked at it again. It was heavy, designed for rough seas. It even had fire hoses that were split lengthwise and nailed to the rails instead of fenders. It was a retired Coast Guard lifeboat with high rails and it clearly would not be moving anywhere until the tide came in again.

"We could both heft it on to a log and roll it down."

"I seem to have forgotten to pack a log this trip," I said sarcastically. "Besides, there are way too many big rocks on this beach to use a log."

Pete saw the hopelessness of moving our stranded vessel. In his mind's eye he saw the silver sides of salmon jumping and falling uncaught into the water — like bright precious coins falling from a torn moneybag.

"What a waste. The salmon are running at peak and I am stuck on this beach."

He let out a long breath of air and shook his head in disgust. "What a waste this is."

"I'm going back to bed." He clomped his way back to the tent in his boots, slipping several times on the wet, green seaweed that grew on the stones. He fell twice, once forward leaving skin on the side of a barnacled rock, and once backward, before he got to the tent. He plopped down on his sleeping bag and the mattress he had made of pine boughs and stared upward at the brown canvas.

• • •

I found a place above the tide line where there was a large, flat rock. A storm-tossed cedar log with no bark on it was jammed just behind it and made a perfect chair. It is a habit of my life to read something in the Bible every day and I sat on the rock and read the part about Elijah and the ravens where it said, "He went and dwelt by the brook Cherith that is before Jordan. And the ravens brought him bread and flesh in the morning, and bread and flesh in the evening; and he drank of the brook."

I visualized the scene of that ancient event and then heard the raucous noise of ravens and crows in my own morning. They cawed and squawked like a noisy neighborhood just waking up. They squabbled and gossiped and strutted in the grass with their wings behind their backs.

Before me, the morning sun rose above all of the tall trees and yellowed the flats and they were golden and alive before me. Gulls and other sea birds circled above. A pair of eagles perched in a dead cedar snag across the flat, their white heads the color of yellow parchment in the glow. A faint breeze brought the scent of the iodine of the low tide and the smell of starfish that were stuck to the rocks above the tide.

Around me I could hear the squirting of clams. Bright daylight shone through the spurts that shot upward through the sand between the small rocks.

A raven strutted nearby. From time to time it stopped and tilted its head as if it were listening. In the light, the black of its feathers shone iridescent purple and green and blue. The sky was reflected in its eyes and once I saw my own distorted reflection in them. The black orbs blinked and the raven cocked its head, looked at me, then at something between the small rocks in the sand. There was a squirt and I could see the wrinkled, flesh colored neck of a butter clam that protruded from the sand.

With a hop and a thrust the raven grabbed the neck with its beak and pulled and tugged at the clam. It pulled side to side and when it did not give it pulled from directly above from where the neck extended from the sand. The raven changed its footing and pulled again and this time the clam was pulled from the loose earth and the raven flew with it into the air.

Thirty feet into the air two other ravens swooped down on the first. The sky became strident with squawking birds. The first raven did a split "S" aerobatic maneuver to evade the other two but was followed close behind like the World War One bi-planes in combat. Another raven flew from under and latched its black beak on the clam from the front. In this aerial tug of war both lost their grips and the clam fell end over end through the air, the long neck fully extended, flopping neck, shell, neck, shell, to the ground.

The butter clam landed on a large rock and shattered, the pieces of shell flying into the air. The birds scrambled for the naked and exposed butter clam. A large male speared and swallowed the pink flesh in a single move. It strutted a few steps to the side and wiped the sides of its bill against a rock, one stroke on one side of its bill and one stroke on the other. It spread its feathers, then strode away, the rest looking to see if there were scraps left behind.

Above the tide line, on the other side of the bay, raucous crows were peeling blue mussels from the still wet rocks. They pried them off with their beaks and flew with them into the air and dropped them on the rocks to break them open. Mussels are lighter in weight than clams and they often bounced and did not break. The crows retrieved them and dropped them again and when the blue-black fragments of shell exploded into the air a dozen birds scrambled to the place.

Across the tidelands near the entrance of the bay were patches of water marked by eelgrass. A flash of a long, sharp, yellow beak revealed a heron in the eelgrass. It speared something in the tide pools, shook its head as it swallowed, then moved forward on thin brittle legs.

"Pete! Let's not waste the day. I want to check out the bay."

He was clearly bored looking up at the brown canvas of the tent. "I'm coming. Might as well do something since we aren't going to catch fish."

I slid my feet over the slippery rocks toward the tide pools where the heron waded. Yellow kelp was attached to the rocks and the little air sacks popped when I stepped on them. I lost my footing with the slipperiness and caught my balance in the sand between the rocks. I made my way by stepping on rocks with barnacles for traction. Ahead, the surface of the pools dimpled with the movement of small fish in the water.

A small surge from the open sea moved the eelgrass back and forth. In the parting of the sea grass I saw a flash of orange from a crab in the flow and shuffled closer. At my approach the heron lifted its body, moving its long wings in slow flight. It made a "crank, crank" sound in its throat in time to its wing beat. I saw other crab in the grass. They were Dungeness crab and of decent size.

"Pete, bring the bucket and the net. We can get some crab."

He left the tent like a bear leaving a cave. He wore his green halibut jacket and blue jeans tucked inside his boots. He rummaged inside of the skiff. Heavy things thumped dully against the sides of the wooden boat. He loaded his arms with our five gallon bucket and a fish net in one hand and the oars and gaff hook in the other, then shuffled to where I stood in the shallow water.

Then I heard, "Aaagh," and saw his legs fly into the air and he came down on his hip directly on a rock covered with leafy seaweed. I could hear the impact of his fall and the slap of his boots against the rock. I heard as the air was knocked out of his lungs. "Aaagh," he said again, this time because of the shock of cold water that soaked him completely and filled his boots.

I ran to him just as he rolled over on his stomach and pushed himself up. He could not speak with the cold. He gasped trying to catch his breath.

"Let's dump the water out of your boots at least," I said.

He sat on a rock and I braced myself and pulled on his boots. They seemed glued to his feet with his wet socks. I wiggled them back and forth and water rolled out of his boots. They finally gave with a sucking sound. I had been holding his boot with both hands and fell backward into the pool of water and the coldness of it took my breath. I stood upright shocked with a cold that was nearly painful.

"Let's just make the best of it, Pete. I saw some good sized crab in the pools."

We moved, slowly parting the eelgrass with the oars.

"There's one!" I pointed at the spot with my net. "You can reach it with your oar."

He pinned it with the blade and I tried to scoop it with the net but it just rolled over the top.

There was nothing for it. I dropped to my knees in the water and grabbed it by the back of the shell. The crab clicked its claws at empty air.

"That's big. I don't even have to measure that one."

It was a male and I put it in the bucket and it thumped into the plastic. The claws scraped back and forth against the sides.

I stood and bent my legs, heels to buttocks so the water could pour from my boots. I felt the water exit the boot and pour over my knees.

We worked the eelgrass side by side parting the grass in the water. I pinned another male and it lifted the front of its shell and raised its pinchers. Pete grabbed it from the back and added it to several others in the pail.

"We have at least a dozen in the pail," Pete said with a grin.

I glanced at the pail and the sun shining through the plastic sides left a shadow of the level of crab inside. A dozen pair of claws were scratching the sides as they tried to claw free.

I pinned another one from behind with the round of the gaff hook. Pete grabbed it from the front and as he did it latched on to the web of his hand with a claw.

"Aaagh."

He held his hand up in the air, fingers splayed like a child says, "Five years old," with the crab still firmly clamped to the skin of his hand.

"Aaagh."

He held his hand over the bucket and shook it and tried to loosen the crab. He shook it up and down, but gingerly as the dungy was still holding on. With a last determined shake it let go and fell into the bucket, a few splashes of Pete's blood also going in with it and merged pink with the saltwater.

"Aaagh."

"You keep saying that," I said.

"I think we got all of the keepers in the pools. I'm happy," he said.

The water that remained in our boots had about warmed to flesh temperature and our wetness no longer dominated our minds. We put some seawater in the bucket to keep the crab alive and carried it to the skiff. We covered the bucket with a life jacket to hide it from the birds and put the oars over the top.

"Pete, I think we have time before the tide comes in. I would like to explore that point on the other side of the entrance where we came in. Look how you can see the light through the trees. I bet up there you could see the ocean and back this way over the bay. I can hear the ocean from here."

Pete squinted and looked where I pointed with the net.

"I'm with you."

"We won't have much time to look," he said as he sucked some blood from the web of his hand. "I think we are at slack tide now and the water will be coming in soon."

• • •

The water was high on our boots as we crossed the narrow tongue of water that marked the entrance to the bay. When we had entered this place the entire area was underwater but with the low tide it was a field of vegetation. I could imagine that in the winter when deep snow covered the grass and shrubs elsewhere and skinny deer pawed the crusted snow for food, this hidden cove would be a haven for deer at the right tide. Each day when the ocean left the bay it would reveal a smorgasbord of green sea grass and varieties of kelp.

It was also a place completely hidden from the eyes of passing boat hunters.

"You know, Pete, if we didn't know this place was here by seeing it on a map, we would never have found it. That opening to this cove is so small, and from the ocean it just looks like the contour of the shore."

He thought about that a minute. "I bet this place never gets hunted."

I pointed up the slope of the side we were facing. "That's the place I wanted to see."

Ahead was a slope that entered the tall trees like a driveway. The surface of the slope was of round, ocean-rolled stones that became smaller in size as the slope entered the trees. The surface was white sand where the slope ended at the base of the trees.

The area was what they call old growth — tall, very large cedar and hemlock trees that blocked out the sun and prevented new undergrowth. The effect was of being in a park. I could not take a step without looking around in wonder.

"Hey, look at that."

"What?"

"That."

Pete stared in the direction I was looking. "I can't see anything."

"There. Look at the lines of that shape. It's perfectly square."

I pointed with the gaff hook, which for some reason I still had in my hand. "Right there."

I took several steps in the direction I was pointing. "Right there."

"Hey," he said, "it's a cabin."

Both of us ran to it. It was completely covered in thick moss, but the shape was unmistakable. As we stood before the structure, it was clearly a cabin of notched and fitted logs but so covered as to render it invisible. It was not large, perhaps ten by twelve with flat slabs of stone leading to the door.

The door had been made of heavy planks and bolted together by those huge hinges blacksmiths make. In the center of the door a ship's porthole had been fitted for light and ventilation. Pete pulled on the handle and the door swung open with noisy protest. When we entered, a bird the color of grey dust flew from the interior through a single broken windowpane. We stepped inside and let our eyes adjust to the dimness.

Although it was not large, it was very well built. It was constructed of large cedar logs and the floor was of thick milled timber. One window facing the ocean let in light. There had been a slight air flow between the broken windowpane and the barely open porthole in the door, which kept mold and rot from the room. To the left was a double bunk and on either side of it was closet space. Before us was a wood burning stove for heat and cooking. Pete tapped the chimney, "It's still solid. You could use it today."

I looked outside at the roof and returned to the stove. "He left a can over the top of the chimney to keep out the rain."

There was a table and bench at the window and I sat on it to look around the cabin. "Pete, this looks like the guy just left for the afternoon and didn't come back yet. Look at all of his stuff."

Pete went to a corner and hefted a double bladed axe. "This is still good. The handle isn't rotten and the blade is a bit rusty but it is still sharp. And here are some of his traps hanging."

Along the windowsill were some old bottles and two glass Japanese net floats. Hanging over the table and over the bunks were two oil lanterns. I sniffed and could smell the kerosene inside of the wells.

"Look at the chair." Pete sat in it with satisfaction. It was made of alder branches that had been woven into an easy chair complete with arm rests.

Pete beamed as he sat in the chair. "This had to be a trapper cabin but you could spend a lot of time in this comfortably."

"I would guess that he would trap all the way around this bay and then work his way up the coast to some others," I added.

"Look at the size of that fry pan. It must weigh five pounds." I saw it on the floor beside the stove. Above it I could see where the nail had given way and it fell at some point over the years.

"I wonder how long it has been since anyone has been here?"

"Years, decades," I offered.

On the wall, above the lower bunk was a calendar. The picture was of a Philip Goodwin painting of a campsite. The hunters were returning in their canoes but in their absence a sow bear and two cubs had been ransacking the camp. Food and cans and boxes were strung over the ground. A skunk had entered the campsite and the cubs were darting away, one climbing a tree. The sow was raised on her hind legs and not sure what to do about the skunk. The date on the calendar was 1941.

Across the cabin floor I noticed a couple of boxes under the bunk. One was of a painted enamel surface that resisted rust. I rushed to it. It had weight and I knew there was something inside.

"Treasure," I announced to Pete.

"What do you hope to find?"

"A Honus Wagner baseball card," I said.

"What is that?"

"I'm just kidding about that. Honus Wagner was one of the first baseball players to have his face on a baseball card. One of his cards sold for over three million dollars."

Pete went to the window. He picked up a tiny cobalt blue bottle. "I'm going to take this for a souvenir."

I sat at the table and opened the box. The smell of "old" emitted from the box but not any odor of mold. Inside the box were three books and some magazines.

"He liked good books," I said, "These are first editions. He had Steinbeck's 'Grapes of Wrath' and Hemingway's 'For Whom the Bell

Tolls.'" I set them on the table and pulled out another. "Here is Dickens' 'Tale of Two Cities.'"

Pete was not interested in the books, as he did not read for pleasure.

I pulled out a 1941 magazine called "Outdoorsman Magazine." The caption on the cover was "American Trapping Goes Modern."

"Pete, I wonder if this guy left the country to go to the war."

"Why do you say that?"

"Everything is 1941. That's Pearl Harbor times. My Dad enlisted then. Did you know that most of the mines that closed in Alaska didn't close because there was no more gold but because the miners all went to the war?"

I pointed at the calendar. "Look at the calendar. Nineteen forty one."

Pete rubbed his hip where he fell on the rocks. "Maybe he just liked the picture."

"No imagination," I said.

I pulled another magazine from the box. It was April 1941. The magazine was, "Hunting and Fishing Magazine" and the cover was a painting that depicted two soldiers in a bomb crater. An explosion was blowing debris near them but one was smiling at the other and gesturing upward with his thumb at a flock of geese passing overhead.

"Look at that," I said in triumph.

I copied the trapper's name from the address label. "I wonder who he was. Did he survive the war? Did he return to Alaska? Does he have family?"

I looked about the interior of this little hut. The man was gone. Gone for perhaps half a century or far longer. But his presence still lingered there. His character spoke from the quality of his dwelling and his work, the things he collected, his solitude. His industry was in the Victor traps that hung in the corner and the hand carved stretchers. His industry was evident in the line of split wood under the eaves and the tight fit of the logs.

But it was his absence that struck me most. Who was he? What happened to him? I tucked the name I wrote from the address label on the magazine into my pocket.

"Tide is coming in pretty fast." I looked outside the door and could see the saltwater enter the cove with a current like a fast-moving stream. A few bubbles floated on the surface and swirled with the flow. "I guess we better go while we can cross it in our boots. As it is we may have to go inland for a ways."

Peter turned to the cabin with the cobalt blue bottle in his hand. "I think I am going to leave it here." I watched as Peter almost tenderly placed it on the sill.

• • •

I sat on the bow of Pete's skiff, straddling it like a horse, my feet dangling over the sides. The first fingers of the oncoming tide that was filling the bay were touching the toes of my boot.

Pete's stern end was still dry and firm to the earth. In a half hour or so there would be enough buoyancy to lift the bow of the boat. Where my hunting and fishing partner sat, he would only need to pull the starting cord of the outboard and we could motor away if we waited. But I knew it would not end that way. As soon as he would feel the buoyancy of the bow lift, we would both be at the stern on the ground hefting those last few feet of ground that held us like a chain.

As I sat looking to the west and the sky, I remembered what another famous painter of landscapes told me.

We were in his studio and there were a half dozen of his paintings on easels. They were all of Mount McKinley and all but one bore the colors of red and crimson and yellow sky.

He smiled at me — unusual as he was a grumpy type. "Can you tell me which paintings are of sunrise and which are of sunset?"

I was stumped. Such color schemes could be either, I thought. All were beautiful. He was a brilliant painter, nationally acclaimed. I looked for clues. What objects had to be westward or from the east. All had brilliant colors, perfectly done. I hadn't a clue.

"I give up. I don't know."

Ernie Robertson got serious. "Here is the difference between a painter who can just paint well, and a master. The master intimately knows his subject and the master must be in perfect command of his medium."

"Sunrises are always pure and the colors are vibrant and honest. Nothing is added to them. Crimson is pure crimson. Yellow is pure yellow. Sunsets are never that way. They always take on the haze and mist and sweat of the day. Now, can you pick out the sunsets?"

I could.

As I sat there straddling the bow of Pete's boat and looked toward the west, I could see that Ernie Robertson was right. As I gazed skyward, I thought of the events of this, my day, and its contributions to the record of this time on the tide flat. I watched the off-red and parchment yellow push its way through the breaks of the trees above the cabin. And I thought, "This is my sky."

# Alaskan Halfway House

I did a stint in a halfway house for recovering alcoholics. Not what you think. I am a teetotaler. I don't drink at all for any reason. I don't pet rattlesnakes either.

I once offended the captain and crew of a Russian expedition that sailed from Vladivostok and were retracing Baranof's voyages to Alaska. My wife and I reserved a shelter on the beach with a fire pit and tables to welcome them and make them feel at home. We brought American dishes and things we knew they had been without on the voyage. The Russians brought a special treasure from the ship that they called "shashlik." It was brought in a multi gallon clear jar and whatever was inside was the opaque grey color of dishwater. The contents reminded me of the old days when you went to the carnival and for a dollar you could examine the mysterious "thing" in the jar. The Russian sailors speared the shashlik on a stick like shish kebab and if you shut your eyes it wasn't bad at all.

Banquets with Russian sailors always include toasts — many of them. All such toasts require the requisite tipping of the vodka glass — not one big toast with one drink to finalize it, but numerous toasts, all of which required the glass. Smart people. They do not toast one's family but rather, each member of it individually. I could see the nearly clear vodka swirl in their glasses with the hazy hint of potato in the liquid. Their hands shook in the exuberance of their words and perhaps with the succession of many toasts.

"You do not drink wodka with us," said a blond sailor looking at me. He said vodka with a "w."

I held up my coffee cup.

"I'm toasting with my coffee," I explained. "I don't drink alcohol."

They eyed me suspiciously.

"No?"

"No. Never," I said. "Nothing with alcohol."

They seemed to doubt that a toast could actually be endorsed or finalized with its absence. The shelter we had reserved at the beach became very quiet. I could hear the waves softly break on the shore. A breeze seemed to be caught in the eaves of the shelter and could not free itself, like a stuck fly struggling in a web.

A short brown haired Russian was still holding his glass in the air and stared over his arm at me. His eyes seemed to say, "So you do not drink with Russians?"

"I just don't drink on any occasion."

He seemed to ponder the strangeness of that, then he shrugged his shoulders in a manner that said, "Crazy American. Let's get on with the toasting."

With my abstemious history regarding alcohol and its effects, it was perhaps surprising that I was hired to manage a halfway house for substance abusers. There was a concern that a non-drinker could not relate to the residents of a halfway house. Truth was, I discovered that most of the clients of the house did not relate to themselves; none ever admitted that they were on the result end of a thousand deliberate choices that brought them to the place they were. Instead they believed they had a disease or genetic condition, like height and eye color that made them victims and certainly not responsible for their drinking.

Perhaps the most telling consideration that landed me the position was the probability that I would stay sober at the house. My two predecessors were currently on a binge.

One was clearly above the world — high as a kite. He was at the center of the bar floor standing between the bar and the booths with both arms raised for attention.

"Time me," he shouted as he double tied the laces of his brand new running shoes, shoes that bore white thunderbolts on the sides. "I am going to have one beer in each of the bars. I will start on Katlian Street, go down Lincoln Street to those three bars, then out the road to The Three and a Half, then to The Kiksadi Club. Time me." He grinned like a pug dog, his tongue out at one side.

"On foot or are you going to use taxis?"

"He picked the longest cigarette stub from an ashtray on the bar top, one without lipstick on the filter, lit it, took one drag and winked at the man next to him. "Running all the way."

"Time me… now!" And he ran for the door, his foot sliding on the spilled booze on the floor as he skidded around the corner.

The other past manager had taken drunkenness to a different form. He sat at the far end of the bar in the shadows and decided he would make a pyramid of empty beer cans that would reach the low ceiling. At one point the bartender tried to clean them from the bar.

"Leave 'em," he said.

The bartender glanced into the milky eyes and saw such malice that he slowly slid back the can he held in his hand.

Another patron of the bar took a seat beside him, grinned, and slowly inched his hand toward the stack, his fingers moving like a spider.

Before the prankster could blink, my predecessor drew his knife and plunged it into the creeping hand, anchoring it to the countertop. The thud of the knife and the shriek were clear over the loudness of the jukebox and the clank of glasses.

The victim would be still affixed to the bar were it not for the fact that the numerous layers of lacquer that made up the bar surface prevented the blade from penetrating the wood beyond retrieval.

Moreover, my predecessor wanted his knife back — the drop point one with the giraffe bone handle. He worked the knife back and forth a few times to free it from the wood, then held down the victim's hand with one of his own and slid out the blade. He seemed not to notice the man's shrieking when he worked his knife free. Stone faced, he stood slowly and moved toward the door.

At the door he stopped and turned around as though he had forgotten something. He strode back to where the man sat, still staring at his quivering, bleeding hand as if it were still affixed to the bar. Terror filled his face when he looked up and saw his attacker return to him. But the assailant ignored his victim as if he were of no consequence and his act something out of the distant past. With a last look at the stack of silver colored cans and one swoop of his arm he wrecked his edifice and with sure, deliberate steps, left the bar.

• • •

We drove to the halfway house in Ben's beat up blue car and its attendant rattling of car parts. Fumes fled the chaos of the engine and escaped through the muffler in a black, sooty cloud. After a cough, Ben mumbled, "Gotta fix that someday."

He drove slowly, maneuvering around the deep potholes, proceeding to the very end of the road and the last building on it. It was the structure on the island most distant from any bar. The air was hot and sticky for our part of Alaska, and we drove with the windows down. A phenomenon of a rainforest is that after just a few sunny days, roads become dusty. In those days we had no paved roads and the grass in the ditches bore a sheen of powder. Brown dust entered the car like a passenger and took a seat. I felt grit on my teeth.

Gravel crunched under the tires as we slowed to the front door and stopped next to a yellow station wagon.

"That's your car. It's for the manager's use for the halfway house. Take it home and use it. Don't leave it here. I do not want any of the clients to fall off the wagon and take it. It's here now only because they need to get groceries and run errands. One of the residents has the keys and thinks he is in charge. Take the keys away from him."

I nodded.

Our car dust drifted toward the open door and windows of the halfway house. It was a converted barracks building left from World War Two when the area was built up in anticipation of a Japanese invasion. From the doorway emerged a thin, sallow-skinned man. He wore a black Billy Jack cowboy hat, blue jeans, and a black t-shirt. (The movie had come out only the year before.) He had one thumb in a loop of his jeans, a large ring of keys hooked in another loop, and he walked slowly as if he had just alighted his horse after a long trek in the saddle. I fully expected him to say, "Yer new in these parts ain't cha," or maybe even, "Fill your hand!"

This was Richard and he eyed me as an interloper on his spread, something to be dealt with later.

"Richard, this is your new manager."

Richard seemed to flinch slightly as if a fly had bitten him. He composed himself before answering.

"Noon," he greeted in cowboy fashion.

"Afternoon to you too, Richard," Ben said with a nod.

There was a shout from inside the building. "Shut that door. What's the matter with you? You're getting dust in the food."

"That is the cook — the one everyone tries to keep happy no matter where you are in this country," Ben said.

Ben wore a cowboy hat himself. It was Nevada style, beat up and old and dusty like Ben himself. He gave me the tour and introductions and left me there at the halfway house, at the end of the last island on the causeway, the last building from town and any liquor store.

• • •

It was later in the day when I took the keys from Richard. At the far end of the barracks was a small room with a twin bed, closet, and desk separated from the other quarters by the day room. In the war it was undoubtedly where the officer or sergeant in charge stayed. This was my place and Richard had followed me there as he explained the operation of the facility.

"I will not be staying here every night as I have a family," I said as

I tossed my rucksack on the bed and placed a couple of things into a dresser drawer. “Actually I will be going in a few minutes. I better get the keys from you now,” I said and held out my hand.

His eyes widened. He did not move. It was as if the chevrons were being torn from his sleeve.

The time had come. His hour of power was evaporating as clearly as if the head of a firing squad had just slipped the blindfold over his eyes and he were being marched out in the rain to a place at a bullet riddled wall.

“Richard, Ben and I appreciate the efforts you have done to keep things going in the absence of a manager. I hope I can count on your continued help as I learn the ropes here.”

I heard the air pass through his lips and thin mustache.

He slapped the keys into my hand and turned to leave.

I watched him walk away and then turn and come back to me.

He paused and shuffled his feet and said, “I was a Green Beret, you know. It’s the war dreams that make me drink.”

He slowly raised his eyes to mine — slowly like two brown bugs climbing a wall. “Two hundred of us Green Berets attacked that hill and I am the only one that lived. I’ll never forget that sight, the cries for water.”

With good theater he lowered his eyes.

I thought for a minute, deciding if I should say what was on my mind.

“Richard, one of the first things needed to stay sober is to be honest.”

He cocked his head to the side to say, “What are you getting at?”

“How did you like Bragg?”

“Oh, we don’t brag.”

“What group were you in, Richard?”

“We didn’t have groups. We were all just Green Berets”

“What was your M-O-S?”

He did not answer.

“Let me explain it this way. You can’t believe how many people tell me they were a Green Beret. Have you ever met a general from the

Army?"

"Naa," he said suspiciously.

"Did you know there were more generals and admirals in the military than there are Special Forces? You would be more likely to bump into a general on leave than an SF man. Richard, there are probably not ten people in the whole state of Alaska who were ever in Special Forces. Today was your bad luck to bump into one of them."

He waited with his thumbs in his belt loops.

"Infantry, Marines and Rangers may attack a hill together but not Green Berets. Our basic unit has only twelve men. Of all the questions I asked, you got every one of them wrong."

I waited for this to sink in.

"We will let this one pass. I want you to stay sober and I want to count on you."

He turned without speaking and left my room.

• • •

I said goodbye to the cook and a couple of men lounging in the kitchen and stepped outside into the sunlight. Because of the dust, the car windows had been rolled to the top and I knew it would be an oven inside. I rolled them down to let it cool inside as I walked toward the shore below the halfway house.

As I turned to go, Richard stood in my way. His eyes were red and bloodshot. When he finally spoke it was like Eisenhower at D Day quietly saying, "There it is then. We go."

Richard looked directly into my eyes and said, "I have a pellet gun. Just a few pumps and you could kill a dog."

I listened.

"You can't stay awake forever. You just watch. I will creep into your room. I can pick the lock. I'm good at it."

He began to breathe heavily. His nostrils flared to the sides and his upper lip bared his teeth.

"I am going to watch you when you are sleeping. You won't know that I am there and I won't do it right away. But I will be there."

His eyes glazed like a serpent's and for the time it takes one to strike, I saw a reflection of myself in them. He pointed at my eyes with one forefinger. "I am going to watch your pupils sliding under your eyelids and I am going to line up your pupils with the hole in the back of your eye socket and the pellet is going to go through the hole and into your brain."

His eyes were glassy like water on a skating rink. He was like a movie producer planning out the scene. He was a Viet Cong sapper crawling in the mud through the perimeter wire and into the hut of the enemy and "taking him out."

His hands were curled around an imaginary pistol. The corners of his eyes were drawn up in wrinkles. Under his hunched shoulders his body was tense and crouched into a spring. The veins of his free hand bulged on the top of his hands.

"Richard," I said quietly, clearly, and slowly, "I changed my mind. I am going to come back and stay the night after all. I will be in my room, Richard. See you later."

I never saw him again.

• • •

It rained the next Friday. It began just after dinner. I was in the kitchen helping the cook with the dishes and heard it tapping on the windows and I looked up to see it slide in rivulets down the panes in the layers of dust like wet mascara.

In the open doorway it smelled of dust as the first drops landed in the powder of the path until it was replaced by the freshness of the shower. The rain, tapping the leaves of the alder trees, sounded like applause.

I went to bed early and listened to the rain on the roof until it was diminished to drops late in the night. By morning it was over and sunlight squeezed between the layers of stratus clouds.

Just after breakfast Ben drove up in his rig. I could hear the car rattle each time he hit a pothole, and as he pulled up and turned off the key there was a bang — like a period at the end of a solid declarative sentence.

"Gotta fix that someday," he said.

Cook made him some eggs and toast and we visited over coffee.

"I want to show you a couple of things, see what you think," I said.

We walked down to the shore where a heavy-looking wood boat lay upright in the tall grass. It was one of those narrow rowing skiffs and was pulled high up on the bank above the tide lines. A pair of solid oak oars waited in the brass-turned-green oarlocks. Green paint on the sides and interior was peeling to a farmer red that was underneath.

I pointed to it as we walked.

"Is that ours?"

Ben scratched his chin.

"Yes. I forgot all about that. Someone that we got sober gave it to us. We never used it."

"I checked it out. I can't see any leaks and it has oars and seat cushions."

Ben touched his mustache and in his mind I knew he was thinking of the person who donated the boat.

"A success story?"

Ben slowly came out of his reverie.

"A husband and wife actually. I found her drunk in a ditch near death and looking like a drowned rat. I don't know how she lived."

We stopped just in front of the boat and I stared at the bulk before us. "Man, that looks heavy. Look at the size of those beams."

Ben studied the craft before us. "But I don't think it's waterlogged. And they got it off the ground and set it on those beams. That's good. There shouldn't be any rot."

"The husband was a logger and had been drinking and fell off a log boom. He was hit in the head by another log and was knocked out. He was under for several minutes before they found him. He was all but dead when they got him. They flew him to Seattle but he came back and actually has most of his marbles."

He looked at me with a twinkle in his eye. "The wife is my secretary. And you met the husband too. He is the head of the board of directors."

There was delight in Ben's face. "Those are the ones that keep me going."

"I was thinking of getting the people off the couch and away from the television. I thought I could get them out in the boat. We would have to row of course and maybe jig for a fish. I was thinking of taking them out one at a time just to visit and encourage them. A completely informal setting."

"Good idea. We would have to keep it in the water. You will not be able to get any of them to do any work to launch it each time."

"I also thought we could get them to take on a project of sprucing it up."

"Good luck with that one," he said. "Maybe if one or two of them has to stay busy or drink."

Ben walked to the side door and shouted inside, "Hey you fellows, come out here and help us launch this."

I pointed to a building several times larger than an outhouse. "I think that's ours too. That has to be the largest smokehouse in town. I thought we could catch and smoke up some salmon."

"And I know one of my clients who caught too many sockeye and might donate some of them."

While we waited for them there was a loud squawking in the alder tree by the boat. A crow with ruffled feathers seemed to drop out of the branches and landed in the grass beside the boat. First its head popped up above the grass and it looked side to side to see where it was. It got up and staggered. "Squaaak."

It cocked its head as if to say, "That isn't how it is supposed to sound." And it tried again, "Squaaak."

Two other crows dropped from the branches above and staggered about, their paths in the wet grass traced a long sentence in cursive. They bumped each other and one toppled over and regained its feet with his bill open.

Two other crows rustled in the leaves above and red berries fell to the ground. The first crow to land in the grass puked a mass of red berries.

"They're potted. They're drunk as Lords. I heard alder berries could do that to them."

Two men came from the house and smiled at the sight. One of them wore a wife beater tank and sandals. He looked like he just woke up.

Ben looked at the two men. "Don't get any ideas, fellas."

One crow hopped to the stern of the boat, swayed back and forth twice, squirted its load and fell over backward into the weeds.

A few other residents joined us. Joe, who wore the wife beater and sandals, wanted no part in moving the skiff. "It's the sandals," he said, "I don't want to squish my toes."

With our numbers positioned around the boat, there was no problem getting it to the water. It slid easily on the rain-wet grass but it took all of our strength to lift it over the rocks at the edge.

It floated high and proud. With the weight of the wood, it was stable in the water. Nick, one of our Indian people, stood on the side rail with an oar to fend off any rocks and there was barely a list to the side.

"I like that boat," I said "She just seems stable and safe."

Ben nodded in approval. "We have no dock so it would have to be Indian moored in place."

Nick looked around him and said in his taciturn manner, "This is a good place. Tucked out of the weather, no rocks."

"Nick could you manage that?"

He glanced into the bottom of the boat. "Yes, we have line and anchor."

Nick never looked up at us. "I will do it."

He emphasized the word, "I" which meant he did not need nor want help. Just consider it done.

When Ben said the words, "Thank you," it meant we left it in his hands.

• • •

Nick was one of the first with whom I went out in the skiff. He was nearing the end in his thirty days in the halfway house and I would not have much time with him. He was one of those Indians who seem never to laugh or display emotion of any kind. He did not engage a speaker with his eyes but simply stated what was on his mind with as few words as needed. He was about five foot six or eight and always walked as if he had a pack on and was trudging uphill. He always walked at the same speed. His hair was short and he wore a jean jacket and flannel shirt whenever I saw him. If you were walking with him and lagged behind he never looked back to see if you were still there.

We were in the skiff about mid channel with our hooks down for bottom fish. He watched the tapping of his rod tip as if it were the ultra-cipher machine sending signals from the secret world to Bletchley Park.

"Ben got me sober and I will not drink again." He stated it as a fact not to be doubted. "But it was my wife who made me decide to go to Ben. My wife is a drunk. A bad one. She is mean with liquor and full of hate. She screams at me and scratches my face." He said this as he looked into the calm water.

I could see the reflection of his face in the water and saw that he was looking into my eyes in the water. We continued our conversation in this way.

"We have two little kids. Someone has to be sober or the State will take them away. The neighbors call the police because she swears and curses and throws things. She had polio in her hands and when the police come and put the cuffs on she pulls her hands out of them and spits on the cops and scratches them."

Nick looked up at me and for the first time directly into my eyes. "You will never see me touch alcohol again. Nothing biting here, want to troll?"

He showed me how to rig up so the bait would remain deep enough below the surface.

"I will row, you catch fish."

I felt guilty with him doing the work rowing. "Let me take a turn."

"Naah. I used to row for the white tourists when they trolled like you are. I can do this all day. You see how my back is bowed."

We caught two salmon and brought them to the cook to stake and broil the next day.

• • •

On occasion my good intentions backfired on me. I had Charles out with me in the skiff and I had rowed to the edge of the sound where snapper and the occasional China rockfish could be had. He sat in the bow of the boat wearing a white shirt and a scowl. He seemed to be one of those who said with his features, "I dare you to make me happy."

Charles was a thin, muscle-less native with a potbelly and fingers that were soft and boneless. He complied with the rules more like a stick of furniture would, than as a breathing client on the way to recovery.

I pulled up a beautiful China rockfish, my favorite of the rockfish meat, and he did not glance at the treasure in the ribs of the boat.

"I like that as much as yellow eye," I said looking at his eyes for signs of life.

I saw none.

"I want to congratulate you as you are finishing your thirty days. You must feel a sense of accomplishment. You will soon have a job and your own place and a future."

He did not speak or look up. His lips turned even more downward and the shades of afternoon cast dark shadows under his eyes.

For the next week Charles sought occasion to argue and bicker with the other tenants. He picked fights and ratcheted them up. To the cook he said, "I wouldn't feed this to my dog."

"Then get out of my kitchen and cook our own."

Bones was hot in anger. He shook his stir spoon in Charles' face. Cake batter splashed on his forehead. "You are a worthless bottom feeder, a waste of good air. You better get out while you can."

He slid into the TV area and sat in the shadows on a couch.

In the middle of a tense scene in the show he shouted, "The TV only has re-runs."

"Then why don't ya mow the lawn? Ya haven't lifted a finger since you came here," someone shouted at him.

Next, he went to the room where he slept and with one sweep of his arm, knocked his roommate's belongings off a shelf, walked on them, and stomped out of the house. A few of the tenants watched him leave from the doorway, his white shirt getting smaller and smaller as he made his way toward town and the binge he had prepared for. "These people could drive me to drink," he told himself.

As Ben explained it to me, "Success is the last thing some of the people want. With success comes responsibility. They cannot handle a future of getting to work on time, rent payments or responsibilities of being in a family."

Ben rubbed his chin. "I saw that one coming the day he came into the program. When he saw graduation coming he looked for a reason to get drunk and blame it on someone else. That is why he picked fights with everyone the last week."

Ben looked at me with his wise eyes. "Those kinds cannot get sober. They will not admit that they are the cause of their drinking."

Then he smiled. "At least you caught some China rockfish."

• • •

July brought with it some huge tides. The highs brought its fingers of seawater far onto our lawn that left waterlogged boards and tree limbs and flotsam behind as it receded. I would pick up empty yellow Joy bottles, net floats, and rubber toys each tide.

At low tide our bay emptied itself and the sea bottom was covered with lime-green sea grass, red sun stars and squirting butter clams. Our skiff lay upright and unmovable in the mud. I wondered if our boat, sucked as it was in the sludge, was an albatross I might regret.

I stood on the rocks above the boat and watched the crows feed on the exposed sea life. I could hear the squirting of mollusks and dripping into the bay. The smell was of rot and silage.

Anthony walked up and stood beside me. "I need a project. I have to stay busy. As long as I am doing something I don't think of booze."

"What do you have in mind Anthony?"

He nodded his head of brown curly hair at the skiff.

"That."

"The skiff?"

"Yes. It's perfect." He pointed with one extended hand as if the hand held an unfolded argument. "Just look at it," he said. "It is solid and it just needs the outside to match the quality of the inside."

"There is a lot of philosophy in those words, Anthony. If you want to tackle the project it's yours. I'll get you the help and material you need to get it done."

"Only to get it out of the water and onto a couple of beams. Then I want to take it from there." He said this never taking his eyes from the rowboat. He was already doing it in his mind.

I looked at our skiff sunk in the mud and saw it as Anthony did — with its peeling paint and old lines and green brass and what it could be. "A wonderful idea, Anthony."

• • •

The high tide lifted our boat well over the rocks and onto the lawn. We wet the grass and with a little help from my stationwagon and a long rope, pulled it above the tide line and slid two large beams underneath.

Anthony was skinny but wiry and strong. His skin was pale and his beard was thin and red-brown on his chin. I got him coveralls and the tools he wanted, and he spent his waking hours scraping and sanding and humming sections of Beethoven and Wagner.

"I feel guilty for not helping you or having any of them help."

"No," he said, "I want to make it my project. When I leave I want to leave something behind me. And it has to be of quality."

He stood back and critiqued the progress of the day. "When I am done the paint will be perfect. The brass will be polished. The lines will be new. We gotta do something about those life cushions though. And the last thing I will do is coil the line into a perfect circle."

"And you can paint the name of the boat on the bow if you can think of one."

"I hadn't thought of that. I will work on that."

Later, I went to the project. I observed the nervous tension in which he held the chisel, the sharp edge flitting back and forth like the tentacles of one of those Japanese monsters in the black and whites. I knew he was fighting his thirst then, and I knew also it was but a skirmish in his war against his alcoholism. Then the blade would steady itself and slide under the weather-lifted green paint to the farmer red below. I backed a few paces and left him in the struggle only he could wage.

We had a stretch of sunny days and his fingers moved like a weaver's as he prepared the wood for painting. On those days of sun he wore a

Hawaiian shirt with faded palm trees and kneeled before his work with his knees on a seat cushion. When progress was swift I could hear him singing the notes of "The Ride of the Valkyries" — "Da da-da da da da da-da da da daaa." And his head would sway side to side with the tune.

When rain came, he prepared a tarp to cover the site. In those days he worked in green rain gear that glistened with wetness and the reflected sky on his coat stayed to watch him work.

As I visited with him one morning I saw that he had taped a poem to the boat rail. His fingers still shook as he worked. From time to time he stopped and looked at the words, then returned to his work.

"I admire the care that you take with your project."

His answering grunt said, "I wouldn't do it any other way."

"I memorize things," he said as he pointed at the paper with his scraper. He looked up at me and continued, "Poems, verses, speeches. Anything worthwhile."

"So do I. All the time," I said, noticing the tremor in his fingers. "Last week I memorized a Bible verse. It goes like this, 'and the peace of God which passeth all understanding shall keep your hearts and minds through Christ Jesus.'"

"Say it again," he said.

I did.

"Where is that found?"

I told him.

• • •

A few days later as the sun grew warm and white seagulls passing overhead carried dark black shadows under them, Anthony finished the first coat of primer. As he waited for it to dry he enlisted the help of Nick to make the bowline for the skiff.

They sat side by side on a log bench outside the kitchen. Nick was gesturing with his right hand and held a spud made from a deer antler in the other.

"There, twist the line the opposite way it is now. There. See how it opens up and you can see three strands of line in it."

Anthony nodded.

"Now take the other end of the line in your other hand. Do you see where we unraveled it into three lines? Now take that first little line."

Nick looked at Anthony's hands, all cuts and scrapes with layers of green, red and primer — hands that now resembled the boat. Veins stood out on the back of his hands. They were steady hands now, browned in the sun.

"Let me do it first and then I will unravel it and you can do it. We will do the eye first and then we will back splice the other end. We will cut it shorter than the length of the boat. That way if it dropped into the water it couldn't tangle up in the prop."

By evening Anthony had painted the base coat over the dried primer. He stood with a wet brush in one hand and the paint pail in the other and examined his work. He ran the brush over one place where the paint had run and nodded his head in approval. He set his tools under the cover of the boat, tapped down the lid on the paint can and washed the brush.

"Ya goin' ta eat?" someone called out to him.

"Coming." And he set a sign on the boat, "WET PAINT."

• • •

Nick left the halfway house the next afternoon, his time it an end. In his fashion, he did not announce his departure to the other residents but as he left, he strode in his deliberate steps to the boat.

"Sup?" Nick asked.

"Nuthin's up," Anthony answered and he wiped his hands on his pant leg.

"I am going now."

Anthony held out his hardened hand for Nick to shake. "Thought so. Thank you for what you taught me."

"It's a good boat. I might have rowed it in the old days. This one was painted so many times I am not sure."

"Did you get any smoked fish?"

Nick tapped his backpack. "I will see you in the store or post office but not in a bar."

"A deal," Anthony agreed.

He watched the Indian walk away in his trudging gate. He tapped the lid of the paint can, washed the brush in the faucet, and propped up his sign, "WET PAINT."

• • •

It was Thursday and I decided to spend the night at the house. We had some court referral clients and I wanted to be there for a night or two. I had never seen a success from a court referral. I would nip any "what can you do to me" attitudes right away.

A warm, untimely wind rolled leaves down the road and flapped the screen door of the kitchen as if autumn had slipped inside.

Anthony was missing at dinner, an unusual thing. During his stay at the house he had only left with me to get supplies for the boat.

I went to the boat where it was still on the lawn and close to being launched. What I saw brought me great concern. Some of his tools still lay on the grass. A paintbrush, thick with Cape Cod grey paint lay on a board beside the vessel. A half full paint can was also on the board with the lid nearby, paint upward on the board. A few dry leaves and a dragonfly were stuck in the paint and the breeze moved the leaves like moth wings.

The tale this told seemed plain. It was like a pile of bird feathers below a nest. It was like a missing baby — its rattle and blue teddy bear by the playpen.

I walked around the building, passed the smokehouse and peeked inside, and went into the kitchen through the screen door. The cook had his back to me and was doing dishes in the sink.

"Bones, have you seen Anthony. It isn't like him not to be here. His tools are still out there."

He faced me, dishwater dripping from his fingers. I could smell the bleach I asked him to put in the rinse water.

"No," he said after a pause. "Come to think of it I didn't. He usually takes his food and eats on the bench outside if the weather is good. He didn't help me with the noon dishes either. He usually does."

His things were still in his room.

I sat in the TV room for a while with some of the clients. They were watching "Ironside" who was locked up in a room by criminals as they decided how they would "take care of him." From his wheelchair he cut the extension cord of a lamp in two. Then he left the frayed ends touching the floor on either side of the doorway. He got a bucket of water and made a noise in the room. When the criminal came in to investigate, he threw the water on the floor under his feet. The water completed the circuit and electrocuted the criminal. Ironside unplugged the cord, retrieved his gun, and my clients whooped it up.

As dusk approached I went back to the boat.

"Hi Boss."

I looked up at him in relief.

Anthony had a big smile on his face. "You were worried about me, Boss."

"I was."

"I sorta went on a walk about. I prayed before I left but if I had any sense I wouldn't have gone in the first place. One of the cleats on the boat was too pitted to bother with so I bought one in town."

Anthony pulled a cleat from a paper bag he had in his pocket and held it next to the rail.

"What a difference!" he exclaimed. "But here is the clincher. On the way back, I had to pass the bar I used to go to and I paused at the sidewalk and nearly went in. You will never guess what I saw."

He had a look of triumph on his face. "The door had a brass handle and there was a sign on it that said, 'WET PAINT.' Can you believe that? Well I remembered that I didn't pick up my tools or put up my own sign. So here I am."

He propped up his sign against the breeze and wiped the excess paint of his brush into the pail and tapped down the lid. He started toward the faucet to wash off the brush but stopped abruptly.

"Oh, I forgot." Anthony walked to the skiff and with the flourish of a magician, lifted a small tarp from the bow. There, in clear, simple, bold letters he had painted the name of the boat — "PEACE."

• • •

The appearance of my new client at the halfway house was a momentary deception. A bright setting sun was at her back as she stood in the open doorway and she seemed to be a cardboard shadow, flat and without features or shape. But then she stepped inside, took on dimensions and became a shapely woman with face and skin and clothing.

Her features were clearly defined — her nose, cheekbones, jawline and broad forehead resembled the old photos of Comanche warriors. Her skin was brown, her hair jet black but not shiny. I would not have been surprised to have learned that she had just finished chewing leather to make it soft for moccasins before she stepped into my doorway and this century and the halfway house.

Over her shoulders she wore a leather jacket made of split moose hide. Beads and porcupine quills had been sewn into the leather across the chest and on the sleeve ends. The smoke smell of the tanning fires that cured the leather remained, but competed with the stink of ten thousand cigarettes smoked in a dozen bars on Fourth Avenue in Anchorage. In my mind I could see her in her different life sewing in those beads by lantern light on a frozen winter night along the Tanana River where the northern lights get tangled in the trees.

She saw me looking at her jacket.

"My people are Athabaskan Indian. Some people laugh and say, 'half a gas can.' We are the ones who live in the interior of Alaska. We live mostly in villages along the rivers and many of us have kept the old ways." She made herself tall and straight as she said this. There was a pride in her declaration. She looked directly into my eyes. The woman was bold and confident in her manner. Every sentence was laid out like a challenge.

"You wonder about me," she said. "I don't have a suitcase so I wear what is important. My people wear leather and we have baskets made of birch bark and birch bark canoes. But now we have store bought too."

She paused long enough to be sure I was interested in what she had to say and continued, "They say the Apache came from us and went south. My family said that I was savage and fierce like them and should have been Geronimo's wife."

She smiled then for the first time and I found it hard not to look.

Before me was a beautiful, sensual woman, but many of her teeth were gone or broken. She removed her leather jacket and placed it on her bag and I saw a dozen or more scars from wounds and slashes that told of a life of violence.

For a second time I could not shake the similarity between her and the old photos of the Comanche. I recalled the stories of their raids on other Indian camps and subsequent slaughter of young and old — how they would arrange the severed heads of the victims in a circle around the fires. The warriors dispassionately looked upon the faces of their victims as they cooked them. My new client's eyes were brown, piercing brown and intense like a kestrel's eyes.

"Talk to me in the kitchen. Cook has gone to bed and there is always coffee around. He made cake too. What is your name? I missed it when Ben dropped you off."

"Tina. Tina Charlie."

"Tina," I thought, "is a name for a slim, blond, high school cheerleader, not the woman before me." This brown skinned native was female, but strong and muscular and powerful looking. I could see her skinning beaver, splitting wood, hauling water from a stream on a sled. For that matter, I could see her holding her own in a scrap with a man.

"Tina." I said. "Forgive me but you do not look like a Tina."

She laughed loudly. "I got sent to a boarding school when I was young and they said, 'Who are you?' One of the names for the Athabascan people is 'Dena.' It means, 'The People.' And some of our people pronounce it 'Tinneh.'

"So, when the principal of the school said, 'who are you?' I said, 'I am Tinneh.' Then he said, 'what is your other name?' and I said my father's name. So, I have been Tina Charlie ever since."

This was a femininity I was not used to. This was no submissive creature that needed the protection of a man. She had all of the attributes of a shapely female, but was completely self-assured and capable of ruling her world — except the world of alcohol.

I explained the rules, how we operated the house, and showed her a place on the female side of the house.

Tina was a court referral. A world of abstinence was not a thing that she had chosen. Her lawyer reminded her that her time spent with us was a thing to be preferred over a jail cell and the time would be taken off her sentence. I had never seen a court referral become sober. My only hold on Tina was that if her behavior warranted it I would refer her back to the court and she could sit in her cell and rake her cup back and forth across the bars.

She became a part of the group, a participant of every activity and conversation. Where she was in the building was revealed by her loud laugh and her dominant presence. I became concerned however because she seemed to seek me out when I was alone and ask questions for which I knew she knew the answers.

I was walking down the hall to the kitchen when she stepped into it from her dorm room. I moved to one side to let her pass and she moved to the side I just took. I moved to the other and so did she. I moved back to the other and she did again.

"We gotta stop meeting like this," she said, quoting a recent movie.

I made a nervous laugh.

Later in the day I was in the kitchen making up a grocery list with the cook and she came into the room. She pointed to the chair beside me, one of several empty ones in the room.

"Is this seat taken?" She asked. And she sat beside me. I could smell the perfume she had just put on. Rose water, I think. It was strong and competed with the bread in Cook's oven.

I caught his eyes and he rolled them skyward.

"We could row out in the boat," she said. "Maybe you could get something." She smiled at me. "I could work on my tan," she added.

These exchanges and encounters happened more frequently and I was not completely dense. On another occasion I needed to get groceries from the store for the house and with the list in one hand I started for the door.

"Oh, can I come too? I want to go with you."

She wore tight blue jeans with a white button shirt unbuttoned part way down.

"Just a second."

I went into the kitchen. "Bones, you have to come with me to the store."

He was stirring something with a wooden spoon. He had a puzzled look in his eyes. I spoke in a louder voice so Tina could hear it. "Remember, you wanted to be sure I got the right stuff this time. You better come with." I nodded my head vigorously as I said this.

"Well I…"

"Come with us." And I jerked my head toward the door so he would get the point.

Bones looked out of the window and smiled at me. "Oh yes I remember. You will just muck it up if I'm not there."

Bones whispered to me as we left the building, "You owe me one."

• • •

That evening I told my wife, "I think Tina is making a pass at me. Or maybe she is just trying to get management curled under her thumb."

"What!"

"Nothing is happening. I just have to be careful. I don't want to be alone with her."

But my wife was furious. "Let's go. I'm coming down there right now."

I held up a hand like a stop sign. "No. No. That isn't necessary."

"I mean it. I'm coming down now."

"You don't want to do that. She could be a handful."

"That's what I'm afraid of."

"No. Stop." I held her back with both of my hands to her shoulders. "I looked up her criminal history. On the surface she can be polite in society. She doesn't look like skid row, far from it. She is clean and polite at the house."

My wife settled down enough to listen.

"Her criminal history is public record and it took some effort but I found it. Her history is pages of violence. She was just let out of prison to come to the house."

"What is she charged with?"

"She was convicted this time of mayhem. She held a woman down in a bar fight and bit off her nose. Clean off at the skull. There was a hole into the nasal cavity."

"Then she laughed at the victim through her broken teeth and let the woman see her nose in her mouth. When the woman knew that it was her nose, Tina laughed again, chewed it a couple of times and then swallowed it so she would have nothing to sew back on."

"Yuck!" my wife said, horrified.

"No kidding."

I sat down in the chair by the door. "I understand they made her a nose from those plastic materials and grafted skin from her leg but the colors don't match and she looks like she is always wearing one of those Groucho Marks masks." I paused and added, "I just wanted you to know."

• • •

As I am thinking about noses, I am reminded of my cook, Bones. His real name was Porter Hambrick and he had one of those noses that moved up and down when he talked. Perhaps his nose muscles were attached too tightly to his upper lip, so when he formed his words his nose went up and down.

Bones was tall and thin, of ancient Normand origin. His face was very pale, like a prisoner of old time just out of his dungeon. His clothing was pure logger — high water, cutoff wool pants and wool socks with deck slippers for shoes. He always wore the grey and white pin stripe shirt and red suspenders. He was about fifty, hard worn by work and drink.

Bones was not one given to smile or engage in extended conversation. In a storytelling group he would be the one quietly listening in the corner, in a chair tipped back on two legs.

Sometimes I brought my two small boys to the kitchen to visit. It was here I saw a tempered joy and affection in his features. Bones would often bake a cake when he knew they would come and always had a treat for them stored by.

There was a place of affection in my heart for this crippled up old logger.

• • •

Once a week an AA meeting was held in the day room of the halfway house. They were held in the evening and were very well attended. I added rows from folding chairs that we kept in storage. Attendance by my people was mandatory but I personally tried to be all but invisible as I was not an alcoholic and did not belong in the group. As the manager of the house, I felt as though I should at least be somewhere on the premises.

Our policy was that our people could consume no alcohol in any amount and to do so was an immediate removal from the house.

During one of these meetings I was in the kitchen when I saw my cook, Bones, stagger in from the side door. He fell and caught his balance by bracing his hand on the wall, then stumbled to the day room before I could catch him. With a loud sigh he slumped into a seat in the back of the room.

As quietly as I could, I made my way to his seat and saw his head nod like a heavy, white pumpkin with his large pock marked nose resting on his chest. He stank of booze.

I put my hand on his shoulder and he started, and looked at me with red watery eyes.

"Bones," I whispered, "Bones."

His head nodded heavily on his chest and I shook him. "Bones, wake up. Let me talk with you in the kitchen."

"W-W-What!"

"Shhh. Come with me."

It took fully a minute for this to calibrate in his head.

"Bones, come now."

He tottered as he stood to his feet and I steadied him by holding his elbow. We shuffled to the kitchen and he collapsed into the chair by the screen door. His arms hung loosely down at his sides, his knuckles nearly touching the floor.

"Bones," I said shaking him, "Bones you have to wake up."

I shook him again.

"Bones, I'm sorry but you know the rules. You're drunk."

"Hunhh?"

"You're plastered."

He lifted his heavy head from his chest and gazed at me, a blurry thing that just crossed his vision. He seemed to focus on my face. His eyes took on a shade of blue that was the epitome of sincerity and innocence.

"I am not jhhrunk!"

He nodded his head at me as if to say, "Get that, Buster."

"I am not jhhrunk." He spaced each word for emphasis, his nose moving up and down like a witness in court affirming his testimony.

"Bones, you are very drunk. You can't even walk. You can't stay here. You will have to leave the house. We have the whole day room filled up with AA people."

Bones just stared at me as if in his mind he was thinking, "I think I know that person. Blamed if I know where."

"I will call you a cab. But you have to leave here. When you get off this binge talk to Ben and me. When you get some sobriety under your belt we can talk about you coming back."

My cook took on a new tack. "Djaa only reason I jhrink is the pain in my shoulder," he said, rubbing the place with a hand and appealing to my reason and common sense. "It is for djaa pain," he said as the blue veined nose went up and down.

Cook stared at me waiting for clarity to enter my occluded mind.

His head swayed and he continued, "You don't know the pain I go through. I used to be able to lift my arm over my head like this," and he showed me. "Now I can only lift it this high."

Bones stared at me as if I were dense. His eyes were an intense blue. He reached across to the table and took from it a humongous bottle of aspirin. He unscrewed the top holding the large cap between his thumb and forefinger and dumped fifteen or twenty white aspirin into the palm of the hand. Before I realized what he was about to do, he tossed all of them into his mouth and began to chew them.

In moments his lips were white with powder. "Sdjometimes a man has to take a swallow of Jack Daniels to ease the pain, don't ya see?"

Bones clearly was trying to council me in my unreasonableness however I did not give his argument the attention it deserved because when he tossed the handful of pills into his mouth, the white bottle cap which he had held between his thumb and forefinger had stuck firmly on his nose. His lips were white and the white bottle cap waved at me with every word he spoke. It was difficult to lend proper weight to someone who says, "I am not jhrunk," when their lips are white and a bottle cap is stuck to their nose and is waving like John Philip Sousa's baton.

I called a taxi and watched him as we waited for it, looking for any ill effects of the aspirin. Bones seemed not to notice the white appendage that was still stuck to his nose and there was no inclination to remove the bottle cap.

I gave the taxi the address and paid the fare in advance. As the cab left the house in the half-darkness Bones looked back through the taxi window. The aspirin top shone white like the moon.

• • •

I once had nearly all of the officials and department heads of the village of Yakutat in my halfway house all at once. Yakutat is an isolated fishing town of about six hundred people on the northern coast of the Gulf of Alaska and the only way in or out was to fly or go by boat across the Gulf. I wondered how it came about that the entire government decided to get sober at the same time, and more, who was running the place now.

It seemed to be that there was a sincere determination among them to reclaim their lives and character. They knew each other as friends and relatives and the atmosphere among them in our house was cordial and supportive.

As it came to be, the group gathered informally in the kitchen each evening over coffee and the cakes Bones often made. Stories flowed from the memory banks of these men — hunting stories, fishing disasters, the glacier that moved so quickly toward the coast that it trapped sea mammals in a fjord, which then became an inland lake. There were stories of clam diggers whose feet became stuck in mud on the vast tide flats with an incoming tide and futile rescue attempts.

They talked about the great earthquake that wiped out so much of the Alaska coast, and they told stories about bouts of drinking.

One evening as Bones leaned back in his chair in the corner holding his mug of coffee, and the men of Yakutat told yarns in the warm kitchen, Emmet Tweedy entered the room.

Emmet was a recovered alcoholic who had given counsel to most of these men and had explained the tools of sobriety.

"Hey, can anyone join you guys?"

They all greeted him at the same time. "Emmet, sit here," and they pointed at a place centered in the room. Bones pointed a crooked finger at the cake pan.

Emmet Tweedy was easy to describe. He was Snidley Whiplash of the Rocky and Bullwinkle show. Snidley was the arch villain and bane of Dudley Do-right, the hero of the Royal Canadian Mounted Police. It would not have taken much effort to imagine Emmet Tweedy being the one who tied little Nell to the railroad tracks. Perhaps, we could think, he came inside our kitchen this night just to listen for the train whistle.

Emmet twisted his thin, black, waxed mustache as he lowered himself into a chair. He had black hair, slicked back, and a thin mustache and goatee. He could have been Snidley auditioning for the role of Lucifer. As he sat down, his smile narrowed his tiny coal-black eyes into shifty little slits.

Emmet Tweedy was fifty-two years old but could have passed for seventy. The wrinkles that covered every micro-inch of his skin were deep and dark, the kind that a washrag can never reach. When I thought of the wrinkles of his face I recalled the salmon we had smoked out back where the screen left its imprint — deep, dark, and permanent.

"I am fifty-two years old," he said after a time. "Twenty-six of those years have been spent in prison. And when you think about it, I didn't start jail until my late teens, and I have been sober for nearly eight, so almost all of my life has been in prison. When I was on the street I only thought of booze, babes, and bags of money. When I was in jail I was always planning on how to get some."

Ardel was the only white guy from Yakutat. He was a skinny,

strawberry blond about thirty-five and was the head of the Public Works Department. "Man, I was never arrested for crimes. I would just start drinking with my buddies and wind up in the drunk tank. In the morning I would have to ask the jailor what I had done the night before."

Emmet waited for Ardel to finish. "Man, you have to watch it with your friends. The wrong ones are worse than booze, let me tell you."

Emmet looked at the floor to collect his thoughts before he continued. "One of the first times I went to prison was because I teamed up with an idiot who didn't have both oars in the water. You wouldn't believe this but it is true."

He straightened himself in the chair and continued. "We were going to rob this bank in a small town and my partner said, 'Two of us would look suspicious. You just wait outside in the car and keep the engine running.'

"You won't believe this but it is true so help me. He goes in with a note and gives it to the teller. He has his hand in his coat pocket with his finger out like he has a gun inside. He's doing his imitation of Machine Gun Kelly. He looks at the teller right in her eyes and he rolls his eyes up and down toward his pocket so she sees it.

"Anyway, Elmer, that's his name, has kinky black hair and huge black eyebrows like caterpillars and the teller thinks he is in a disguise, only it's him himself. Finally, she gets the point, 'There's a gun in my pocket.'

"The note says, 'This is a stik up hand over yur kash.' The teller is a blond but even she can tell this guy doesn't have both oars in the water.

"'I am sorry sir. Can you see that sign? It says, 'First Bank — Your Quality Bank.' We do not honor anything that is not first quality. We just never do. I'm sorry but this is policy. You will just have to correct your spelling and we will honor your request. You can use the desk over there. These are the words you misspelled.'

"Of course, she called the cops. So, there is my partner over at the check stand writing. I can see him through the window. He is licking the lead pencil and printing with his best penmanship.

"Then I hear the sirens coming down the road. I waited as long as

I dared and got ready to peel rubber. Just as I am about to hit the gas and go, he runs from the bank and does a head first swan dive into the back seat just as two squad cars hem us in."

Ardel stared at Emmet to see if he is pulling his leg. Floyd, the head of Sanitation and Utilities removes his glasses and watches Emmet for signs of mirth.

"It is true so help me. But you want to know the kicker? He winds up being my 'cellie' for the next two years. Now, I ask you, who do you think I pick to do the next job with. You guessed it. Maybe we are both in that elevator that doesn't go all the way to the top."

Emmet looked at the floor again. "Maybe I hang out with idiots because it makes me feel so smart when I am around them."

Across the room I notice that Ardel, of Public Works, is laughing and holding his crotch and I think he might wet himself laughing.

"I was with him on a job in Idaho," Emmet continues. "This one was all my fault. There are basically two types of safes to crack — peel or punch. This one was a rough one because the safe was in the main room of the business with a big picture window in front and anyone could see it from the sidewalk.

"Well my idiot partner came up with the idea of using a screen to put behind the window and he hung a couple pictures on it so it liked like an empty room and it seemed to work fine. The problem was that he did not tell me that this was a peel type safe. They are made of layers of steel laminated together. The only way to get into that kind of safe if you don't know the combination, is to peel every layer of metal, one at a time, until you got inside. That can take all night and you might not get it done before someone comes in to open the store. And you don't have much getaway time.

"Anyway, we are working in the dark and I am tired so I tell him to take a turn at it and I was going to the kitchen to get something to drink. Well there is a window there too so I don't dare to turn on a light but I find the coffee pot on the burner and turn it on and get it hot and settle back for a cup.

"I am so tired of peeling with that crow bar I lean back on a chair and take a couple swigs and I am about to fall asleep when I shriek, I mean, shriek. My insides are scalding. My throat feels like all the skin is gone. I am gasping for breath and think I am about to die. I am looking for a sink with water and my partner has rushed back to my side.

"'Quiet! You shouldn't scream so loud. We are going to get caught!'

"Well, we did get caught. They arrested me in the emergency room at the hospital. What I drank was the acid that they clean coins with. But no problem — I had nearly two years in an Idaho prison to heal."

Norris, the head of the Electric Department, nodded his head and smiled. "It is lucky you have a voice to be a counselor." Norris is a thin man and his hair is flat on his head as if he had just taken off his hardhat. (I have never seen a fat electrician.) Bones rocked back and forth and smiled.

"I just never learned. I was with the same guy in the Dakotas. It was in one of the badlands towns — one of those with one or two streetlights. It had a saloon called 'Wild Bill's, named after Wild Bill Hickok, the gunfighter.

"We drove through real slow to scope out the place. It was one of those nights when there is a light rain and the street is slightly wet and it all smells fresh. Now we ease by in the car and at the intersection the light is green and Main Street reflects green on the wet pavement.

"'Hey,' Elmer yells out, 'It's an omen. The whole street is green. We have the green light. It's an omen, I tell ya.' Elmer looks at me and he is waving those black, bushy, Groucho Marx eyebrows at me. He is grinning at me like a fool.

"'The town does look empty — no one to watch us do a job. 'Nice,' I think. 'Yes, but any movement from us and we will stick out like a sore thumb,' I tell my idiot friend.

"'Hey, I tell you, it's an omen. Can't fail,' he says and he is hitting the top of the steering wheel with both hands. 'I'll show you the place we are going to hit. I scoped it out last week. The place to hit is the office for the mill. The town closes up at night and I saw the safe — a piece of cake. It's a punch safe. Easy in, easy out.'

"'Let's go around the block again,' I tell him, 'I want to be sure about this.' We make a big sweep around the area and we pass a school grounds and I yell, 'Stop!' and he slams on the brake and I nearly hit my head on the window.

"'What!?' he yells.

"'There. Over there on the playground.' There is a slight wind and it is swinging the swings back and forth as if people were swinging on them. Only there is no one on them of course.

"'Right there on the swings,' I tell him.

"'I don't see nuthin,' he says.

"'That's what I mean. You can't see them. It's like someone is watching us.' He lowers his push-broom eyebrows at me. 'Have you been hitting the sauce?' I am exasperated. 'Never mind,' I tell him.

"Well we decide to do it. Everything like clockwork. He gets in in the afternoon and uses the bathroom, loosens a ceiling tile and gets into the crawl space above and waits until midnight when he crawls down and unlatches the front door. He reminds me this is a piece of cake, what could go wrong?

"It's just like he said: a punch safe. You just hold a punch (which I brought with me) over the center of the combination, and then you whack it with a sledge hammer (which I also brought with me).

"Well, because of the picture window we don't dare turn on a light so we are working in the dark. I hold the punch over the combination and I tell him, okay now give it a whack.

"I can hear his clothes moving as he draws back the sledge hammer, and I hear him grunt when he swings with all his might. Wham. Right on my hand. The hammer makes a thud sound because it is meat that it hits.

"I scream. I mean, I really scream. My hand is busted up good. The top of my hand is smashed and I feel blood squirting out my fingertips. Just in case he didn't hear, I scream again. 'Yaaah!'

"'Shuush,' he says, 'Someone will hear. You always yell on these jobs.'

"Well, we have come this far and I have a busted hand in this so I say that we will finish the job. 'Okay,' I tell him as I switch hands and hold the punch in the other one. 'This time be careful.'

"I hear the swish of his jacket and his grunt as he gives it all his might. Wham! He did it again. He smashed my other hand. I screamed, really screamed.

"He is awfully quiet there in the dark. 'Are you still there?' I yell into the blackness.

"After a time, with a note of sadness in his voice he says, 'I guess this is it, Emmet. You got no more hands. Even if I held the punch, you couldn't swing the hammer.'

"'Oh, I could manage that tonight,' I tell him.

"Well they busted me at the emergency room. When we left the building, we forgot to shut the front door all the way and when the cop looked inside he saw the punch and hammer on the floor, and the blood where we tried to crack the safe and put two and two together.

"Jail in the Dakotas are not what it's cracked up to be."

Harold, head of the Police and Fire Commission, is laughing with tears streaming from his eyes. Emmet is holding his hands in the air like claws. He stares at them as if he were reliving the night in the little town.

Virgil Brown, the director of Tourism and Commerce shakes his head. "Did you ever pull one off?"

Emmet smiles, his eyes gleam like silver dollars.

"When we got out of jail in the Dakotas it was cold. We were arrested in summer and got out in the winter and a howling wind was blowing the snow off the highways. It was a blizzard and the highways were bare and we walked down it with one foot on the pavement and one on the snow on the shoulder in order to walk a straight line 'cause you couldn't see twenty feet. We were so miserable looking that we caught a ride with a trucker right away who took us all the way to Montana. We figured we would go there where we weren't known and maybe even go straight, no more jails, only booze and broads."

Emmet leaned forward and placed both his hands on his knees and we could see his face in the light. The wrinkles looked like he wore a hair net over his face.

"The temptation was too much. We found ourselves in a small mining town in central Montana and it was payroll week. Everyone in the burg got paid the same day and this town, we heard, only believed in cash, no checks stuff.

"My partner, Elmer, can't stand it. 'This is so easy. The people here don't even lock their doors. The bank is like cowboy times. Are you thinking what I'm thinking, Emmet?'

"'No. I definitely am not.'

"'Yes, you are. Your fingers are itching. Look at 'em. Nobody around. Punch safe. Easy peasy.'

"Elmer holds his hand out and like a promise. His brows look like Bert the muppet. I think for a minute. 'This time you hold the punch.'

"'Deal,' he says.

"This bank was so easy. The town's entire payroll in one bank. The streets were empty and we got into the old bank just by sliding a credit card through the side. This was perfect. It was cold outside and if someone were to come down the sidewalk you could hear their steps in the crunchy snow a block away so we didn't even worry much about the picture window.

"Elmer held the punch and I gave it one swing and presto, we were in. The door creaks open on rusty hinges and the entire payroll for the whole town is right there in front of our faces.

"In silver dollars!"

The kitchen burst into laughter.

Emmet spread his hands out in a gesture of, "We should have known."

"I should have known — Montana! Silver dollars. These people don't want paper. They want something that feels like value. They want their money in silver."

The whole kitchen is caught up in the dilemma. Ardell of Public Works is holding both his hands on his stomach and rocks backward in his chair, both his legs lifted off the floor.

"Now we got a problem. How do we get away with a gillion dollars of coins? We fill our pockets. We had a couple of backpacks and we fill them too. There were a few bank bags around and we fill them up. We have hardly made a dent in the loot. We trudge out the door. We must have two hundred pounds of coins apiece. We can hardly walk but we make it to our car, which we hid in the alley.

"We dump it all in the trunk. 'We gotta make trips. We'll fill up the car,' Elmer gasps as his eyes bug out with the weight.

"So, we make trips. We can hardly move with the weight. I am puffing with the strain and my eyes blur. At the car, Elmer runs his hands through the coins and chuckles insanely like some kind of King Midas or something. He is getting into the coins thing.

"We are on our fourth trip when we hear the sirens. It was too good to last. Apparently one of our bags was leaking silver dollars on the sidewalk. Not a normal thing even in Montana. Someone saw it and called it in.

"So here comes the squad car behind us and we try to run from the cops. Hey, try outrun a cop with two hundred pounds of coins on you. My legs are like rubber. I am out of breath and I am seeing visions.

"The cop doesn't even chase us. He just drives right behind us about ten feet back. I look over my shoulder and the cop is smiling.

"I can't take another step. I can't lift my legs. I am out of breath and can't even talk, I just puff. The cop drives alongside of us and quietly says, 'Need a ride, boys?' He says it so sweet and smarmy. (I hate a smart aleck cop.) 'Need a ride boys? I have a place you can stay.'"

Bones brought him some coffee and he sipped before he continued.

"When I got out of prison that time I just became a drunk. I went from binge drinking to daily drinking. I couldn't control when I started or stopped, either one. I would do short stints in jail for disorderly and nights in the drunk tank but never big stuff. I lost the mind to plan out anything more than the day I was in. I could only think of the next drink.

"My partner, Elmer was just as bad. He also got this thing for coins. 'Feel 'em,' he would say, 'they are solid, and cold and heavy and they don't get soggy. That's what I want.'

"Finally, a cop showed mercy on me. Not what you would think. I was drunk in a ditch and shivering and had soiled myself.

"'People have been making it easy for you to stay a drunk. They give you a flophouse bed and meals at the mission station. They even wash your clothes. Not me. I am just going to leave you there. You can stay in that ditch until you are miserable enough to leave that life. You still have enough brain left to make a choice.'

"And he walked away.

"That was eight years ago and I haven't had a drink since he walked away."

"What about your partner?" It was Bones who spoke, his first words of the evening.

"Elmer never stopped drinking. He died a few years ago just before I got clean. He was stumbling drunk walking down an old road in the Dakotas outside of Minot because he had heard there was a rodeo going on. He fell into a ditch and passed out and died there. No one saw him in the snow and the snowplows covered him when they did the roads and they never found him until spring.

"They said his hands were in his pockets when they found him and they figured that they were freezing. But I heard that his fingers were coiled around a couple rolls of quarters and a few silver dollars."

Emmet stopped speaking. Moments passed and like a preacher who applies his message to his parishioners, he gazed into the faces of the people in the room.

"You can be me, who finally decides he will do whatever it takes to get out of that life, or — you can stumble through life with a few silver dollars clasped in your frozen fingers."

• • •

There was a bang and the wheezing of a car engine outside the house. Ben's car seemed to have emphysema. The car door slammed and I heard a voice say, "Gotta fix that someday."

I went to the door. "Hi Ben."

"Hello. I have a new client for you. He just finished his thirty days sobriety and now needs a halfway house."

I shook his hand and saw that his eyes were clear and expectant. His clothing was clean and neat. I noticed his shoes. They were nearly new running shoes with white thunderbolts along the sides.

# Slim and Hal

Slim got out of his truck at the harbor parking lot moving just like the paper past-due bill he had just crumpled into a ball and tossed on the dash: slowly, noisily and unfolding itself. His feet showed first under the door, then his long legs, joint by joint. Then his arms came out like a structure of an erector set. His head was next, bent low under the doorframe and his torso followed. He was too tall for the compact vehicle but it was cheap when he bought it and good on gas. He got his deep-sea rod, tackle and rain-suit from the back and started for the ramp but then returned to the truck. He retrieved the twenty he had hidden in the ashtray. Hal was grumbling the last couple fishing trips about always putting in the gas. "Well, why shouldn't he? It was his boat," Slim reasoned.

Slim was thin as a scarecrow and his clothes hung loosely down from his shoulders and scrawny hips. In his rain gear and large black hat with the wide brim to keep off the rain, he could have passed for one. His skin was pale, moon colored, cheese-like, and between the hat and his collar his skin hung in wrinkles at the neck like a paper bag cinched up and tied. To add to that effect, the harbor light above darkened his eye sockets in shadow. Slim usually moved slowly and talked slowly and his presence unnerved people when he oozed up to them but did not talk.

At the top of the ramp near the shelter where fishermen often worked their nets, he stopped and listened as he gazed over the harbor. Daylight would begin shortly after four in the morning this time of year and the first faint hint of light showed over Mount Verstovia. Otherwise, the town was in darkness. He heard a dog bark twice from a house across the harbor and a sea lion made a loud exchange of air as it made its rounds in the harbor.

He saw Hal's car in the lot and thought he would give him time to get the boat ready for their fishing trip. "No use disturbing a man when he's working."

Someone was trying to start an outboard motor. "Hal," Slim thought.

Slim listened. "Rup-up-up-up. Rup-up-up-up," Over and over. He listened for several minutes. The skinny man in baggy clothes figured that he would wait until Hal got it going before he went down. When finally the "Rup-up-up" ended in a long hiss, like an exhausted person giving a last breath, Slim descended the ramp. "If this trip is going to come off I better get down there."

He moseyed down the ramp, noting its steepness with the low tide. "If we timed it so we came back at high tide it won't be so steep coming back up. I'll mention that one to Hal."

An explosion of air startled slim and he jumped back to the middle of the dock. A huge bull sea lion broke surface and swam to the edge. Its nostrils were flared. His black eyes blinked and focused on Slim. Even in this light Slim could see red where the white of its eyes should be.

"You must be out looking for a missus. Well it ain't me."

Slim kept to the middle of the dock. It was said that a bull sea lion had grabbed someone on the dock by his shirtsleeve and pulled him into the water. He tapped the edge of the dock with the end of his fishing rod. "You just keep your distance, hear."

He walked up to the boat. Hal was hovered over the motor, both hands working like a squirrel eating a pinecone.

Slim dropped his tackle box on the dock next to Hal. The thump was loud in the harbor.

"No use trying to scare me, Slim. Ah seen ya comin' down the dock. The sun rises quicker than you walk."

Slim bent down near the motor like a doctor checking an abscess. "Won't start, huh."

Hal glared at him. "You could tell that all the way from your car. Na it won't start."

"Flooded," Slim pronounce as a verdict.

"No, it isn't flooded, Slim."

"It is."

Hal raised his head and stared at the apparition who stood above him.

"Is," Slim repeated, "I could smell gas all the way up to the car."

"Then, why didn't you come down to help?"

"I just like to see you suffer, Hal."

Hal slumped over the motor.

"Did you pump the ball good and firm?"

"Did that. Here, feel it."

"I believe you."

"How about — did you open the air vent at the tank?"

"Of course. Do you think this is my first rodeo?"

"Spark plug?"

Hal pushed air out of his mouth. His eyes were small and porcine. "The spark plug is good."

Slim shoved his cheek out with his tongue.

"Well, only one thing left, Hal. Is the key on?"

"Hey," Hal said, pointing, "What's that over there?"

"Nice try. You just don't want me to see you turn on the key."

Hal had one of those lower lips that stuck out, especially when he did not want to admit something. Slim pointed at his lip with his forefinger, nearly touching it.

"You otter put snuff in that lip. You could be a professional, I'm telling you."

"Ain't you the talkative one this morning. You must have saved all of your words of the month to use on me."

"You're welcome, Hal."

He placed his tackle and rod in the bow, untied the lines, and stepped into the boat. "I hope you bought bait, Hal."

Hal started to say something like, "If I waited for you we'd never have none," but he just stuck his lower lip out instead.

Slim sat in the bow of the boat with several life preservers under his back and extended his legs toward the stern. "Why did you get me up so early? It's dark as a coalmine still. Oh, watch you don't hit that sea lion."

Hal sat beside the motor on a milk carton with a life cushion on it. He was hunched up, round like a ball in his shortness. His left hand was on the tiller and he maneuvered slowly out of the harbor leaving no wake behind the boat.

"It's that stretch just before we get to Vitskari Rocks that always bothers me. It can get so rough there. I want to hit slack tide so we don't get beat up."

Slim lay back on the preservers and studied his friend. "Do you know who you remind me of, Hal?"

Hal slowly took his eyes off the black ocean ahead and looked at the apparition in the bow of the boat. He had been looking for floating logs in the water that he might hit underway. The tides had been very high and logs had been lifted from the beaches and floated in the open water.

"No, Slim. Who."

Slim reappraised the ball of a person at the motor before he answered. "The Beagle Boys."

"What?"

"The Beagle Boys. You know, the Beagle Boys."

"You can say, 'Beagle Boys' til you are tired. I don't know the Beagle Boys."

"Sure you do. The Beagle Boys." Slim said the words slowly and emphasized each word so even Hal could understand.

In the lessening darkness he saw Hal's lip thrust out.

"Don't you know literature? The Beagle Boys are the ones in the cartoons that are always trying to steal Scrooge McDuck's money."

Hal's memory banks were in overdrive. He wondered also who McSlim in the bow would have rooted for — Scrooge or the Beagle Boys.

"You mean those guys in the masks, black hair, big and round?"

"The same," Slim said in triumph. "You look just like 'em."

Hal seemed sad. He focused ahead as he passed out into Eastern Channel. The swell of the open ocean gave a loping motion to the boat.

"Ya know, Slim. You might be right. My old lady told me I look like Black Pete."

"Now you got me. I don't know Black Pete."

"He is the bad guy in the Mickey Mouse cartoons. I don't think my wife ever thought much of me."

He looked sad hunched over the tiller with his black curly hair, like a big ball under his halibut jacket.

Slim was quiet for a time. He sat up and wrapped his arms around his knees to hold himself in a sitting position. "I'm sorry, Hal."

"Slept on the couch again."

Slim looked forward of the boat and watched the water ahead, more so not to look at his friend. The water had a swell but was smooth. The incipient daylight placed shadow before the rise of each swell.

"Watch that log, Hal."

He swerved the boat and steered around it. "If it weren't for the shadow I wouldn't have seen it. If we were a half hour earlier it would have been too dark to see it."

"Ya know, Slim. When the wife tol' me I reminded her of Black Pete, I was dumb enough to think she was sayin' sumthin' nice. I was thinking she meant like a famous outlaw or hansom pirate or sumthin'."

They were passing Six Mile Rock and the ocean swells were four feet but far apart. The skiff easily climbed the slopes and slid smoothly down the next. There was no chop on the swells and the surface of the water was as smooth as mercury.

"Then I saw the cartoon. 'What ya mean by that, callin' me Black Pete. I ain't at all like him.'

"'Just look at yourself,' she yells at me. 'There you are in your wife beater and you haven't shaved and you got a gut and,' she looks at me and she sneers and her nose wrinkles up like she smells something. 'You're dirty and you smell.'"

Slim was holding the line attached to a side cleat for balance and he picked at it with his fingers as he listened.

"My own wife, Slim. Anyway, I looked in the mirror. And there he was — Black Pete. When I rubbed my bristles on my face I really did see dirt fall off. I even got teeth like a bulldog on the bottom. I guess I am not much to look at. But I put food on the table and I don't beat her none."

Slim was not sure what to say. He picked at the line he held in his hands and looked off to the bow. The light was still grey. The sun had not yet risen over the horizon. A couple of pigeon guillemot sea birds dived into the swell ahead of the boat with their beaks full of needlefish.

Hal changed the subject. "See the swells here. That's why I wanted to be here at slack tide. This area always has seas coming from two directions and the chop on the swell can beat you to death. I timed it for slack tide so there would not be any tide to run against the sea and no wind to blow the tops off the waves. This is smooth going."

Slim was back to his taciturnity. He just nodded and smiled.

Hal took his hand off the throttle long enough to put on his rain slicker to break the wind of the boat's speed.

A few horned puffin with their red and yellow parrot-like beaks swam near the skiff.

"Know sumpin' I allus wondered 'bout them puffin birds when they come up with a whole beak full of needle fish. How can they catch the second ones without losing the first ones in their beaks?"

He looked at Slim in the bow and gave him time to comment. He did not.

"Well, I wondered," he said, emphasizing the word, "I," and added quietly, "all to myself."

"I heard you," Slim assured him. "I just don't always answer."

They arrived at Vitskari Rocks, a shallow, rocky, rough water area marked by a buoy to warn mariners. "I want to get us near where we got all the fish last time." He positioned himself east and west by lining the marker buoy with the peak of Mount Edgecumbe. He then placed Biorka Island on his bow and a place below Verstovia Mountain off his stern.

"We're here," he said as he shut off the engine. The last spray from the bow hissed on the surface.

Slim sat upright on the cushion and loosened the hook from the eye of the rod. "My ol' lady called me, 'Lurch.'"

He reached into the package and grabbed a still frozen herring and ran the circle hook through the body twice. He let off the brake and let the sinker take the bait to the bottom keeping his thumb on the reel so it did not spin too fast and tangle. When hit finally hit bottom a hundred feet below, he cranked it up from the bottom a few turns and set the brake.

"Lurch," he repeated.

"You mean the butler guy on the Addams Family what goes slow up to ya and doesn't talk, that one?"

"Yep, that one. The wife watches good stuff on TV."

"Your wife really calls you, 'Lurch.' Wow."

After a long pause Slim drawled, "You got one nibbling on your hook."

"I know. I'm holdin' the rod ain't I? I can feel it."

He stared at the tipping of Hal's rod. "Yeh, she did say it and it weren't no joke neither — it was the way she said it — 'Lurch,' like I was a joke or an insect, or like I should be working in a mortuary or sumpthin'."

Hal tried to change the subject. "Did ya hear 'bout the guy who was at the kitchen table the other day and all at once he grabbed a knife and stabbed the corn flakes box over and over?"

Slim listened, his eyes on the jolting of Hal's rod tip. "Arrested him. Know what for?"

Slim lifted his eyes from the rod tip to his friend's eyes.

"Yep. They hauled him off. Found out he was a cereal killer."

Slim gave no indication that he even heard his pal. "Ya got one on there, Hal. Ya gonna reel it up or no?"

"Hey, you zombie, I'm the one holdin' the rod ain't I? I can feel it."

Then the tip of his rod bent down, all the way down to the water. The first eyelets were fully under water. Hal jumped to his feet, the first time he had risen the whole trip. He wrapped both his arms under the rod and hoisted back with all his might, his face contorted with the effort.

"It's a big one." He hoisted his back as far as he could and quickly reeled the slack back down to the water.

"You aren't hooked on the bottom are you?"

"Na. I can feel it jerking." Hal stood in his roundness in his yellow rain coat with his thin legs braced against the sides and continued to hoist and reel.

"You remind me of one of those M&M candies," Slim thought to himself, "One of the yellow ones with the letters written on the side," but he would not say it aloud.

The rod seemed about to break. "Let off some drag," Hal shouted.

The skiff listed to the side and Hal was like a yellow marble that rolled to the down side of the boat.

"Hey, it's taking the line and swimming away with it."

"Can't be. That's a halibut on your line, sure. They don't swim they just fight where they are."

"Look at the line, Slim."

He braced his arms under the rod and let the fish fight against the drag. He pulled and reeled and the fish took the hook and ran with it. The line was no longer under the boat but thirty or forty feet off the side.

"I think it's coming closer to the top. I see something white coming up. Hey what is that?"

"Slim, Look. What am I seeing? Look." Hall was puffing, out of breath. "What, huh, huh, huh, is that?"

Slim stood to better see. "Its two things." He studied the water more closely. "You got two things on your hook."

Then Hal could also make it out. "That's a shark. It's a shark, I tell you. Look at it. A shark has my halibut."

Slim watched the scene with his mouth open. A huge dorsal fin broke the surface, then they could make out the shark as it thrashed in the water.

"Look, Slim! Look at it!"

The shark slashed its head side to side like a knife fighter left and right. The water foamed white in the frenzy. Then with a flick of its tail it disappeared into the blackness.

"Sharks don't eat halibut, least I never heard of it. They have plenty of salmon sharks that will take salmon, but I never have heard of 'em taking a halibut."

Hal lifted the hook from the water. Only the head and gills and a chunk of its length remained. A crescent bite showed where the shark jaws had severed the flesh. The incision was clean. A few white and pink tendrils of stringy flesh hung from the head.

For a moment they imagined the drama that had occurred far below the surface of the sea, where colors faded to shades of grey — a struggling halibut, its white belly flashing above a wandering shark; the attack in the depths, an assault committed in utter privacy. Was the attack a meal or malice?

"Man you don't know what goes on where we can't see, do ya?"

Hal collapsed on the milk crate, gasping, his open mouth working like a first caught fish does as it lies on the dock. He balanced the rod upright on the bottom of the boat with one hand and stared at the chunk of meat on his hook. The head swayed back and forth in rhythm to Hal's breathing.

"That was a big one, Hal. See how far apart the eyes are on the head. Bet it was well over a hundred."

Hal's lower lip was thrust out as he continued to catch his breath. "You said I look like an M&M."

Slim was horrified that he might have said it out loud. He thought back in his mind. I know I didn't say it out loud. I know I thought it but I don't think I really said it. "Nah, I don't think I said that. You must have heard something else."

"You said it. I heard it."

He lowered himself on to the cushions in the bow. "I didn't know I said it."

He leaned his rod against the side where a nibble would make the tip slide along the edge and the scraping alert him to a fish. "I'm sorry, Hal. You are my best friend."

He looked away from his partner to the water where the shark had been and formulated what he would say next. Pieces of halibut floated to the top. Around the place low flying gulls swarmed, dipped to the surface and flew away with pink threads of flesh in their bills.

"It's not so good at my house either." His rod slid along the rail and he tested it for a bite, then replaced it on the side. "The city shut off the power to my house last week and I'm up to my neck in bills."

"All I hear over and over is, 'Do you know what it's like to go to the neighbors and have to ask if you can store some things in their freezer. You think they don't know what's going on. They do I tell you. Do you know how embarrassing that is? Huh?'"

"That woman will not let up." He looked up to his friend in the bow. "And she is yelling at me with those white curlers in her black hair like Frankenstein's wife. I can almost see sparks of electricity coming off her, only I know we don't have power."

"'My mom told me not to marry you. I should have listened to her,' she says. "And then she yells at me, 'Why don't you answer me? Why don't you talk? You're just avoiding the issue.'"

"Hal, you know me. I just don't talk much."

He jigged his rod a few times and continued, "So we don't have lights and have to use lanterns. Now she is yelling that the house stinks like kerosene.

"Sometimes I wonder if life can ever get worse."

Slim jigged his rod up and down and leaned it again on the rail. The sun was rising red just over the skyline and seemed to melt on the surface of the calm water. A gull glided down low over the boat making a pass at the package of herring not quite daring to grab it so near the two men. Hal retrieved a herring from the bag and ran his hook twice through the body and let it down.

The two men quietly fished, each of them captured by their own thoughts. A quarter mile away in the only other boat in the area, a father and his son fished. The man's voice carried clearly across the water to Hal's boat as if they were speaking next to them. "You got one on, son."

The sounds alone told the story in the boat. The sound of a tackle box slamming against the side of the boat told of a boy jumping up, knocking it over in his hurry.

"That's it, Danny. Hoist it up. Reel down to the water. Hoist it up. Reel down. Good job."

"I see it coming up, Dad."

"Good job. Just a few more hoists."

Another thump from the distant boat said without words that the father was retrieving his gaff hook.

A splash and a "thunk" and then the flapping of the fish against the metal bottom ended the narrative.

The chatter of the boy in the distant boat floated clearly over the water and entered Slim and Hal's vessel like a visitor and took its place on a milk crate.

Hal smiled through the bristle of his face, his lower lip no longer protruding, but a part of a wide grin. His two lower canines showed in his overbite. His eyes smiled into thin slits.

Slim propped himself up by his elbows on the life jackets, turned and gazed at the distant boat. He was surprised at the distance, for the sound carried so clearly on the crisp air. The boat was, however, far away.

Colors could not be seen on the far boat. All was black and white like a memory from decades before. The red and white of the Lund were dark grey and light grey. The two fishermen were but silhouettes. He caught a glimpse of something bright in the boat — a belly of a fish, a sandwich in cellophane, a father's hand messing up a son's hair as he gazed into his brown eyes?

Slim turned back and saw Hal in the stern. "What are you grinning at you ol' fool?"

But Slim also grinned.

"I never saw it so calm here. There isn't a ripple for miles."

Slim nodded slowly in answer — about the speed a fisherman jigs his line.

Hal suddenly looked up. Something made him do so. His eyes caught sight of Slim in the bow. Slim's eyes were wide with whites all around the pupils. His mouth was wide open. He was pushing himself up with one of his hands and with the other was in the act of pointing.

Hal spun around in the direction of the finger. He sucked in his breath. The sound it made was that that the wind makes when it passes over power lines in the winter.

There. Close. Very close. Only a few boat lengths away a humpback whale burst straight up out of the water. Its bulk ascended higher and higher — ten feet, twenty, more. Hal fell backward from the crate and scrambled to the stern of the skiff lest the whale fall on him in the boat.

The ascent of the whale continued upward, like a three-story building rising from the ocean. Its dorsal showed above the water. Just before the humpback reached the zenith of the rise, three killer whales rose on three sides of the humpback and their white teeth clamped to its flesh in midair. Their rise from the water was timed so that as the humpback was still rising, theirs began to fall. In each mouth was a bit of hide and flesh. As the killer whales began to fall into the water, their body weights tore huge strips of flesh from the whale. The baleen whale was stripped like a banana. The outer skin was grey-black with a layer of white blubber under that. The meat of the humpback was crimson and exposed in the air.

The tear sounded like bacon when it is dropped into a hot pan. The intensity of the event muted all other senses — the smell of raw meat, the moan of the whale, the body heat of the attacked mammal.

The splash was gigantic and fell into the boat drenching Slim and Hal. Hal's hair hung from his head like strips of black seaweed. He spit water from his mouth. Saltwater stung his eyes. An inch of water lay in the bottom of the boat.

There was one splash. Only that. The whales did not fall on the boat. There was no struggle to the death on the surface. The attack did not continue elsewhere on the surface of the sea.

The friends did not move for a time. Would the whales next come up under the boat and toss it high into the air like a piece of weightless bark? Would a huge tail slam the boat to pieces or sink it altogether?

Slim placed both his hands on the rail and hoisted himself up on his shaking legs. He rose first, bent over, cautiously, then to his full height. He slowly stood — as someone does when he walks on new ice, uncertain it will hold.

The ocean was calm. Dead calm. They expected massive turmoil and struggle — killer whales swim in wolf packs. Hal recalled a pack of wolves would take a moose and hamstring it so it could not walk or crawl away, and eat it alive for days. They would eat on the living moose and return the next day to consume more of the helpless animal whose eyes were fixed ahead in shock trying not to think it was being eaten away.

"Hal, there's nothin' happening here."

"Look how calm it is. You can see for miles — nothin' as far as you can see. There is no spray, no slash, no churning water, nothin'," He paused. "Like it all didn't happen."

Hal lifted himself up from where he fell from the crate. "I'm afraid to stand up in case they come up under us and knock us out of the boat."

"Look how red the water is, Slim."

Slim paused a moment before he answered. "It's the sunrise, just laying red like blood on the water. It isn't thick like blood."

"Like it never happened, Slim," He repeated.

"Yeh, only it did happen. See we're drenched from it. You and I were a part of this."

They stared in every direction. Nothing living broke surface anywhere. In their minds they wondered what was happening under the sea out of sight.

There was a small place off the port side of the boat where thousands of tiny bubbles hissed and popped. A dozen gulls circled and dipped at the place.

Hal thought it was like a dream.

"Fella once told me, and I don't know how he knew this, but a bunch of killer whales circled a blue whale and the killer whales rammed it in the belly with their heads until it knocked the wind out of the blue whale and its tongue came out. They say the tongue of a blue can weigh a thousand pounds. Anyway, when the tongue came out, the other killer whales grabbed the tongue and they tore out the tongue and ate it. They let the blue swim off to die of starvation and ate its tongue. You just don't know what goes on where you can't see it."

Neither of them spoke for a time. The sunrise took its blood red color from the water and exchanged it for gold.

"Mind if we reel up. I don't know what we might hook today?"

Slim slowly nodded. It was a taciturn nod that spoke a full paragraph — "I think I got enough for one day."

# Christina

She came from a tiny Eskimo village on the Northwest coast of Alaska where the Bering Sea slammed the shore and the sound of its pounding deafened the cries of the gulls as they dipped in the troughs after needle fish. At a certain place where the rock cliffs were worn almost into a cave, the ocean would boom and white foam, like torn undershirts, floated at the edge. In that village was a single electric power line and when the wind came off the ocean the wire sliced it in two like a body and the wind moaned in the wire and shuddered until it died.

On the seaside of her village, houses clung to the steep rock cliffs, houses that were like grey dead men's hands whose boney fingers were the pilings that grasped the stone. Below the houses on the ledges of the cliffs, gulls, common murres, and tufted puffin lay their top-shaped eggs in stone recesses and hovered over them against the wind. In good weather and at the right time, the women of the village went down the cliffs in ropes and gathered the eggs into baskets made of sea grass. The sea birds swarmed and circled overhead like seasoning in soup and cried their alarm. They would dive with open beaks and veer off at the last instant helpless and distraught.

Along the seaside row of houses was another row set farther inland separated from the other by a single lane dirt road. That road was no more than sixty yards in length and had been made for the use of the only vehicle in the settlement — an old fire engine given to the town decades before. It had not run in years and the red paint had blistered and peeled and flaked off and the metal rusted the color of red-brown walrus. The ladders that remained on the truck were white, like ribs. The fire hoses had been run out and left in a pile beside the fire truck and the vehicle remained like a disemboweled creature at the far end of the little street.

Only walking Eskimos used the road and a narrow path had been furrowed by their feet exactly down the center of the road. Thin blades of weathered grass grew in the old wheel ruts of the road on either side of the path and bent with the wind.

Her name was Christina Oogaruk and she lived in a house with her parents, which faced the sea and was the color of grey sky. It was built from timber and beams that had floated in the current for a thousand miles and had been storm tossed to the shore near the village. The boards used to build the house were heavy, saturated with seawater. When the nails were pounded in, water was pushed from the wood. It had never been painted.

Christina slept in a small room next to her parents' bedroom. On her bed was a caribou hide blanket with its smooth hair side up. Clothing hung on the walls from pegs, and pictures, mainly cut from magazines, were pinned to the walls. One picture was of the campus of the school in Sitka showing smiling faces of students happily carrying books. In the photo, a student in a blue cloth jacket was throwing a snowball at the others. On a table next to Christina's bed was a tablet of lined paper, some schoolbooks and a lamp with seal oil for fuel. Christina always thought the glow from the lamp was the very same color and shade of the moon when it was full and she would smile and consider they were all reading the same page.

On the floor by the door were a few cardboard boxes that were packed and tied with twine. Each bore a shipping label that said, "Christina Oogaruk/ Sheldon Jackson School/ Sitka, Alaska." On the top of the boxes was a near empty backpack, which waited for last things to be packed. As soon as the salmon run was over, but before the men left to hunt the tundra for moose and caribou, Christina would be making the journey to Sitka for school.

At night dreams crept into Christina's sleep like stalking wolves. It might have been that the wind howled in the darkness the same pitch and sound of the wolves of the tundra or of the sled dogs. In her sleep she would hear the headman's fierce dogs nearby as they snarled and fought with a ferocity that frightened her. She could imagine the bared white teeth in the moonlight and blood tossed from gashes received in the fight. In her sleep Christina dreamed that she was walking on the path and the dogs lurched at her legs with dripping fangs. Then, just as their teeth were about to set, the ropes around their necks would reach full length and stop them short. The jolt would lift the animals into the air and spittle would fly from their mouths. In her dreams she always looked back to where the rusty eyebolts were attached to the building and wondered how long they would hold.

Toward morning the wind ceased and Christina could hear gulls in the air and ravens walking on the roof above her head. The sky was clear of clouds and the beams of morning light entered her room through the window pane and rested on the center of the wood floor like a piece of yellow parchment ready to be written on with the acts of the day.

She put on her blue jeans and sweatshirt, for it was still summer, and over it she wore her red kuspuk. A cloth kuspuk is worn over one's fur parka called a parkee to keep it clean but she wore it just because she liked the colors and wore it often. She would smile when the children of the village skipped along beside her and would say, "It's like Joseph in the Bible and the coat of many colors." She would smile and say to them as she would touch each of the colors, "Green is for the tundra when we roam and yellow is the color of the lights of home. Red is for the berries of late July…" Then she would pause before the last line and reach for the nearest child to tickle her, "And blue is for the malamute's eye!"

As she slid on her mukluks she heard shouting from the street, someone calling to people in nearby houses. It was her older brother rousing the crew of his whaleboat. "Whales! Get up! Let's go!"

Then, without a knock, he thrust open Christina's door. "We have whales just off shore!" He rushed inside and grabbed his harpoons and Winchester and the very long lengths of line made of walrus skin. He already had on his gut skin rain gear, preferring it to modern rain gear because it was lighter and in it he could better maneuver his harpoon. "I'll help you," Christina said, and she lifted three of the sealskin air bags and threw them over her shoulder. They were huge over her small frame and she maneuvered to get them through the doorway. Together they ran out the door and along the path to where the rocks sloped to the water's edge and to the umiaks, which were lined along the shore. In the bay of the village the morning sun shone on the spray of the spouts of several whales. The bowhead whales were near enough that the sound of the exhaled breaths could be clearly heard.

Some of the men were already at the boat and they rolled the umiak over to its bottom and began to slide it to the water's edge. One of them attached the outboard motor to the stern. Someone else tossed in the paddles with which they would silently approach the whale at the end of the stalk. Christina's brother tied one end of the walrus line to the harpoon head and the other end to the air bags and they pushed off into the sound.

Christina stood at the shore and watched the men in the umiak cast off. She was a classic Eskimo with a round brown face and high cheekbones. Her black hair was made into a single braid at the back. She was young, not yet out of her teens. She was strong and capable of the hardship of the village. Her brother waved and she smiled with perfect white teeth and waved back.

Her father arrived and stood beside her. He was frail, thin and grey. Tufts of white hair protruded out of the sides of his old ball cap. He was bow legged, as were many of the older Eskimos, and as Christina saw his face she saw that it was set and unreadable. His eyes were moist and cloudy. He seemed to soak in the scene of his departing son and lock it into his memory.

Christina's mother arrived also at the shore beside them. She too was quite old as Christina was the youngest and last of several children. She also wore a kuspuk over her coat and wore a green scarf around her hair. She was of the old generation and had six vertical black tattoos that extended from her lower lip to her chin. She put her arm around Christina and said, "The men catch whale. You and me we go catch eggs."

• • •

They climbed the cliff overlooking the ocean, Christina moving at the pace of her mother who paused from time to time for breath. At the top, the ground was mostly moss with a scattering of grass, heather and blue bellflowers. Nearby a section of caribou antler lay bleached on the ground. Looking out to sea the water was calm, and in the far distance a thin layer of clouds marked the unseen shore of Russia. There were no trees to tie off Christina's rope so she wrapped it twice around a very large rock at the edge and placed a fur between the rock and her rope to prevent chafing. Her mother lined the basket with grass to keep their eggs from breaking. The morning sun was on Christina's back and she saw her shadow before her disappear over the cliff.

Her mother placed the bag over Christina's shoulder. "You be careful," and she smiled, "I don't want you to break the eggs."

Christina smiled at her little joke. "I will, Mama."

Christina walked backward off the cliff playing out the rope around her back, holding it with both hands. As she descended her feet dislodged pebbles and small rocks and she could hear them as they bounced on the rock sides and landed at the bottom of the cliff. She did not want to count the seconds it took to hear the final fall.

There were hundreds of seabirds on the cliffs and Christina shooed off the guillemots and began to fill her basket with their spotted blue-green eggs. There were some common murres also and she gathered several of their eggs and placed them carefully into her basket and pressed grass around the eggs.

Her mother shouted from above and pointed at the bay, "Look, they are about to strike!"

Christina glanced seaward. Only a hundred yards out she could see her brother's umiak glide to striking distance of the whale's black back. She could see her brother in his gut skin coat stand up in the bow, his harpoon raised in his right hand. She saw the whale blow and could clearly hear it. The steam of its breath exhaled high in the air and she knew that the men in the boat would be able to smell the starfish odor of its breath. But then just as he began his thrust, the bow of the boat moved and his target was just on the other side of the bow. He took one step to the left and thrust.

He thrust deeply and as designed, the harpoon tip separated from the shaft. They could hear the crew's shouts of triumph over the calm water. The whale sounded downward and the huge tail, wider than the boat was long, raised skyward and sank down into the depths with a spray that soaked the men in the boat. The line rapidly played out, the rope loudly dragging over the bow. Then over the water she heard a gasp and saw her brother bend over and scramble with something on the bottom of the boat. His hands moved franticly. Christina in horror knew what was happening. When he had stepped he had entangled himself in the bite of the line and it was wrapped around his ankle. The line was feeding out at speed as the whale descended into the depths. Her brother tore at the line trying to free his ankle.

Then it seemed that everything happened at slow motion. Christina knew what she would see. The bow of the boat tipped nearly to waterline. Her brother was pulled feet first into the air, his lower body still on the floor of the boat. In an instant as if he weighed nothing he was pulled from the boat. He went feet first over the bow and then downward into the black water. Fathoms of line followed him, then the air bags, and then everything went underwater. In a moment even the splash was gone. The crew ran to the side and stared into the blackness. Absolutely nothing was to be seen. Where he went down ten thousand tiny bubbles boiled to the surface and disappeared with a hiss into the air.

"Mama!" she shouted, horrified, "Mama!"

From above her mother had seen it too. As if her son could hear her she shouted his name, "Walter!"

"Mama," shouted Christina again.

Her mother seemed to scream but no sound came. With both of her hands she slapped them to her ears. She began to stagger at the top of the cliff.

"Mama, Mama, don't fall."

She continued to stagger at the edge and then dropped to her knees staring at the black water biting the back of her hand.

"Mama, stay there! I'm coming."

She could not remember climbing to the top. She only recalled sitting beside her mother with both arms around her and they both convulsed in sobs. They held each other and rocked back and forth, their eyes fixed on the bay.

The eyes of the men in the boat hunted the water. Those on the side of the boat where the captain was pulled in looked directly downward into the depths hoping for any sight of the whaler. The others looked toward the horizon, searching for the air bags when they came to the surface. Arms hanging limply at their sides, they were helpless to do anything. A whale is not attached to the boat by the harpoon and line, only to the float. A good strike kills instantly, the whale sounds as it dies and the crew wait for the float to come to the surface and then begin to retrieve it. This was the nightmare leaving the pillow of every whaler and entering the real world, pulling one of them under with a whale.

Nothing on the surface. Twenty minutes.

Other boats had entered the bay. The headman's boat bypassed the stricken crew and was in pursuit of other whales. Two other whalers however took position around the boat and searched the horizon for air bags at the surface.

Christina's father arrived on shaking legs beside them on the bluff. He was silent and searching the waters with his watery eyes.

"We can see better from up here," he said. He sat down heavily beside the two women. With a sigh he softly said, "It has been too long now."

He ceased looking to sea. He seemed to stare at the moss on the ground.

Thirty minutes. Nothing.

"Ho ho!" someone shouted. He stood upright in the bow and pointed a distance away. Three skin floats tied together came to the surface.

They started their outboard and drove rapidly to the site. Hand over hand they pulled the floats and line into the umiak. With the ease with which they pulled it was clear that there was no whale on the other end. Then with a shout of agony they pulled the young man in his gut skin parka into the boat. The rope was still firmly tied around his ankle but beyond that the line was cut free of the whale.

Christina and her parents ran from the cliff edge toward the shore where the umiak would beach. Her mother followed and staggered and fell on the way and her father held her up under his arm.

Walter Oogaruk was dead. His eyes were like opaque marbles, open and unseeing and his skin was the texture of cold clay. When they pulled him aboard, seawater poured from his mouth. They saw that his knife was missing from his sheath and that the line that had been attached to the whale had been cut. The crewman who steered the umiak saw the fear and desperation in Walter's eyes and he closed them with the palm of his hand.

As they laid him gently on the bottom of the boat and crossed his hands over his chest it became clear that there had been more terror in the death than had been reflected just in his eyes. The fingernails of Walter's hands were attached at the base but peeled back from his fingers like a book cover. As Walter was going down he had clawed at the rope until at the last moment, when too late, he remembered his knife. One of them bent his nails back on his fingers so the family would not see. The boat reached the shore with the crunch of small pebbles on the beach and sadly they lifted their captain from the boat and laid him on the beach.

• • •

Walter was buried the next day. A ship's bell, taken from an old wreck, was slowly tolled to announce the walk to the gravesite. In the village, house doors were being softly shut. Shuffling, uncertain feet squeaked on the frosty boardwalk and in the distance was the loud sighing and exhaling of whales in the bay. The sun rose molten gold and evaporating steam from wet roofs ascended into the air. As the people began the procession from their houses, the morning sun produced dark shadows before the mourners that proceeded them into the cemetery. Walter was carried in a coffin made of dry driftwood and his own crew bore it. They passed down the path side by side with the coffin between, the dogs along the way silently following the procession only with their eyes.

At the cemetery, two black ravens cawed from a grey scraggly tree, their calling muted as though entangled in the limbs. In the far distance a marsh hawk hunted, rising up and dropping at some unseen target. Otherwise all was quiet save for the brown grass that swished against the boots of the mourners as they walked by. They passed through the arches of the cemetery gate that were made of bowhead whale ribs and into the enclosure. The men set the coffin beside the open grave and stepped aside.

The missionary had come in a small bush plane for the service and stood waiting for the people to arrive. He was old, his skin pale as birch bark, and his hair was white and carefully combed. He wore a wool halibut jacket and held his open Bible with both hands. Slowly, one at a time, he looked at all of the people before him and nodded sadly to Walter's parents. "Albert… Mildred… Christina," he said quietly. "Friends. I cannot tell you how much I sympathize with you for the loss of Walter. I have known him since he was a little boy. I remember when I first saw him, he was wearing a blue striped shirt and he came to Bible school. He was a good boy and honest and pleasant to all." The missionary looked solemnly to the people. "It is hard to find comfort in this other than to say that Walter is in Heaven today."

He looked at the people before him and held out his open black Bible with one hand, the covers and pages of the well-read book draped limply down over the sides of his hand like a dead black bird. "The Bible says so. Walter is not in Heaven because he was good — and he was. Walter is in Heaven because he was born twice."

Here some of the people looked up at him in surprise.

"The Bible talks about a man named Nicodemus who was a good man and religious who came to Jesus because he knew that there was something missing in his soul and he wanted to go to Heaven. And Jesus told him 'marvel not ye must be born again.' You see the best of us are born sinners and need to be born again. I am going to talk with you about that when I come back again. But today I want to share with you that Walter understood what Jesus said and was born again and you can meet him in Heaven too when you die."

The missionary spoke a few more minutes and talked about Walter's life and achievements and it was time to lower the casket into the grave. He was lowered by ropes taken from the very same line in which he had been entangled and when the casket rested on the bottom of the hole the men released the lines, lines that were no longer needed, and left them entangled in the grave on top of the casket.

Solemnly the men shoveled the dirt into the hole. When they finished, the grave was covered over with smooth beach stones that Christina had brought in the early morning from the beach. His harpoon and lance were placed upright in the ground and crossed at the top over the grave. On a large flat stone in white paint was written, "Walter Oogaruk, Captain, Son, Brother." Over the grave Christina lay her caribou blanket.

• • •

The clouds were what they call a mackerel sky when Christina left her home for Sitka. Thin strips of broken white clouds schooled on the horizon and the sunrise left its redness on their sides. In truth the sockeye salmon run had ended and around the houses the drying racks were bright red with salmon that were split in two and lapped over the racks for curing in the air. As Christina left the house, village women were still cutting more salmon with their ulus for drying. Stellar jays perched on rooftops and posts and made their calls, calls that sounded like rusty springs, and waited for scraps.

There had been a light freeze in the night and a thin layer of ice covered the puddles along the path like cellophane. In the sky, first flocks of brant and snow geese passed overhead and positioned themselves on the ponds of the tundra where they waited for the fall gales upon which they would hitch a ride to the south.

She stayed behind for a few minutes for a last look before she went down the path to the airstrip.

"Christina!" shouted several children, "we're going to walk with you."

"Wonderful," she smiled.

"Tell us again where you are going."

"I'm going to Sitka for school. When you finish all of your school you can go there too to learn more."

"But that is so far away," they protested.

"Yes it is very far. We live in the Northwest part of Alaska and Sitka is in the Southeast part, a thousand miles away." Christina knew as she said it none of them knew how far a thousand miles was. "I will think of you every day that I am gone."

"When will you come back, Christina?"

"You see those geese? When they come back in the spring I will come back from school too."

A little Eskimo boy in blue tennis shoes and a Levi jacket pulled on her sleeve. "Hey," he said, "You have on your kuspuk like Joseph in the Bible."

His name was Alfred Eemok. His hair was jet black and his bangs were cut square across his forehead. He laughed and two of his teeth were missing. "We need to change our poem about it."

"But why?" Christina asked.

Alfred stopped on the path. He did not want to think and walk at the same time. He said, "Because it isn't 'red is for the berries of late July' anymore." He smiled at her. "It is red is for the salmon on the rack now."

"You are right, Alfred. Let's fix it." They continued walking and Christina put her hand on her chin in thought. "To make it rhyme we need something blue to go with rack." She recited their rhyme about her kuspuk. "Green is for the tundra when we roam/yellow is the color of the lights of home/ red is for the berries of late July/ and blue is for the malamute's eye."

Christina looked at the children. "If we change it to 'red is for the salmon on the rack' we need something that rhymes with rack."

The children began to suggest words, "Lack, pack, hack, and sack."

"I know," said another child, "How about 'back,' when Christina comes back?"

Here Christina said, "Yes! Blue is for the sky when I come back."

The group arrived at the airstrip and Christina turned to the children. "Time for you to go to school. Don't be late."

The little Eskimo children turned toward the village waving as they went. Christina watched them until they were nearly out of sight. Then she remembered and shouted to them, "Stay on the path!"

At the dirt strip where the plane would land she glanced across the open spaces before her. As far as she could see all was red and yellow and orange. She knew the red was from the blueberry leaves blushed by the frost. There was yellow and orange from the cranberry and willows. The moss was silvery near the rocks.

A de Havilland bush plane landed and taxied to the group and cut its engine.

They unloaded cargo and Christina's father began to hoist up boxes to the pilot. "Here, father, I'll get those," she said. He seemed small and frail.

"Let me do it," she said. Christina saw blue veins on the back of his hands as he lifted a box. "It's good for me to do it."

He looked at her with his milky eyes. "I put some carvings in the box for you to sell in the stores in Sitka. The people like Eskimo carvings. Mother made some dance fans and baskets for you too. And your Auntie made a doll for you to sell for money at school." He gazed at Christina fixing her into his memory. "Write to us."

"Ah Dee!" she said, "Ah Dee, my heart." And she hugged him and wept.

Christina's mom stood beside her, smaller than her father. She wore her parkee and the wolf ruff of the hood surrounded her head like a halo. She looked up at Christina's face and smiled like a conspirator. "I put some Eskimo food in the box. I don't think you can get any in Sitka."

Christina looked down at her and she was like an Eskimo doll with her ivory face and slanted eyes and smile and tattoos. And she loved her. "I will come back like the swans."

Christina boarded and as the plane taxied away she saw several ptarmigan running as they do, running in the low brown grass parallel to the runway. They were still mostly brown but taking on the white of winter, shedding off the summer and putting on a new season.

• • •

The first time that I ever saw Christina was in our living room in Sitka. She was sitting in our old rocking chair holding our Raggedy Ann doll rocking slowly back and forth. She wore mukluks and blue jeans and a beautiful kuspuk and smiled as though perfectly delighted and content. I never saw such a contented smile and her slanted Eskimo eyes seemed but slits in her round brown face.

But I am way ahead of myself.

My wife and I, not much older than the college students ourselves, were hired as, "head residents" of the dorm. That is, we were called dorm parents and in fact as we began to know and care greatly about our "kids" they called us "Mom" and "Dad."

My wife had arrived a month before me as I was in Special Forces and was doing a short tour in South America with the Army. When I arrived in Sitka she already knew all of the "kids" and I was catching up.

She brought in popcorn and hot chocolate and introduced me to Christina. "This is my husband," and she said my name. "He is brown and dry because he has been in the jungle. He has lots of stories that he can tell."

Christina just smiled and did not say anything.

"I think I got more bug bites and thorn scratches than sun though," I said.

Christina just smiled as if she was just hearing some new but interesting information.

I tried to get her to talk. I was not sure if I was looking at a shirt or a short dress that she wore over her blue jeans and I told her how pretty it was.

"It's called a kuspuk," my wife said when it was clear that Christina was not going to comment. "It's worn over the fur parka so it doesn't get dirty."

"It is beautiful with all of the colors," I ventured, trying to bring her into conversation. She smiled. It seemed that the thought of the colors of her Kuspuk reminded her of a place and time far away and pleasant. But she did not respond to me.

Over the course of the next half hour I asked about her village and family, anything to get her to talk. But she just seemed to be very shy and gave only the shortest of answers to my queries.

I talked about South America from where I had just come. "We parachuted at night with scuba tanks into a bay of the ocean so we would not be seen by anyone. That was frightening jumping in the dark with just the moon shining on the water to let you know that the ground was close." I was not sure there was any point of comparison for Christina to know the significance of that. She listened intently but did not ask any questions about what I might have been doing there.

"We spent a day in black, chest deep swamp water holding our rifles over our heads so they would not get wet. Huge lizards with webs of skin between their toes would run by our faces so fast they did not sink in the water."

Christina listened carefully but still did not talk.

"On the swampy shores were thousands of holes the size of your fist in the mud. They were tarantula holes and each one of them held a tarantula." Christina rocked in the chair as I talked.

After a pause to give her time to say something I continued, "There were places in the jungle you would get dizzy and you would think that there was something wrong with you and you would almost fall down. But then you would see that the ground itself was moving because there were thousands of soldier ants, each of them carrying a leaf." Christina leaned forward with the doll in her arm.

"It was very hot in the day and at night it would rain so hard you would not be able to talk if you wanted."

Still she did not speak but she smiled contentedly. "Maybe Eskimos do not talk," I thought.

Then Christina stood up and said to my wife as though I were not in the room, "I need to go and study." And she left.

"Is it me?" I asked when she left, "Could something have happened in her village with a man? Am I doing something wrong?"

"Be patient. She has to get used to you."

It continued this way for several days. Our other "kids" came to visit us from time to time but it was Christina who came to our living room nearly every evening.

She still sat in our old rocking chair, the one with some of the spindles wrapped in thin copper wire, and rocked and held the Raggedy Ann doll and smiled at my attempts at conversation. I got nowhere asking about village life and what they ate and esoteric customs of the people so I talked about some of my experiences. I never talked about the war in Southeast Asia itself, only observations of a culture foreign to her.

"One day in the war, an old woman threw a deadly poisonous snake at me. They called it a tri-pacer because you would die in three steps if it bit you." She leaned forward in the still rocker in concern, her mouth slightly open.

"One time we Green Berets were flying in an airplane flown by Air America. We knew the pilots and they liked Special Forces. We were crossing a part of the South China Sea flying back to our camp when the pilot called to me to come to the cockpit. He pointed down at the ocean and said, 'Do you see that whitish color on the water?'"

It was huge whatever it was.

"Then the pilot said to me, 'The white is one mile wide and six miles long and the sonar says the white is a thousand feet thick. Know what that is?' Before I could venture a guess he said, 'It is a mass of mating sea snakes, more poisonous than cobras.' He seemed to shudder at the thought. 'If you were to fall in there you would be dead before you stopped going down.'"

Our pan abode living room was quiet. After a minute she uttered a great sigh and said, "I have to go study."

• • •

The next day was Friday and it rained. It was warm in our apartment and the windows were open and the rain on the salmonberry bushes sounded like a loud hiss. The gutters overflowed and water splashed in puddles outside. Christina sat where she was accustomed. She wore her beautiful mukluks over her blue jeans. She smiled at me with her dark eyes and for the first time she talked! Really talked.

She looked at the place where I had been wounded and she quietly said, "My father was a soldier too. He was in the war, the one with the Japanese and the Russians and the Germans."

"What was he in? Where did he fight?" I asked.

"He was an Alaskan Scout. My uncle told me that they were famous. They called his group, 'Something Cutthroats.' I can't remember exactly the name. There were only sixty-five of them at first and they were all trappers and miners and hunters and Indians and Eskimos. They were picked because they could live off the land and were very strong. They took their own clothes and rifles and they spied on the Japanese."

She drank some cocoa and continued. "He was on the island of Attu in the Aleutians after the Japanese invaded it. He paddled in a rubber raft at night in the rain. He wore those clothes that look like grass and crawled right among the Japanese soldiers and they never saw him. My father said that at the end he was all night crawling into the enemy camp. It rained in the night and the Japanese did not pay attention so he crawled right among them. He could hear fighting far away in the dark but nothing close. In the morning it was foggy and he could not see but in the fog he heard small explosions on the tundra, too small to be cannons from the ships. The fog lifted and then he could see all over the sides of the hills that the explosions were from grenades. The Japanese were killing themselves with them before the Americans landed from the ships."

Christina seemed to call up the vision in her mind. "My father said that the soldiers around him stood up quickly. They looked across the valley and saw what was happening and they bowed to each other and they poured something into their canteen cups and drank it. They took grenades out and hit them on their helmets and held them to their chins. My father said that since he was so close some of the pieces of metal and pieces of bone wounded him and he was taken to a hospital ship until he was better."

She looked down at the floor. "My father does not talk much." Christina changed the subject and continued to talk.

"Our village is dry," she said. "We do not allow alcohol to be taken in or to drink it. Some villages are wet and people can drink but those villages have problems. Eskimos drink and then go on the ice when it is thin. Sometimes they do suicide."

"We just have one street in our village, not like Sitka. But there are no cars, just people. When you walk on the road you must stay in the middle on the path. The path is exactly the length of the ropes that tie the dogs." She thought for a moment and said, "Sled dogs are good but you must watch the other ones."

• • •

As the year moved deeper into autumn our little Eskimo girl became a part of our family. The tundra swans that dotted the potholes of the northern interior in their twos just weeks before, combined and flew overhead in their flocks and Christina would run to the door and watch them pass.

Then one evening winter eased into the campus. Northern lights flamed across the sky. Curtains of green and then yellow light blew across the sky, swaying back and forth as though God left a window open. The colors changed from green to yellow to red and back. The campus was quiet as though all creatures held their breath at the sight.

From the channel was the sound of the marker buoy as it moaned in the darkness. Then from across the campus in the dark was loud whistling, not like calling a taxi but a long trill. From other locations on the campus we could hear more whistling. Christina appeared beside us. "There are other Eskimos here," she said. "At home we whistle at the sky to make the lights brighter." I could tell in the dark that she was delighted. From other parts of the campus people whistled.

As winter continued it would be whenever the borealis flamed across the sky and it would seem that if you just listened carefully you could hear the winds in the heavens that caused them to rustle, somewhere in the darkness far away there would be the lonesome whistling of an Eskimo. At times it would be in the trees toward Mount Verstovia. Other times the whistle would come from the shore close to the moaning of the marker buoy near the harbor.

One evening I was sitting in my chair reading Steinbeck or Hemingway, I can't remember which, when I heard whistling outside. I set down the book, put on a jacket and went outside to see the lights. But instead of a borealis I saw the sky was not clear, but overcast and a very thin rain, almost a lonesome mist was falling. I heard the whistle again, this time from behind our log cabin dorm near the tree line. I walked around the building keeping to the shadows and stood in the dark and waited.

A figure emerged from the area of the salmonberry bushes. It moved toward the windows of the students' rooms.

"Can I help you?" I asked in a tone that was more of a challenge then a question.

"Oh!" he said, "I was just walking by."

"Come over to the light."

He stepped to where the lights from the window shown.

He was a thin Indian about thirty or forty, too old to be around the students with any propriety. His hair was long and straight hanging halfway down his back. He seemed to be wearing a brown leather coat, the kind they wore in the old west with the fringes down the sleeves and from the hem at the bottom.

"You need to move along. You shouldn't be hanging around the dorms at night, especially in the dark."

"Yes," he answered, "I was just passing through."

And he left, walking slowly away, taking his time as I watched until he was well out of sight.

• • •

I all but forgot about the incident. The school year progressed and students seemed more committed with classes and studies. We saw less of the students in our little living room and more of them on the campus paths. Christina also visited us less frequently but that just seemed to make the times that we had together more precious.

Snow fell on the campus all of that night and most of the morning. It was thick and moist and clung to the bare tree branches and in the distance, the lights of the town shone pink in the sky. Children sledded down the front lawn of the campus, their parents standing at the bottom to stop them from sliding all of the way into the street.

Below the campus in the channel, the marker buoy moaned in the swell, its muffled note guiding returning boats to the harbor through the snowfall. At the top of the ramp were bloodstains in the snow where harvested deer had been dragged. Seeing pink blood in one of the drag marks, my wartime thought was, "That one was lung shot."

I was walking across the front lawn of the campus and I saw Christina and with her was the Indian who I saw behind the dorm. She wore her parka of muskrat, martin, seal and bear with the ruff of wolf hair. "Hi, Dad," she shouted. She remembered that she was with someone. "This is my friend John George." She said.

"I think I met you before," I said. He seemed to not know what I meant. "Behind the dorm the other day. You said you were just passing through."

"Oh." was all he said.

I said my name and extended my hand and shook his. His hand felt like a glove full of marbles with his knuckles. He smelled of stale alcohol and cigarettes and his hair was long and greasy. "My name is John George. I'm visiting Christina." I saw he was missing a tooth.

"Well, enjoy the snow, Christina. There is a sled at our apartment if you want to use it."

"Thank you," she said with a smile. They walked toward the school cafeteria, he on the sidewalk, she trudging happily beside him through the knee-deep snow off the walk.

• • •

A couple of months later I saw Christina again with John George walking across the campus. They held hands as they walked, she jabbered away at something, he walked looking straight ahead. Her parka was open as they walked up to me.

"You don't have your colorful kuspuk on," I said. Her kuspuk was ubiquitous prior to this.

She looked at me, then to him with a "should I tell him look." She smiled shyly and shuffled one of her mukluked feet. "I'm going to have a baby."

I know my mouth was open. I looked over to John George. He still carried that unwashed, old alcohol, cigarette odor about him. I really did not like him. He did not smile, did not seem embarrassed, did not seem like a proud father to be. He did not speak in reference to what Christina had just said.

"Congratulations," I said. "I assume you are the father to be?"

"Yes." He said, and did not add a syllable after that.

Christina, seeing nothing was coming forth from the future father turned to me and said, "We were talking about this. We decided that we are going to get married."

I was taking all of this in in gulps. There before me was my little Eskimo girl, with this Indian in his greasy leather coat who did not show the emotions I would have expected in the circumstance, and a baby to come to boot!

"We want to get married here in Sitka right away. My parents are too far away and too weak for such a journey."

"Will you be my father and give me away at the wedding?"

I looked over to John George. "Do you love her John George? Would you take care of her?"

He gave me the faintest of nods.

"Of course, Christina, I would be greatly honored to be your dad."

"We already talked to 'Mom' and she knows. We already talked to a preacher in a little church and he will do the ceremony."

"When?"

"Soon," she said, "I don't fit into my kuspuk already."

"Just tell me when and what you want me to do."

I hugged her and held her at arm's length to look at her. She was in love with this guy. There was joy in her eyes. I guess she could see a great deal in his heart that I could not. I would not diminish her joy.

"Congratulations, John George. This is a beautiful precious girl who you will be marrying." I looked in his eyes to let him know that this little girl was precious also to me.

• • •

The ceremony was in a tiny church on a morning that sent sunbeams wiggling through the stained glass to sit in the front pews. In the other pews there were but a few people, some of the college kids, a few others. An organist played and I led Christina in her pretty dress and an armful of flowers down the aisle. Her dress was pretty but her face was radiant.

John George stood there in clean new blue jeans and a newly ironed shirt, thanks to my wife, with his hair done neatly in a ponytail. He smelled clean and looked handsome with his chiseled brown features. He smiled as Christina came down the aisle.

The pastor told of how God had established marriage as an enduring holy bond. He spoke of fidelity and caring for the needs of each other for all of their lives. He spoke of children being the gift of the Lord and the solemn duty to raise them up in the nurture and admonition of the Lord. When the wedding was over the ladies of the church, although they did not really know the bride or groom, made a beautiful luncheon and visited with the couple and sincerely wished them happiness.

When it came time to leave the church students threw rice and cheered.

• • •

When spring came to the campus it arrived just as winter had arrived months before, with a huge wet fluffy snow that covered the old church bell on the campus front lawn and left the old cannons half buried in snow. It was a Currier and Ives snow that seemed so much like a Christmas card that the Orthodox Church in the center of town rang its bells just for the fun of it. Christina and John George were packed and waiting at the airport and we wondered if the plane would land at all. For several hours they had been plowing and sanding the runway and clearing the snow off the runway lights. The visibility was near zero. Twice from the north of the airport we saw the hazy glow of the plane's landing lights coming in on final in the snow storm and then we saw it veer off at the last moment. Once more the pilot tried, this time landing where the numbers would have been and braked to a stop at the very end of the strip.

Christina with her belly could not close her parka all the way. "I will be glad to get back into my kuspuk," she said rubbing her belly.

John George wore his buckskin jacket. In his hands he carried a heavy parka for it was still very cold at Christina's village where they would live. "Thank you for the coat." He said to my wife.

"We will let you know how to write to us when we get to our village. We will stay with my parents until we make a place," Christina said.

We hugged. My wife cried. I just looked at the two of them, locking the image into my memory.

We never heard from them again.

• • •

The geese had come and gone for a couple of seasons. We waited to hear from them. They had no telephone in the village in those days and used CB radio for emergencies. We considered sending a letter in the blind but did not.

One day I met someone from the area who knew the village and our Christina. He was a very old trapper who came to the Pioneer Home to live out his last days. He had served with Christina's father in the war and visited the village when the ground was frozen and he could travel.

He told me — and this is just what he said — that John George became a drunk. "Imagine a drunk in a dry village. That still wonders me." He combed his white beard with the fingers of his hand. The old trapper looked at me with his tiny blue eyes. "He never really fit in at the village him being Indian and they all Eskimo with their foods and habits."

"It seemed that when the cargo plane arrived he would get his booze and get sauced and he would crawl into that ol' fire engine they got at the end of that street. He would pass out in there. Sometimes when he would disappear for a day or two they would find him there with the ends of his legs sticking out of the door."

"The Indian and Christina had their little girl. They named her Pearl. She was about two." The trapper looked at me and his eyes began to water and he paused and cleared his throat. "She died," he said. "Beautiful little thing."

"It happened that that Indian was staggering drunk and was walking down the path to where he slept in the fire truck and staggered off the path and the dogs near to got him. There he was cursing and swinging his arms and fists at 'em, when little Pearl saw her daddy going down the path."

"She loved her daddy, Lord knows why, and she ran down the path and was calling, 'Daddy, Daddy.' Christina didn't see her go and she couldn't hear because of the wind in the wire. And the little girl went off the path and in a minute the dogs were on her." The trapper stared at his patched tin pants and continued.

"Christina saw what had happened too late. She screamed for Pearl but the wind caught away her shouts. She ran to little Pearl and lay across her body to shield her from the bites and the dogs tore at Christina's legs and hands. There on the path under that red kuspuk was a mother and child. Only the mother lived."

"I was there at the funeral. John George staggered at the grave. He was drunk again. When it was all over Christina put a Raggedy Ann doll on the grave. They say she would visit the grave and hold the doll and rock back and forth and say something to little Pearl and she would put the doll back on the grave and go away."

The trapper pulled on his suspenders and sat back, "One day John George was gone. Some say he hitched a ride on the mail plane and went to Anchorage where he lives with the drunks on Fourth Avenue. A fella told me he actually saw him one morning very early. He had bags under his eyes and the flesh of his cheeks were puffy and sunken. But it was him all right with his fringed leather coat all grimy and greasy. He was passed out on the steps of a liquor store. He seemed to be breathing ok so they passed on."

The trapper combed his beard again with his fingers and I saw that two of them were missing at the second joint. He saw me looking at them.

"Number four Victor double spring," was his answer to the question I did not ask.

"Darn fool thing to happen to an old trapper what should know better. But it happens. I was on the North Fork of the Kuskokwim and the weather was freeze, thaw, freeze, thaw when I got my fingers into the trap. The jaws and even the chain were frozen in ice and I did everything I could to get the jaws loose. My pack and axe were too far away to help me. I knew I was goin' to freeze to death if I didn't get out soon so I just cut my fingers off with my knife.

"I saved the fingers in my pocket for a while in case I might be able to put them back but that was a no go. I did have enough brains though to cut them off at the joints so there wern't no sawin' on the bone.

"Got some advice for you should you ever get into that fix though. Save some skin to lap it over. I didn't do that."

"We were talking about Christina. What happened to her?" I asked him.

"She disappeared." News from the villages is sometimes scarce. "When she went missing they looked out on the tundra as far as a person could walk and there was nothing. She would always be at little Pearl's grave or she would sit on the rock cliffs in her red kuspuk and stare out to sea so of course they looked there first of all."

The old man looked at me and paused as if he wondered if he should tell me the rest of what he knew. "One of the boats returning from a seal hunt thought he saw a length of red cloth on the rocks. The colors were bright against the rocks, but with the surf they could not get close enough to be sure what it was. They tried again but whatever they saw was gone."

And that is what he told me.

# Flying Stories

When I was a boy in Northern Minnesota, living in the coldest town in continental United States, flying and airplanes were far beyond hope and dreams.

In winter everything was frozen. All about us seemed to be brittle. The insulators on the barbed wire fences were bearded with hoar frost and drifting snow sighed as it passed through the wire. We thought that if we were to find a frozen, hibernating frog in the mud and drop it to the steel-hard highway, it would splatter to fragments like a broken dish.

At the airport, small planes were tethered on the field and frosted white, and lay half buried in hard crusts of snow that held them like jaws. Sometimes the wind blew in from Canada across the frozen Rainy River and farmer's fields and snow drifted over the parked Cessnas and Piper Cubs. Snow would seep through the slits in the windows and fill the seats inside like ghosts waiting for a flight.

Every year winter would surrender to spring and it would arrive in its gentleness. In the calmness of the day when I would venture out to play marbles where ground appeared, I could hear the trickle of melt under the snow. You could hear groups of raucous crows, dozens of them, cawing and squawking, but it was too early for mating and nesting and you knew that winterkill had been found here and there in the thaw.

Snow would recede to patches and to strips along the roadway where the snow plows had left it densely packed. But on the runway I knew that the spring sun on the black pavement would have left it clear and melted.

Then, as though thawed from winter, I could hear the first airplanes in the sky. I would place a hand over my eyes against the sun and watch until they were gone. When airplanes flew low overhead I would always wave, and a few times the pilot would tip his wings, and there a connection occurred between a dream and a young boy standing in the brown grass.

"Somebody up there sees me," and I felt big and important.

Our family was certainly not "well to do" as they say, and the idea of flying or being a passenger in one of those miracles was beyond possibility. Just to be close to one of them, to just look inside, to sit on the seat and pretend… just to slide my hand along the hard, fabric skin of a Citabria airplane tethered to the airfield would be no less a thrill than to stroke a sleeping dinosaur.

Up in our town just below the Canadian border, many people lived in the "sticks." They had no telephones or roads, and as the radio said, "they were not served by regular communications." Each morning and evening the radio announced messages to them.

"To Albert Red Horse on Loon Lake. Mother is doing better. Have package for you. Will see you at break up."

"To Simon Bill at Pike Lake. Your pelts sold at auction. Good price. In bank. Fred"

"To Esther at Squaw Point, Martha had her baby. Girl."

I would imagine the pilots flying toward those many destinations.

I loved those paintings of Philip R. Goodwin. I could always see me in those white canvas tents with pine boughs for loft and Hudson

Bay blankets over me. I could smell bacon frying and mixing with the fried potatoes. And I could just hear in my mind a companion shout, "I got one." Were those airplanes going to a remote cabin or fishing lake?

One time a man in our church brought his Piper Cub plane on skis to where our youth group was on the ice. It was New Years and we had a game night and during the next day we tobogganed on the shore of the frozen lake. Mr. Titus flew us up, one at a time, and showed us the area. Along the river that separated us from Canada were several moose bedded down in the willows. We circled above them and we were low enough that when the big bull turned his head I could see his bent down nose and ears and its blue shadow where it lay in the snow. Although it had already shed its antlers in the late fall, I could clearly see the bell shaped flesh that hung under its throat that indicated it was a male.

"What you could do with an airplane," I thought.

The demands of school and growing up and working in the grocery store and logging, ushered the possibility of flying into the attic of my mind. Then one day the call of war climbed up the creaky ladder to the attic of my memory and brushed off the cobwebs, and flying and skills of the air became an integral part of my life.

• • •

I was never a pilot until after the Vietnam War, but flight, getting to a place, and then getting down to the ground or back again into an aircraft filled my world for the next three years. I was a Green Beret. My task was leading troops in combat to achieve missions on the ground. It was others who brought us in or gave us air support or, often in horrendous circumstances, got us out.

I did about 126 parachute jumps. That was not many jumps compared to most of my teammates. But my jumps were memorable. Most were called "combat jumps" which meant that you jumped with full gear and usually at night. Over time I had three "May West" openings, which meant the main chute did not fully open and that I had to pull the reserve chute. I landed in trees twice because of untimely winds and needed to cut myself down.

I parachuted into the mountains with winter gear, skis, and my rifle one dark winter night. We were so packed down with equipment we looked like houses leaving the plane. The relative wind of the four-engine plane grabbed our bulk and tossed us into the darkness like an angry giant. I could only hope to land on a level surface and not on a cliff edge.

We had one night mission that required us to jump with scuba gear into the backwaters of Noriega's Panama. We spent a day and a night in chest deep, shark infested water near a castle built by Spanish Conquistadores before we could continue the mission among snakes, tarantulas, and the thickest jungles of my experience.

On one night combat jump I thought I saw the moon shining on a field hundreds of feet below me and headed for it thinking it was the landing zone. But it was not a field far below me after all, but the top of another chute only twenty feet below. On a night lit only by the stars I could not tell. I landed on his chute and both of our chutes began to collapse. Franticly, I ran on top of his chute to the edge, my feet sinking deeply into the marshmallow-like surface, and jumped off. I jerked and snapped on the shroud lines and hoped to re-inflate my chute before we hit. Just as it billowed up again I landed unhurt.

Three times I stood in the door ready to jump because the engine of our airplane was on fire, once we were over the Pacific Ocean, once we were over a mountain range, and one time we were over a city.

Once, we were pulled from a firefight by ladders that we made in camp using braided metal cables. It is extremely difficult to climb a rope ladder suspended in the air wearing a full rucksack and more so when you are wounded. Through a small opening in the trees the door gunner tossed the free end of the ladder down to us. The other end was clamped to the floor of the hovering helicopter. In the intense firefight, two of the three cables were shot through by bullets before we made it into the helicopter.

Late in the war, we usually rappelled into our target areas because the Communists monitored any opening in the jungle large enough to land a chopper. To get us out under fire, we had the choppers throw us ropes that were tied to the floor of the aircraft. We would tie off into the ropes and when the helicopters would ascend we would hang in the air below them. On a certain mission I had been wounded twice and we spent the night evading the enemy. In the morning we found a break in the trees and a helicopter arrived under heavy enemy attack, and threw down ropes to pull us out of the battle. I had been shot in the hand and had difficulty tying the knot, but managed a sloppy overhand and snapped into it. The communists rushed us just as the chopper gained in elevation. I was shooting down at them and they were shooting up and I was shot once more this time in the back of the head. I did not pass out but continued to fire at them. The chopper, instead of rising high enough to clear the trees, began to fly away horizontally. I was dragged through the trees and nearly pulled in two.

• • •

My first real introduction to flying and how to use the controls was in a Cessna Bird Dog airplane. I had been wounded and was not quite ready to go back on "the ground" so I was assigned to our intelligence section. Four of us Green Berets were taking turns flying reconnaissance missions in those little two-seat planes far behind enemy lines. The euphemism for that was, "deep into enemy denied and controlled territory." Army "fixed wing" pilots did the flying from the front seat while one of us would sit in the narrow back seat and look for targets and strategic intelligence, mark our maps, and take pictures.

We would fly in pairs. One plane would fly at a thousand feet above the target for a broad view and to coordinate the rescue of the low flying plane should it get shot down. The second plane would fly at ten feet. The low level plane would tilt its wings vertically to pass between trees. We flew the contour of the ground. We even flew under bridges. We looked for hidden roads, targets, truck parks and bivouac areas. Of the four of us, one was killed and one was wounded within the first month.

I would hold a Leica camera out the window and snap pictures. Green tracers would go in my window and past my head and out the other side. You could hear the impact of the bullets as they hit the fuselage and I wondered how many it would take to kill the engine.

The great danger was having the pilot killed and leaving us in the back seat with no controls. We improvised and drilled a hole in the control tube, which ran along the floor and under the pilot's seat. In that hole we inserted a pipe to use to control the ailerons. For cross wind we decided we would use the doors to compensate. Those flights were all done under extreme pressure and danger and prepared us for any eventuality in civilian flight.

I recall landing after one of those missions at Kontum airfield, hearing the tires screech down, the tires hissing on the hot tar runway and stopping at our hangar. We would count the bullet holes in the fuselage and see oil dripping to the tarmac from the bowels of the engine. We would talk about the truck tracks that disappeared at the bank of a river and reappeared on the other side, indicating a submerged, hidden bridge, "Did you see the sunshine in the trees at the bend of the river? It looked like the sun on a windshield."

My stay in those recon flights was abbreviated when I joined two other Green Berets on a "strike company" of mercenaries to fight behind enemy lines. I actually felt safer there than in the back of that Bird Dog.

• • •

After the war we wondered what we would do with the rest of our lives. Staying in Special Forces was a strong draw. We took advisement however, to give civilian life a chance as we could always go back. I decided that whatever occupation I chose, flying could be of use. One of my Army buddies and I decided to go for the airline transport license. We picked the best flying school in the country and applied the GI Bill and worked to that end.

We gained the skill and smoothness required for a commercial license and built up our hours — cross country flights to remote places, breakfast at Carmel by the Sea, Lunch at The Red Baron in Santa Clara, or dinner at a "ghost town" in the mountains.

We also decided we would train far more than anyone else in the "pack." We would add aerobatics (some people called it stunt flying but we considered it the ultimate of precision flying) and flying gliders, airplanes with no engines.

Our choice for aerobatics was a dirt strip away from any city, in dry barren farm country. There were two parallel strips of runway. The first was of gravel, very short and narrow. With the heat and humidity of the area and the presence of any amount of wind, it took a level of skill just to land on that strip.

Next to that gravel strip was a parallel one that was little more than dry ruts on the edge of a farmer's field. It reminded me of the captions on David Shepherd's paintings of airplanes hidden in farmer's fields in World War Two; "Somewhere in England." When we would rev up our engines for the short field takeoff, thick clouds of dry earth masked the sky.

Between those two tiny, remote airstrips was tall brown grass, and all around and on the strip, rabbits and gophers milled about on the runway. We flew Citabria airplanes with their light fabric skins and powerful engines. In the sky we practiced every maneuver until it was second nature. This lent reflexive skills for Alaska — "What would you do when flying near the face of a mountain cliff and a down draft plunged your airplane a thousand feet? What would you do with sudden turbulence that all but rolled your plane on its back in the air?"

• • •

It was at the foothills of the coast range where I watched California Condors effortlessly soar, not effecting a single wing beat. They had a huge wingspan, far greater than the golden eagle's. They would catch the updraft as the wind from the ocean met the hills and slid upward into the sky. Those winds were but elevators for the condor. As I closely watched, I could see a draft of wind lift a wing and then watched the huge bird bank into that wing and anchor it there. It would circle at that point, rising higher and higher, never flapping a wing a single time.

It was there at those foothills I learned to soar. We flew glider planes, Schweitzers with their long wings that mimicked the condor.

Gliders had no engines. They had to be towed behind a plane with an engine. At a certain altitude we would pull a lever that disconnected the glider from the tow plane. The tow plane would bank left and descend as the glider would claim elevation and bank right. The only sound was the wind passing over the cowling. There were only two instruments, an altimeter and a piece of string tied to the cowling. As long as the string pointed directly at me I knew that my control of the craft was correct.

We would see a farmer's fresh plowed black field and knew that the air there was warmer and would rise, and when I looked above the field I could see the birth of a cloud. I would glide to the place and when I could feel the column of air lift my wing, I would turn into it and go up with it. We would proceed cloud to cloud.

In flight I always looked for either a rising column of air or a place to land that I could glide to. Flying in remote Alaska you always thought, "If I lost my engine now where would I land?"

• • •

One day my old teammate and I were flying together doing touch and go on a sand bar outside of San Francisco. I had to go to work on the swing shift so he let me off. "I am going to do a few more and call it a day," he said.

I just arrived at work and had my time card in hand when the foreman came to me and said, "Your roommate just crashed and is in intensive care at the hospital."

He was a mess. Both legs were badly broken, internal injuries, facial cuts. He was in long recovery. In the interval, I married and moved to Alaska. Mike recovered, continued to fly, and became a superb pilot. He flew Africa, South America, crop-dusted, taught and continued his career in central Alaska.

• • •

The small city where we moved to in Alaska needed "bush pilots." There were eight logging camps in our area that needed supplies on a daily basis. Loggers and the many other people required to run a logging camp needed to come and go to town. In addition to loggers, there were hundreds of people who wanted to experience unspoiled wilderness. Many visitors wanted to be taken to remote lakes and cabins and the largest bush flying company was willing to hire me. I just needed a final check ride from the government.

• • •

The pilot designated by the government to administer my check ride and sign off on my license to be a bush pilot had never had a license himself.

When Alaska was still a territory, Karl Manning was already a skillful and accomplished pilot with years of experience. He and an airplane were one unit. He needed but to think and the craft obeyed like an extension of his brain. Flying, for him, began one day when he saw a floatplane fly low over his homestead and he thought how useful such a thing would be. He bought a kit plane that he saw advertised in a magazine and ferried the parts from the barge company to his cabin with his skiff. There, under a shelter made of bark slabs, he built his own airplane and taught himself how to fly. "How hard could it be?" he thought dismissively. He read the books. He taught himself incrementally, mastering each phase before taking the next. He would taxi to take off speed, lift off, and then settle down. He would do it over and over again until he was comfortable enough for the next phase. In time flying was second nature to him.

He ran a trap line in winter and put skis on his kit plane to check the lines. In the autumn he and his children put out a set-net for salmon at the head of his bay and Karl flew salmon to market that was fresher than from any other source. On one occasion a sockeye salmon flopped from the weigh scale at the market in town. He hunted sheep and goat in the mountains, landing on lakes thought inaccessible by others. He harvested moose and caribou in the North Country using balloon tires to land in the tightest places. He guided hunters. He took his clients to remote, unhunted areas that his passengers could say without argument they were the first to walk. He flew for logging camps and brought supplies to fish camps, mining sites and tiny villages.

When statehood occurred, Karl Manning was grandfathered in

with every fixed wing license he could ever need.

Karl was just what you saw. He had no pretense. The Federal people stated that as a person who represented the government he should wear a tie. So he did. He wore boots, grey wool pants with red logger suspenders, a hickory shirt and a navy blue clip-on tie for quick removal. He never spoke of his skill or experience.

He had an eye that looked slightly off to one side. Students did not want to be caught looking at it and it left them the impression that he had on a monocle. He would look at them sternly and point at them with his yellow pencil and warn, "Passing this test and getting a license will not give you judgment or experience, but I hope it will keep you alive long enough for you to get it." He was quick to admonish, "Alaska will kill you if you let your guard down a single time."

• • •

I visited him at his house to set up a check ride. Karl was what they call, "lanky." He was six feet of boney frame wrapped in many lengths of powerful sinew. He had a slight stoop when he walked and talked as though he carried heavy loads on his back and his mind forgot to take them off. He walked with long, sure strides that were sixty years of moving to a destination.

We talked about my experiences in the air and my background. When I spoke he nodded his head the entire time letting me know that he was following every word I said.

"It is refreshing for me to see a pilot who has judgment before his test," he said emphasizing the word "before."

"I would like to hear about your experiences in the Bird Dog when your test is completed. We could share some techniques. I am free tomorrow at nine for your test."

• • •

It is anyone's guess what the first sound of morning was in our Alaska town. It may have been sparrows that shrugged droplets of dew from their dry feathers as they stepped to a grey branch and trilled and sang.

But if you were like many and slept through that, the first sound to invade your consciousness would be the bush plane. As often as not, they began their day with dawn, around four in the morning. Most bush planes were on floats or were "amphibs," that is, they could land on either land or water. They used the channel of water that marked the edge of town for their airstrip. They landed and took off throughout the day and it seemed their last flight in was to pull the drapes of darkness behind them to end the day.

The workhorse bush plane was the de Havilland Beaver, able to carry two thousand pounds of load. But it was the Cessna 185 that woke you up. The prop blades are shorter than on other bush planes, so to take off, the prop had to turn at a higher rpm. The speed of the blade nearly cracks the sound barrier.

I awoke to the sound of a Cessna 185 taking off and flying low over my house and I remembered my appointment with Karl to take my check ride.

That morning's entry into the ledger of time was a wound and a scar. It was one of those bleak and dark mornings that could have been painted by one of those Soviet Russian painters, for it seemed that brown or soot grey contaminated all of their paints. So it was this morning. Something hovered and brooded.

I arrived at the airfield early and saw that Karl had a student ahead of me. I stayed out of the way and watched from the parking lot.

Her name was Sally and she wore her hair that morning in a pony tail that extended out of the back of her ball cap, and she wore a sweatshirt with a cartoon of Snoopy and the Red Baron printed on the back. She held her checklist in her left hand as she completed her outside inspection and they climbed into the tail dragger. I saw the ailerons and stabilizers move side to side as she worked the controls. She glanced down at her preflight checklist and I heard her run up the throttle. Through the window I saw Karl pull off his tie and put it in his pocket. He bent his head down and appeared to be writing on his clipboard. I could imagine the yellow pencil moving like a small stick in a beaver's mouth. They taxied downwind to the beginning of the runway. I could see her silhouette hold the microphone as she announced her intentions on the radio.

I walked to the edge of the field to watch the takeoff. I could see the spray of the waves as they broke at the end of the runway.

The plane accelerated and just before the lip of the runway she lifted off. Perhaps the spray at the end of the strip startled her, but for a reason known only to her, she pulled up abruptly, very hard. The airplane shot straight up and did a full stall just above the runway. Sally must have then stalled one wing into a hammerhead stall. The Cessna rolled to one side and accelerated nose down into the ocean. The engine seemed to scream in protest and it was over.

It seemed that emergency vehicles and boats instantly materialized. I ran to the lip of the strip and saw Sally at the surface only twenty feet from the edge. She gasped, her lungs too full to scream. She sputtered and gagged as she dog paddled toward the edge of the runway. Her ball cap was gone and her red hair hung in thin red threads across her face and streams of blood the color of her hair lined her forehead and cheeks. As I scrambled to get down to her I could hear her shriek, "Aaugh, aaugh," with her last effort to make safety. There at the water's edge she hugged a basket-sized boulder with both her arms and laid her head on it as she gasped for breath. Her back and shoulders heaved with every breath.

There at the rock, with both arms tightly around it, her gasps turned into sobs and I knew that she would survive the ordeal. Both of her legs were broken. When a plane hits the water the foot pedals vibrate at tremendous speed and always seem to break the legs of the pilot. She would live.

I ran to the crash site. Nothing. Not even bubbles. No debris. Karl did not come up nor did the airplane. The Coast Guard came and looked. Boats came and searched. Divers went down and sought. No trace of Karl or of the airplane was ever discovered. Perhaps a fast current carried it all with Karl still strapped in his seat, like the aircraft carrier pilots buried at sea inside their planes.

• • •

Sally, the red haired pilot, healed over time. She had a limp for some years, but over the years even that went away. But Sally had spunk, sand in her craw. She learned that her mistake cost a life of a great pilot and true Alaskan. It was in physical therapy as they were working on the foot that the vibrating pedal had so fractured, she made a decision. "I cost the life of a good man and the only amends I can ever do is to do my best to fill his void."

She mastered her fears suffered in the crash. Sally became a great pilot in Alaska's environment. In time she became a pilot in a major commercial airline.

Over the place where Karl disappeared they extended the runway out to sea making it one third longer than it was. It is still considered by some to be a short field for modern jets. It is unknown if truckloads of rock and gravel may have covered his secret resting place at the end of the runway. I think however, that he would have smiled, just the corners of his mouth a little bit, at a secret irony. He would think it fitting the airstrip was being built on the shoulders of an accomplished pilot.

As for me, the government spent nearly a year finding and appointing an examiner to replace Karl. I made several appointments with the new examiner and he would forget or just fail to show up for his check rides. The Feds admonished him and he assured them he would be more circumspect with his students. By then there was not an airplane available for anyone to rent with which to fly. My life took another direction and I flew then only for pleasure in pursuit of a campsite that I imagined as a boy while looking at a Goodwin painting.

*Artist Ernest Robertson*

# Fog Flying

Fog slithered over the airport like a living thing. Although it was the middle of the day, its thickness so greyed the sky that the two automatic lights turned on in the parking lot. Thick bands of mist coiled themselves around the bases of the light poles and crawled upward where tendrils of fog, like fangs, engulfed the lights.

To the north, the landing light of the Alaska Airlines jet poked through the haze seconds before the jet touched down. It appeared to have made an escape from a grey fist of sky and to have just made it to safety. The rumble of the tires sounded smothered and muffled where it touched down and the rumble lagged behind the jet as it continued down the runway.

From the parking lot Pastor Lindstrum heard the pilot apply the brakes and heard the loud hissing of the jet as it turned around at the end and taxied to the terminal. His heart thumped. He could hear his heart beat as if it were a sound from outside his body. His car keys dropped from his shaking hands. He placed a hand on his chest.

Would other people be able to see the beating of his heart? He felt guilty because he had hoped the flight would bypass the town and not land today. Now he had no choice but to fly.

The preacher from the small Baptist church shut his car door and glanced at the nearly empty parking lot. Who would fly in this? In the thickness of the fog the two lights in the lot could be barely seen but glowed like the eyes of a ghost. In the direction of the open sea the sky was very dark, blue-black. It seemed certain that a weather system was moving in. The air around him left a layer of moisture on his glasses and he took them off and cleaned them on his white shirt. "I do not want to fly in this soup," he thought to himself. "If there was any way out of this I would take it." The hand that held his car key had a tremor and he missed the slot twice before he could lock the door. He put on his backpack and made for the terminal.

He had checked in with the ticket agent earlier and she informed him that the weather was marginal. Well, the jet landed.

Pastor Lindstrum stood next in line at the counter just as the passengers leaving the airplane entered the terminal. A short man with red-blond hair turning nearly white near his ears left the line of offloading passengers, looked left and right, and walked directly to the ticket counter to the head of the line. His porcine skin was pink and covered with liver spots and sparse blond hair. A large, hard belly proceeded him as he barged to the front of the line.

"They said on the plane that we would not make it to Juneau tonight. I need to get over there. I have a business to run."

The agent spoke quietly, "I'm sorry, sir. But the weather there is below minimums. We are on hold here."

"Well they landed here. Why can't they go on? I paid for my ticket."

"Sir, the weather here is just marginal. Juneau is below minimums. We are on hold here. If the weather improves in Juneau we could try it. We can only wait for improvement."

"Lady, I have meetings in Juneau. I can't wait for bureaucrats to make up their minds. Talk to someone. I know people in Juneau."

"I am sorry, sir."

"So you won't help me then. What is your name, lady?"

An older woman in an airlines jacket appeared before him. "Sir, if you have pressing business—"

He interrupted her. "My name is Van Flood. You know my name. I have businesses all over this country."

"Mr. Van Flood. I am afraid that we have no choice but to wait for better conditions. If you have pressing business you could go next door to the Alaska bush pilots. They enjoy more generous minimums and might fly today."

"Well, you just lost my business," he grunted.

"You're welcome," she said as he spun around and left the ticket counter.

She looked up and saw the skinny pastor, next in line. He came forward on weak legs.

"I heard what you told the other gentleman," Lindstrum said. His mouth seemed dry as he spoke. "I am afraid that I have to get to Juneau too, but I am sure nervous to fly today."

"We can only wait and hope for improvement," the agent said.

"You can't imagine what you just said. I have to go to Juneau to see someone on a deathbed in which he can only hope for improvement. The family doesn't think there is any hope. I need to share the gospel before he dies."

"I think your best course is to go with the bush pilots too. They are very good pilots and they certainly would not fly if it was not safe."

"Thank you, ma'am." Lindstrum saw her understanding smile. "I am kinda embarrassed for being nervous. Must be the fog."

• • •

The sign over the door of the hangar read "Wings Southeast." The logo was painted on an oval plywood board. Old rope that had been used in the past to tether airplanes on the tarmac was used for a frame. The logo featured a white-bodied snow goose with its orange beak and small black eyes in flight over an Alaskan landscape. Outside, to the right of the hangar, were three airplanes on floats. A young man in short hair and a brown leather jacket was loading bags into one of them.

Inside the hangar, to the right of the entrance were several airplane propellers displayed on the wall. One of them had numerous nicks and some severe damage to its leading edges. "I'm glad I wasn't on that flight," he thought. At the counter, the red-faced businessman was talking loudly, his arms gesturing as if he were warding off mosquitos. Lindstrum took a seat to wait.

The preacher looked around the room. Maps and charts of this region of Alaska were attached to the left-most wall. On one map he saw colored stick pins on various locations with string connecting the pins. Lindstrum assumed they indicated certain scheduled flights. There were framed photographs of sportsmen on one wall. One showed a smiling angler holding up a salmon. Another photo showed a hunter standing on a pontoon of a floatplane displaying the cape and head of a mountain goat.

Nearby, on a chair that had once been seat "26-A" on a retired commercial airplane, sat a tall, slim, middle-aged man. He wore grey, pinstriped wool pants cut off at the lower calf and his long john covered legs extended from inside them. Over his long john top were suspenders that said "Alaska Logger." At his feet was a packsack with a hard hat strapped to the top. Looped over it all was a pair of heavy, black boots. His stocking feet rested on the top of the heap.

Lindstrum looked over to the logger.

"You on this flight too?" the man in suspenders asked.

"I haven't checked in yet, but if it is going to Juneau I am."

"Same as me, except I will get off at Bay Logging Company. It's on the way."

The logger pulled out his pocketknife and began to pare his nails.

"They call me Muk. It's short for Nessmuk. Well, who would call their kid Nessmuk, I ask ya? But my dad liked the name. There was a fella who wrote books about the outdoors a hundred years ago. He really lived the life. He was a little fella and he couldn't carry a lot of regular store bought stuff so he kinda invented everything for himself. He was the first ultra-light camper I guess. He invented a special pocket knife, like I am using now, the double bit axe and the Nessmuk style skinning knife.

"My last name is Sears. Nessmuk's real name was George Washington

Sears. My ol' man claimed we were related so he named me after him. Nessmuk was his pen name he used in his writing. What's your name?"

"My name is Lindstrum. Paul Lindstrum. I'm afraid I'm not named after anybody, unless it is the Apostle Paul in the Bible."

Nessmuk stopped paring his nails and studied the skinny pastor. "That's a good one," he said. "What do you do? What's in Juneau?"

"I am the pastor of a little Baptist church here. There is a man on his deathbed in Juneau that needs to hear the Gospel. I don't know why but I am plain nervous on this flight. Look at my hands."

"Not to worry. I do this flight all the time."

"In fog like this."

"It isn't a big deal. They do it all the time."

Muk put away his knife. "Know why I am in my stocking feet with my boots tied to my rucksack? I'll tell you. It's because I respect these people. I have cork boots, you know, nails poking out the bottom of my boots, so I can walk on the logs without falling off. I don't want to put holes in the plane. It's a respect thing I have for them."

"That pilot is going to come out and tell me, 'Muk, put on your boots.' These are good people and I want them to know that I appreciate them."

"Why were you in town, Muk?"

"Jammed a tree limb into my thigh. It went right through and came out the other side. I couldn't even pull it out. These people here came and got me with the limb sticking out both sides of my leg. We shortened the limb some but it still was a sight getting into the plane."

"When did this happen?"

"Four days ago."

"You mean you're going back already? Why so soon"

"Need to get back to work. Healing is for sissies."

Muk leaned over to the preacher, pointed toward the counter with his chin and whispered, "Look at that will ya. Look at his arms waving around like someone who fell overboard and doesn't know how to swim. Think of it. He wants a ticket. They want to sell him a ticket. Should be easy but look at it."

Lindstrum gazed at the unfolding drama and smiled.

Muk reached over and lifted his injured leg with both hands and set it on the floor. "I need to get up or I won't be able to." He stood and limped to the counter and returned with a map of the area and sat next to the preacher.

"You are probably nervous because of the fog. We aren't going to be flying in it. We will be flying under it." He emphasized the words, "in" and "under."

Lindstrum's eyes grew round with horror at the thought.

"I will explain it to you just like the pilot did for me. What if we never took off but had a runway all the way to Juneau. Well, the airplane would just be a car. And what if we taxied with the pontoons on the water all the way to Juneau, well, we would just be a boat. Now neither of those things would bother you would it."

Muk showed him the map. "See we are going to fly the map. We are just going to fly over the water and anytime we want we could set down and become a boat, see?" Muk's finger traced the shoreline and channels and passes all the way to Juneau. But we will lift off the water and be an airplane and fly just high enough to see the map below us but not high enough to be in the fog. Here, take this map and follow us the whole way."

"Thanks, Muk." But the map was a blur before his eyes just like the fog outside.

Nesmuk Sears smiled at the preacher, a smile with perfect white teeth and eyes that so crinkled at the corners it could be heard.

The logger tipped his head toward the preacher again, this time in confession. "I actually did all of the schools, got a license as an architect, had a suite of offices in a skyscraper, dined with the millionaires. One day I just said to myself, 'This is not me. Money is a cold friend. Does the person smiling at me in the fancy restaurant care anything for me or am I just a cog in his network?'"

He lifted his leg on to the backpack again this time pulling it up by the pant leg. "So I chucked it in. I gave the keys to my partner, and put my share of things into an account — I'm not stupid, ya know, and decided to come to Alaska and be a logger.

"I love this life. I like the smell of pitch in my clothes. When I wake up I hear ravens in the trees and I see brown bear foraging on the beach at low tide. I smell breakfast in the mess hall. And the cook will look at me and say, 'Good morning to you today. What'll ya have, Muk?'

"Hey have you ever had fried potatoes mixed with onion and green pepper with a few eggs setting up on the top and you are tipping the plate so the syrup from the flap jacks doesn't run over on to the spuds? Forget that corporate stress. I just want to worry about getting syrup mixed with my eggs."

They laughed out loud. Lindstrum thought of saying, "Well, why don't you use two plates?" but he then realized that the morning battle of the syrup was his daily reminder of conflict left behind, an expression of the only kind of conflict that could confront him now.

The businessman completed the purchase of his ticket and took a seat at the far wall. He looked left and right at those in the room and seeing no threat, placed his case on his lap and tapped his fingers on it like a computer.

The lady at the counter was trying to get Paul Lindstrum's attention.

"You know, preacher, I would pay them to let me work for them. I mean it."

"Sir, I can help you now," she said with a smile.

For a fleeting second Paul Lindstrum had the same feeling he had when they finally called his name in the dentist office. He glanced at the logger and approached the counter.

"I just need to get a ticket to Juneau," he quietly said.

As he was buying the ticket the pilot came out of the hangar and into the waiting room. He wore Xtra Tuff rubber boots over his blue jeans and a brown jacket. His ball cap bore the logo of the snow goose and name of the company.

"Muk, put your boots on. They aren't going to hurt the floor of my plane." His tone was pure affection with a note of, "you goof."

Muk extended his hand and reached for his boots. "My friend at the counter is a little nervous about flying in the fog. I told him you would put him at ease."

"I will do that," he said. "Let me help you with that boot. I don't think you are up to it yet."

The pilot got to his knees, removed his ball cap, and put it on the chair so the bill would not be in the way. Sandy brown hair hung over his ears and forehead and his smooth movements made him appear young to Lindstrum who watched from the counter, very young. The pilot looked up from lacing a boot and saw the preacher.

"I'm Jack, your pilot today. Should be a good flight. We have a better ceiling down the line and there is no turbulence. Funny thing about fog — fog and wind never seem to go together. I see Muk got you a map. We aren't going to go through the fog and over the mountains. We are going to fly around the outside of the island and mountains. You can follow the course we take through the passages on the map. You will probably see a few bear and deer along the way."

The pilot stood up. "We are ready to go folks. Just the three of you. If you will just follow me…."

"I'll take the front seat," said Van Flood walking quickly to the door.

"No," the pilot said. "That one is for the preacher."

"Weight and balance you know," he said as he looked back at Paul Lindstrum and winked at him.

Van Flood glared in the direction of the pilot but realized that bluster would not change things.

"We are taking the smaller plane as there is only the four of us. Let me help you get in first, Muk. Ladies with small children and Muk are pre-boarding."

When they were seated, Jack gave the preacher a head set. "You will be able to hear me talk to the tower and other traffic. You can hear me talk to you with the headset on. To talk with me just push the black button."

Jack did his preflight and run-up in front of the hangar and taxied for takeoff. "As soon as I lift off we will fly toward town and the shoreline. We actually have more ceiling there and can work our way north."

• • •

A small breath of air from off shore lifted the ceiling of fog as they lined up on the centerline of the runway. The pilot pushed full throttle and they were a hundred feet in the air before they were over the end of the airport. Below them, where the water met the edge of the runway, was a white lace of surge breaking on the rocks. All around the Cessna were various shades of grey, light grey fog that fled before the breeze, middle grey of the airstrip and rocks, and a dark grey, almost black, of the ocean below. The pilot retracted the wheels and gently banked the plane toward Sitka with its fish canneries and native village. They banked left and followed the shoreline, a shore that was outlined with breaking wavelets and easy to see.

"We have a much better ceiling here and it looks even better as we go. See, the light is brighter through the haze ahead." The preacher fumbled with the microphone and pressed the correct button.

Jack continued, "I like to get as much altitude as I can. The higher up, the more of the map I can see below us." He placed his hand spider-like with his fingers close together on the map that the preacher held in his lap. As he raised his hand from the paper he spread out his fingers.

"I can see that."

They approached Starrigavin bay and Jack pointed the place on the map. "To the front-right over there is the entrance to Katlian Bay. We don't want that. That bay ends in mountains. Not good."

"I can see that on the map," the preacher said, fully interested.

"See the direction we are headed now? Just ahead is another long bay to the right. We don't want that one either. Same story. We are going to follow Olga and Neva Strait on your map. Can you find it on the map?"

"Yes. The straits look as narrow as a road."

"Exactly. We will follow the straits for about twenty minutes, cross a large sound and then follow the water course after that." The pilot traced the route on the map with his finger.

Jack took his index finger off the map and pointed through the windscreen. "Look below us. The splash by the rocks there. That's a pod of whales." He looked closer at them. "Those are sperm whales. The black cod fishermen tell me they are extremely smart. They say they can find their long lines on the bottom of the ocean and they run the lines through the space between their teeth and strip off all of the cod that are on the hooks just like a comb can remove all the ticks from a hound's hair. The fishermen tell me there are only a few lips and gills left on the hooks."

"I had one fisherman tell me that they were pulling up their gear into the boat and a sperm whale started to strip the fish from the line right from the side of the boat. They could feel the boat pulling and tipping side to side by the whale."

The air was smooth and without the slightest turbulence. Only the soft purring of the engine could be heard.

Paul craned his neck and looked back. Nesmuk was rubbing his wounded thigh in his sleep, his mouth was slightly parted, his chin resting on his chest. He looked farther around and saw Van Flood also asleep, both arms wrapped tightly around his brown leather briefcase.

Leaving Salisbury Sound they saw twenty or more sea lions bobbing among the kelp.

"Hey, do you know the collective for a bunch of sea lion? It's a thing of mine when I am flying. Keeps my mind awake."

"When they are in the water they are called a 'raft,' when they are on land they are called a 'colony,' when they are mating they are called a 'rookery,' and if they are all females they are called a harem."

"Who remembers that stuff?" Then Lindstrum considered, pilots who want to stay awake do. And pilots who want to keep their client's mind off flying in fog do.

A few brant geese were feeding in the grass below the plane and Jack continued, "A bunch of geese on the ground are called a flock but when they are flying they are called a skein."

"You won't believe what the collective for porcupines is — they are called a 'prickle.' Can't go wrong on that one."

"I have two for you. Lord knows why I know them! What do you call a bunch of crows… beside names?"

Jack thought. "I give up."

"A murder."

"You're kidding."

"Really. A murder of crows. Agatha Christie must have thought up that one. I know one more. Ravens."

"I don't know that one either."

Lindstrum smiled in triumph. "A bunch of ravens is called a constable. No wonder you never see ravens and crows together."

They continued their flight through the passage over the thin ribbon of water that divided Baranof Island from Chichigoff Island. The fog had risen to a height that had to be considered to be cloud but still erased most of the mountain heights.

"Look below us, Pastor Lindstrum."

"Paul."

"Thanks. Paul."

"See that fishing boat with the poles up. He must have not looked at the tide book for this part of the passage. This area is the narrows. When the tide is not slack the water of the whole ocean pushes through that opening. When the tide is going either way this area has a current like a river. See over by those rocks. Those are whirlpools. In places along here there are rapids. The current is at least eight knots. That troller can only do about nine knots. It is barely moving against the tide."

"We are coming up on a place where I need to be careful. Around the next bend is an area where the mountains are tight against the narrows. When I go around the corner I want to see daylight under the low clouds. If you think about it, we are really flying in a tunnel. Below us is the water. On the sides are mountains and above is fog. I need to see the other end of the tunnel the whole way before I am comfortable flying through it."

"The problem I need to watch for is that with the mountains pressing close to the edge of the narrows there might not be room to turn an airplane around in that width and go the other way. At least not in normal flying."

"We're coming up on it now."

Paul Lindstrum felt his chest tighten. He realized that he was holding his breath.

Jack flew to the extreme right of the passage. Paul stared at the nearness of the trees alongside them. Perched eagles in the bare trees were close enough to see the black pupils in their unblinking eyes.

"I am edging to one side of the passage to give us turn around room if we need it."

The narrow passage bore left around a point of land and the plane followed the passage. The pilot leaned over the dash and peered ahead. In the distance, fog extended all the way down to the water. There was no daylight ahead.

"Well preacher, we need to do Plan B."

Paul pressed the black button as firmly as if he were pinching a bleeding artery. "W-W-What's wrong?"

"Not to worry, Paul. I need to turn around and land somewhere."

"Are we in trouble? Will we crash?"

"No, no, nothing like that. I just don't want to do the pass until we have better ceiling. There is a bay behind us where I have landed before. We will go there and wait for the fog to lift. If we get a little wind it could clear in a half hour. Just about the right amount of time for one of your prayers." He looked at Lindstrum and smiled reassuringly.

"I am going to do a maneuver that might seem a little freighting to you. But it is completely safe. My father flew those Bird Dog airplanes for the Green Berets in Vietnam and he taught me this maneuver. You can nearly turn an airplane around in its own width and go the opposite direction."

"Might be fun for you."

"I doubt it."

Lindstrum smiled at the pilot. "I will pray for you."

Jack turned his head back and shouted at the passengers in the back. "I need to do a maneuver that might seem unusual to you. It's perfectly safe."

Paul looked back but both men were fast asleep and did not hear.

"Here we go now."

Jack pulled the throttle completely off. The drone of the engines stopped totally and only wind over the wings could be heard.

"I need to let the plane slow down to maneuvering speed," he said over the mic.

Hearing the engine sound completely stop Van Flood sprang from his sleep thinking the engine had failed. He shrieked.

"Auugh, auugh, auugh," he screamed. His voice cracked the third shriek. He dropped his brief case and grabbed the back of the front seat with both hands and thrust his face near the pilot. "What, what? Are we dying? Are we going to crash?"

"Sit back! You're in my way," Jack shouted back at him. "Sit back. It's o.k."

Van Flood's face lost its pink and became as pale as paper. He moaned and cried. He grabbed his valise from the floor and set it on his lap and hugged it with both hands and rocked back and forth. He shut his eyes tightly and wailed.

The Cessna quickly lost airspeed. It seemed nearly to stop in flight. At that point Jack put on full flaps. The plane seemed to have invisible brakes. When the flaps were full, Jack applied full left rudder and made a hard turn to the left. The plane reversed its direction in the space of its own wingspan. When the turn was completed, he pushed the nose down, gave full throttle and reduced flaps. The craft recovered its airspeed and he leveled off the plane and retraced a mile of the passage.

"There is a beautiful cove near here where we are going to land," he said to Paul over the intercom, "We will set down and wait for weather."

Van Flood shouted over the seat, spit spluttering as he did so, "I will have your license! Where did you learn to fly? I am an important passenger."

"Please sit down Mr. Van Flood. This is all perfectly normal and safe. We are going to set down in a cove for a while and wait for the fog to lift."

He retraced their flight down Peril Straight for another mile and bore left down a side finger of water. From the finger of water to the port side of the Cessna was a quiet bay and they made an approach to it. At the far end was a stream and a few salmon jumped at its mouth. A pair of mergansers swam near the grass in the water.

The approach to landing was smooth and when the pontoon touched the skin of water, it sliced it like a scalpel. They glided to a spot on the shore and Jack shut off the engine, got out of the plane and stood on a pontoon with a rope in his hand. Just as they approached the shore he stepped off the plane and tied it off to a dead tree snag.

"We'll just sit here for a while and wait for improvement in the weather. You can stretch your legs if you want. This little spit of land here is pleasant to walk. I can blow the air horn when we are ready to go."

Muk lifted his leg with both hands and swiveled his body toward the door. "I think I stiffened up from sitting there." Jack stretched his hands out to help him off the plane. "That was a cool maneuver back there. Could we do it again?"

Jack grinned at Muk. "We could have actually continued down Peril Straight. I know every rock and snag and bend in the narrows. But I sure don't want to clip a set of trolling poles pulled up on a fishing boat in this fog." He thought for a minute. "It's hard on my pontoons."

"I think I will just get the stiffness out of my leg and sit down again."

Jack turned to help Van Flood. "Don't you ever do that again. I'll have your license. I mean it." He glared at him like a boar hog with its beady eyes. He ignored the pilot's offered hand, holding his leather case in both hands instead.

Van Flood's foot slipped off the pontoon and went calf deep into the water.

The preacher placed a hand on the entrepreneur's shoulder to steady him. "I'm going to do a little stroll — get some fresh air and stretch my legs. Care to join me, Mr. Van Flood?" He glanced at the pilot and winked.

Van Flood grunted, his head down studying the ground before he placed his feet.

"You could probably leave your briefcase on the plane. I am sure it is safe."

Van Flood glanced over at Muk. The logger leaned on the pontoon strut and smiled at the businessman with his beautiful teeth. To Van Flood the smile was that of a cannibal sizing him up.

"I'll take it with me."

Black, water-rounded stones that turned underfoot edged the

small spit of land. Where the receding tide had exposed it, lime-green sea grass covered the stones and was treacherous underfoot. Paul was several steps ahead. "It is much better walking up here. Real ground with grass on it."

The pilot put a hand to his mouth and shouted at them. "Forgot to mention it but with the salmon at the mouth of the stream there could be bear around."

Paul waved his acknowledgment toward the plane.

Van Flood stopped at the crest of the little finger of land. His face was flushed and he wheezed.

"My name is Paul," the pastor said, offering his hand.

Van Flood looked at the hand as though measuring its cleanness. He assumed his business persona and shook his hand. His hand was moist. "Theador Van Flood. You may have heard of me."

"Do they call you Ted?"

For a moment he clinched his teeth at the familiarity. "They call me Mr. Van Flood." He paused making a concession to circumstance. "You can call me Ted if you want, but not in public. In the city I cannot have such informality."

They walked for several minutes along the spit of land. Short alder trees with many limbs lined the crest. A well-used animal trail marked its spine and here and there among the edges of larger rocks were entrances of small animal dens.

"So how much are they paying you for this trip, Preacher?"

He thought for a moment. "Actually nothing."

"What?"

"That's it. Nothing. I hadn't thought of that until now."

"You have a screw loose, don't you?" Theador Van Flood stopped walking, his feet splayed on two rocks. "Are your people cheap?"

"Actually I have a very small church and my people are not wealthy. I never told them I am doing this trip. My wife and I are paying my own way." He picked up a bleached tree limb and set it off the trail. "It is as simple as this. Someone down the line needs me. So here I am in this fog."

"But you must have a good salary."

"Actually no, Theador. God sees to our needs here. You might say we have sent my pay check on to Heaven."

"Preacher," Van Flood began, turning Lindstrum around with one pudgy hand, "Life is here and now. My money is in the bank, in fact, several banks. I am building big holdings. My name will be known."

Lindstrum looked at the businessman's arm. A breeze was blowing the blond hair like the fine hair of a caterpillar. "Can I tell you a story?"

The businessman seemed more interested in looking where next to place his feet.

"When I was a young teen I read about a man in one of those books — maybe it was a Ripley Believe It or Not thing. I can't remember. But the man and what he did has never left my mind. He lived in one of those provincial countries that you don't hear much about. The man was a fabulous carver, very well known in his locality but the world had never discovered him and his great talent.

"He was acquainted with the work of the great masters of sculpture — Michelangelo, Leonardo da Vinci, Donatello and Rodin. He liked the classics of Greece and Rome. He studied the graceful simplicity of Michelangelo's 'David,' and the Pieta, the one with Mary holding the dead body of Jesus in her lap with its great detail and composition. He studied the work of those men and thought to himself with clarity and candor that he could do equally as well as they did.

"He looked at 'The Thinker' of Rodin. There was nothing ornate or difficult about the sculpture — just a simple composition but it had something, a theme that stopped all who wandered by.

"What one creation could he do that would have all the elements that he found in all of those works. He paged through books that portrayed the marble and bronze themes that endured more than a thousand years. Then his eyes fell on one marble sculpture that most fascinated him. It was a gladiator with his weapon, who had been caught in a net that had been thrown by his opponent. It was of one piece of marble and every string that made up the net was carved, suspended in free air with the man inside. That is the caliber of work that he would do. He would carve himself with his work and tools in his hands. It would be intricate and so real viewers would speak to it not knowing that the work was not its creator."

Van Flood was quietly listening. "Let's sit down on this log. I'm not used to walking on uneven ground."

"The carver sought out and bought the perfect wood, just the same hue as his own skin. It was flawless and the grain in it was imperceptible. For weeks he worked in his studio. The lights were often on through the night and the soft tap, tap, tap of his hammer could be heard at the sidewalk outside his window. He had his maid slide his meals to him under the door for there was room for a plate to pass, and he did not want to be disturbed.

"He stood back and examined his progress. The proportions were perfect. Where the artist had a scar, so did the sculpture. Where he had a mole so did the statue. Where he had a crooked finger, so did the carving. The only concession he made to effort outside himself were the eyes. They were glass and matched his own and he wet the lids until they were pliable and set them in and he was satisfied.

"I see the air is blowing your hair a little, Mr. Van Flood. We might get some clear sky after all.

"One day he let in his maid to see her reaction. She held the carver's meal in a tray as she entered and stopped short in a start. But then she continued on. She was used to the master's good work and thought no more of it.

"The artist was certain then that he had not accomplished what he wanted to do. He locked himself into his studio once again and stared at the figure until he knew what he must do.

"Again the lights of the studio glowed through the wax paper window shades. Night after night he labored. But passersby no longer heard the tapping of the hammer and chisel nor the sliding of the carving knife. He worked with the quiet of a monk in an abbey. From time to time however, they heard him groan. But sometimes he sang.

"What the artist did in the solitude was to pluck every hair of his body by the roots, one at a time. He drilled tiny holes and placed his own black hair in the holes — his nose hairs, hair from the back of his knuckles, his arms, eyebrows, the tops of his toes and that on his head — all of his hair.

"Then he carefully removed his own teeth from the front of his mouth, upper and lower. He first wrapped the jaws of his plier with cloth lest he crack and ruin the teeth. He wet the lips of the parted mouth of the figure and placed them in the mouth and the lips dried and set over them.

"The sculptor then removed his own finger and toe nails, made tiny slits — receptacles for them in the wood — and attached them in their place.

"The carver stepped back from his masterpiece. He had finished it. It would make his name known, not just in his province or his own country, but everywhere. This was the monument of his life, his accomplishment. His final act before he let in his maid, was to place his tools in the hands of the finished piece, his brown cloak over one shoulder, and his glasses on its brow.

"It was midday and he placed his triumph across from the door where his maid would see it first when he called for her. She came through the door hesitatingly. She had not seen her master for nearly a month. She held a tray with his noon meal with both her hands. She passed through the doorway and shut the door with her foot as she passed and then looked up. She saw before her the finished statue of her master. 'I brought you your favorite today,' she said to the carving.

"But the carving did not answer her. She spoke again to the image and she also sought where to place the tray. 'You have worked long and hard and I have not seen you.'

"But the statue did not answer and she thought it strange for he always spoke to her, although sometimes when he worked in earnest he was curt with her.

"She was puzzled at his stillness and silence. She looked again at the image and thought it strange that he did not move at all.

"Then her mouth parted as she realized what she was seeing. She heard laughter from the shadows in the corner of the room — her master's — and she dropped the tray of food on the floor, the soup bowl bounced on the floor and the hot soup spilled on her naked foot and she did not notice." Van Flood had not spoken or interrupted the preacher.

"The breeze is chilly. You have goose bumps. I can give you my jacket. It is a bit small for you but you could put it over your shoulders."

"No, thank you," the businessman said. And he added, "I appreciate your offer, Pastor."

They both stood and began to walk back toward the Cessna. The horizon seemed to be lighter and the hills beside them were exposed partway up the sides.

"Why do I think there is more to the story? What happened to the artist?"

The pastor seemed to pull an image from his memory. "I can only tell you my impression when I read of the carver. In my young mind I could see the masterpiece — the fame and accomplishment of a lifetime. But then I could only imagine what the maid must have seen as she peered into the shadows. There in the dusk on a chair was her master. He was hairless and toothless and blood covered his fingertips and toes. His mouth would have been still swollen and bloody and empty air puffed from his mouth as he had to learn how to form his words.

"See, in building his name he destroyed himself."

They heard a blast of the air horn. The sound bounced off the trees and back to them again. A small flock of teal burst from the grass on the far bank, a flock they had not noticed before.

Van Flood walked pensively with his head down picking his way over the round rocks. "You certainly spoke like a preacher. What is the clincher, the punch line, Pastor Lindstrum?"

He did not answer for several steps. "The punch line, Mr. Van Flood, is that I cannot remember the name of the artist." He stopped and looked at the businessman. "I don't think anyone does."

• • •

"I think we have our weather. It looks bright in that direction. We shouldn't have any problems now," Jack reported as they approached the plane.

The passengers boarded. Van Flood was subdued. His case was on the floor at his feet. He looked at the pilot. "I'm sorry for how I acted back there. It was not called for."

The pilot smiled. "We all have our days."

They taxied in a circle inside the bay to rough up the water, then took off, banking right as they gained altitude and flew down Peril Strait toward Bay Logging Company. The fog had lifted to a thousand feet and the increased light from above it showed that it had a thinness.

"Peril Strait bends right and is quite wide here. We will be flying by compass across it. We will get to the other side in about six minutes. Muk's camp is along that side in a quiet, peaceful place." Jack turned his head and shouted behind him. "About time to comb your hair, Mr. Sears. There might be a pretty girl on the dock."

"I'll wear my hat."

They landed and taxied on water that did not have a ripple. In the shallow water near the dock they could see all the way to the bottom. On it were white empty clamshells and red and purple starfish and urchins. He shut off the engine and coasted to the dock turning parallel to it with the rudder and tied off.

There were people on the dock, some to get the mail, food supplies or machine parts.

"Let me help you off, Muk," the preacher said with one raised hand.

"I got it." He said.

"No, let me help. It will let me feel useful."

The owner of the logging camp met Muk. "About time you got back, Muk. You sure go to great lengths to goof off in town."

"That's because you work me like a dog."

The owner shook his hand and hugged him. "Glad to have you back. I don't want you to over-do it though. See me when you are settled and we will figure something out." The owner turned and tended to other business.

"Muk, let me walk you up the dock."

The logger pointed out things of interest as they walked.

"Muk, I enjoyed meeting you. You are a good man."

"You are okay too for a skinny guy."

"I was wondering. Do you think anyone in the camp would like church services here each week? I could fly up each Sunday after our services. Or come up on a Saturday. I could take the bush plane in."

"I thought you were afraid of flying."

"Well it was the fog, really. Flying in soup when I can't see the mountains right beside me frightens me to the core. I get chills down my back."

Muk listened quietly. He stopped and leaned on a dock piling and rubbed his leg.

"Muk, duty will make me fly in the fog. If I am needed I will go." There was a pause and he continued. "Even if there was a good chance that I would crash I would make the trip."

"If you would do that for me, young fellow, I would listen."

"I have a card. It is kind of messed up and dirty from being in my wallet but my information is there."

"And all you have to do to contact me is to write, 'Muk' on an envelope and get it with cargo going to Bay Logging and I will get it." He paused, thinking, "Oh. Let me give you something. Something from Muk. It looks like you chewed your nails on this flight. You otta take care of them. Here is a good knife for that." He pulled it from his pocket and whipped it clean on his pants leg. "See ya, Preacher"

"You too." The preacher started to walk away. "Oh, keep the syrup off your eggs."

Muk waved. His hardened hand that extended from his coat sleeve seemed too large for his body.

• • •

Peril Strait had a swell with a surface chop so they began their take off run from the dock and were airborne before they reached the entrance to Bay Logging Company. Below them, the logging camp receded into small rust colored squares of roof. A single row of homes and a schoolhouse lined the shore. The tide was out and children played in the white sand and two dogs barked at the children.

A grey gravel road followed the contours of the valleys into the interior of the island. Far from the camp the hillsides were the color of moist earth where recent logging was taking place. Nearer the camp the areas of logging were already lime green with new growth.

They flew under the fog along Peril until they hit Chatham Strait. There the fog was as thick as a dare to the north and they proceeded directly across the six miles of its width.

"We will fly the compass across until we see the Indian village and then follow the coast north. I want to keep some altitude as the ferry and some tugs with barges use this route."

Fog hung over Chatham Strait like a shredded flannel blanket. Jack needled through the openings banking left and right and adjusting altitude as necessary.

"Look there, Mr. Van Flood." He shouted to the back seat but kept his eyes ahead.

Before them a tug worked against the waves below. The cable from the tug was lost to sight in a patch of low fog. "There," Jack pointed through the thick haze.

Although the barge at the end of the towline was as large as an apartment building it was barely discernable in the mist. He shouted so Van Flood could hear. "Those container vans are stacked six or eight high. That is as tall at a five-story building. Look at the top of them. See that white on the very top. That isn't fog. That's salt spray from a storm they went through somewhere that hasn't washed off yet."

Van Flood stared at the sight and watched it as they flew by, lost in unshared thought.

"I cannot imagine being in a storm that would throw spray five stories up," the preacher said.

Van Flood spoke. His first unsolicited words of the trip. "Can you imagine what it must be like to be in the tug attached to that barge by a cable having the barge thrown around?"

The minister looked back at him. Van Flood shuddered.

They arrived at the long channel that led to the airport at Juneau and flew low under the fog. They cleared with the control tower, landed and taxied to the terminal.

"We are here, gentlemen." They stepped down to the tarmac and although it was not raining there was a wetness from the fog on everything.

Paul extended his hand to the captain. "I absolutely appreciate you taking the time to reassure me. We will certainly fly again together."

Van Flood offered his hand also. "It has been…" he sought for the word, "an experience."

The pilot thought on the word choice and then laughed aloud.

• • •

"Preacher, I have a car in the lot. Let me give you a ride to your appointment."

The day was darkening. The traffic lights were brighter for the twilight but seemed to wrestle with the haze about them. Although the Lexus was nearly sound proof the hiss of car tires on the wet asphalt could not be ignored.

They drove to the entrance of the hospital and as Paul Lindstrum stepped from the Lexus and turned to thank him, Theador Van Flood 111 also stepped out. As he walked over to the preacher he stopped and looked up.

"Hey. Look." He pointed to the sky. The fog was becoming filmy and thin and light penetrated it to the lot. The fingers of fog that had clung to the lamppost lost their grip and slid down. A slight breeze pulled it from the parking lot and it slunk away.

"Just like Muk said, 'fog and wind don't go together.'"

Van Flood pulled a crisp business card from a gold metal holder. "I don't know how it will go in there but if you are free I would like to take you to dinner. There is a Mexican restaurant on Franklin that looks like nothing on the outside, but the food is wonderful." He continued, "You can tell me one of your stories."

"I would love to have dinner with you. I can tell you the story of the man who wanted bigger barns."

Theador Van Flood 111 smiled. It was the first Lindstrum had seen. It was a good smile. A wonderful smile. And it looked good on him.

# Great Whites

In a certain village on a tiny island in the central Pacific, the people never learned the name of the typhoon that struck them. To them, it was remembered as the one that blinded Uncle as he ran from the house to the pens, blinded him when the thatch from the roof thrust into his eyes like tiny arrows. In the bay, the sails of the fishing smacks were shredded into tendrils like those of jellyfish. It was the typhoon that sucked hogs into the air, and the wind, mocking, mimicked the squealing of the pigs.

In time, the fury of the storm spent itself and shuffled off to the north following the currents. Its edges first arrived in our town in Alaska as a couple of days of balmy warmth, humidity, and calmness. People leaving their houses paused and sniffed the air like dogs. At the door of the drugstore the pharmacist mentioned to a stranger standing nearby, "I think we will go to the Bahamas this year." But he did not know why it was he said it.

Then the rain began. First it was a couple of drops on the porch, which sounded like pine cones falling on the roof. Then it dumped. And dumped. For six days we lived in a wall of water.

"Reminds me of 'Nam," said someone at the store.

It was worse than the rain we usually get in autumn that swells the streams and carries the unique smell of each headwater to sea, and over the nares of waiting salmon massed in the bays. This was spring and the deluge was untimely. The atmosphere was warm and tropical.

Under the awning of a restaurant a man with every other tooth missing like a moss-covered white fence, cupped his hand to his mouth and shouted into my ear. His breath was sour and moist and hot. I only heard over the roar of the rain, "some… gravel roads… south… washed out… like stream bed…." He stepped away and looked at me with his moist, light blue eyes and nodded his head to make sure I caught the information. It always amazed me how often those who lived on the street or in the derelict boats knew facts as fast as the officials.

"You mean that the rain washed out some of the roads?"

He nodded, his approval expressed in his broad grin.

"Well, here's one. Go down the main street," I told him. "As I was coming in this morning I saw that the sewer system was so flooded, the water was lifting those iron manhole covers up in the air."

"No kiddin'. Thankee." And he shuffled off to see the sight.

I was going to tell him (I wanted to tell someone but he was already gone) that on my way to town in my pickup, I also saw yellow water shoot from overflowing culverts as if they were huge fire hoses and spray high into the air like a cough. I also stopped to look at the water from the bridge and the stream that had been gentle a few days ago, sourced only by melting mountain snow, was swelled into torrents. In the rapids I watched bucket sized boulders rolling in the streambed as if they were marbles. But the homeless man was gone.

I went into the restaurant and ordered breakfast, lots of eggs and hash browns. I had black coffee and as I waited for my meal, the foreman from public works was just finishing his. A younger man in a red hardhat and wearing hip waders rapidly approached him. His boots squeaked as he walked. His eyes seemed tiny in his earnest face as he stood dripping before the department head. "Frank, the folks upstairs think the rain has loosened the soil to the point of instability. They just want you to know."

"Well, I can't stop the rain. They are too late anyway. My people just told me that the main road has been cut in two or three places by landslides. My people are already on it."

Then, the downpour abruptly ended. The roar on the roof that had been constant stopped. The waitress paused mid-stride with my plate in her hand and looked up at the ceiling. The sound of forks against plates seemed inordinately loud. I heard splashing from the overloaded rain gutters. People emerged from their shelters like soldiers leaving their bunkers after a bombardment. I imagined that throughout the island animals were doing the very same — deer leaving the shelter of a depression in the dwarf cedar, goats leaving the lee side of the mountain, birds emerging from the fluff of their expanded down and changing back into sparrows. Daybreak and bright sun announced a new day.

In the parking lot as I left the diner, last sullen drops fell from soaked trees. A few songbirds trilled. The air smelled fresh-washed. All about me was the sound of earth draining itself.

On the way to the flying service where my airplane was tied, a few dozen birds were pulling earthworms that had been driven to the surface of the lawn by the flooding. The warmth of the sun evaporated the wetness of roofs into steam and I smiled because the rising steam on the roof of the fire hall gave it the appearance of being on fire.

From the parking lot of the flying service I saw my partner already doing the preflight of the plane on the ramp. "You beat me."

"Just barely," he shouted up at me. "I nearly didn't make it because of the slides, but the one between my house and here only blocked one lane."

I grabbed my rucksack and thermos and hurried down the ramp.

"I think this could be a good day for us," he said. "We only have some freight to take today and no passengers, so most of the day is ours. This will be perfect for you to get experience. You can only get so much training by landing and taking off on these regular runs."

I tossed my gear into the back seat. "I imagine that with this break in the weather every animal that has been hunkered down will be out."

"Exactly. After this rain and now the sun to shine on them we should see animals everywhere. And I have some places to show you where no one ever goes. They will require all of your ability to get to them."

I wondered at this last. I considered myself a good pilot. I had aerobatics and precision flying which most pilots do not have and I was confident in my ability. What I lacked and was keenly aware of, was local knowledge, significant time under my belt and the experience Alaska can throw at you. The pilot I was flying with had thirty thousand hours of bush flying. I didn't have two thousand.

We loaded the cargo into the hold for the day. My mentor's full name was Joseph Tibbs. Everyone called him Joey. He looked like everyone's little brother — when you went out on your own you left him with his model airplanes and comic books and brown hair that sat on his head like a pelt. You come back and there he is — grown up, accomplished and mature.

Working Alaskans like to speak with familiarity with those in their world. They are not impressed with titles, even, "mister." He was, Joey. "Joey can get us through, you can count on Joey."

One logger was telling me, "We were coming in to Iron Mountain and there was a fierce cross wind right 'cross the runway and we had to land. There weren't no way 'round it — we needed to get there. We weren't carrin' no serum to Nome or nuthin' like that, but we did need to land there. The wind was strong 'cross the runway. That ol' red windsock was full up like a balloon about to pop. Well, the wind was trying to blow us sideways on the final approach. So Joey faces into the wind some and we were flying sorta sideways on the approach. I figgered we'd flip for sure — tires don't roll sideways, ya know. I was skaired, I tell ya. I braced myself in the plane. I got one hand against the roof and I'm holding on to my seat with the other. Both o' my legs are out there stiff as posts against the floor.

"He shouts at me, 'Looks funny, I know. It's called crabbing. At the last second I will straighten us out.' So there we were with the nose facing at two thirty with the runway being twelve o'clock. Just as we are about to touchdown he straightened the nose and we landed on solid ground. I cudda kissed 'im. But the side wind was so bad after we landed it wanted to tip us over, so Joey had to taxi with the downwind wheel off the ground for a bit. Another day at the office I figgered."

Joey's father was a pilot before statehood and Joey was behind the yoke of a Cessna before he was out of second grade. He soloed before he was nine. Like many Alaska kids he was accomplished in the field of his father's occupation. A nine-year-old boy would have the savvy and sea time to run the family fishing boat alone. The hunter's young son could identify trophy game at a glance and could find it and hit it. 'Don't shoot that one, Mister. That caribou has points but no spread. That one has good palms but only one shovel.' The contractor's son could run the excavator and loader. And Joey mastered flying in Alaska.

Thirty thousand flying hours in Alaska and he wasn't out of his twenties.

The one thing I noticed about Joey was that he was not a character. There was nothing eccentric about him, nothing to draw attention to himself. His brown hair was short and always neatly combed. His clothing was always clean and neat. He could have been the person you spoke with across a desk. He never spoke of his skill to a client.

"Let's make our call at False Island first but go over the mountains. We can look for goat and work around the cliffs."

I flew north, gaining in altitude as we went. We crossed a large bay where a river poured itself into the ocean. At that place a cloud of brown muddy water extended far into saltwater. The tide was out and deer fed on kelp and seaweed exposed on the flats, their profiles golden in the sun. The wetness of the rain remained on them and their sides glistened in the morning light.

"Looks like they had a decent winter," Joey said. "The does seem to have lots of twins."

I nodded. "The grass is greening up. You would think they are tired of sea grass all winter."

Joey pointed to a place in the tree line but I could not see what it was. "Did you know," he said, "that bear kill more deer than all of the hunters combined? They like the fawns, like over there," he said tapping the windscreen three times. "They are small, just right for a little lunch."

As we climbed, the grassy flats fell away below us and the river seemed like a grey line made from a lead pencil. The forest was dense with evergreens, underbrush, and deadfalls and below them, all lay in deep dark shadow. Against the darkness of the ridge, white waterfalls thrust out from the hillside into the air through gaps in the trees and cascaded to streambeds hundreds of feet below.

First the willow, then the alder trees disappeared. Then the remaining cedar and hemlock thinned out and dwarfed at tree line. After the tree line, the earth turned to alpine tundra. Here and there dwarf cedar trees grew, their scraggly limbs pointing the direction the prevailing wind had gone after bending them all their youth until they were fixed in the direction, never to stand straight again.

This level of the mountains was free of snow and black tail deer ventured into the meadows and fed on some of the new green grasses.

I continued to climb through the passes to the peaks of the mountains. The cliffs were harsh and vertical and black. The plane bounced in the air as though I had run over large invisible curbs. "I hate turbulence," I said to Joey.

"You will get plenty of that flying around here. I was going over the mountains one time and I hit awful turbulence. It was throwing my plane all over the sky. It just threw me around. All I could do was slow to maneuvering speed to keep the wings from getting torn off." He looked at me as he said it. "You are helpless to stop it. You just keep your heading and gut it out.

"It was the most God awful turbulence of my life. And I have been in some. I couldn't turn back and you just can't go ten thousand feet higher with our little planes. I hit my head on the roof of this plane. It knocked me out cold I don't know how long. I came to with just grey rock right in front of me. I had blood streaming down my face from where my head hit the roof and streamed down my cheek and into my mouth."

He traced the route of the blood on his cheek with his four fingers as he talked. "I had just enough time to maneuver away from the cliff. Anytime it gets bumpy now I cinch up my seat belt a couple of notches."

• • •

We were among the peaks flying just below the tops. I followed a cliff edge and circled around the summit, ending where I began. A hawk anchored itself in the sky a few hundred feet off my wing. On the other wing a shriveled cedar clung to the edge of the mountain, its roots tightly grasping the rock with its gnarled grey fingers. In a juncture of branches was a nest of grey sticks and a second hawk filled the space, wings spread over the edge. The whole appeared to be just another section of rock. Had not the sun shone on its beak I would not have noticed it.

Cresting the top, the ground passed underneath only twenty feet below the plane. The top was flat and the meadow there was golden with grass of last fall. Potholes that were in shadow were still frozen and did not reflect the day.

A strong downdraft on the far side of the mountaintop made the airplane drop far enough to bring our stomachs into our chests.

"Goat over there." Joey pointed across the valley to the next mountain. The snow on top lay in patches. "See the small white patches. Those are goat. Head over and get close."

I banked and flew to the place and the patches of white took on shape and legs. A few of the goats turned their heads and gazed at us as if we were strange interlopers then began to move away along the edge. A nanny without a kid climbed upward on the face of a sheer cliff.

"Get closer. If you fly safe you will be timid. Fly like you were dueling the Red Baron. You fly well but you need to get comfortable next to the rocks."

I flew as close as I dared and I saw the nannies and several kids on a wide ledge and the place where the grass was greening and there was moss and growing flowers. The nannies seemed to herd the young goats and placed the cliff edge between them and the airplane.

Joey pointed to the next point of land. "There is a big billy. Wow! He is big. Fly close."

We made for the place and got as close as I dared. He sat on a ledge, unmoving. I flew very close to the edge. I could clearly see the black horns and eyes, even the thin black line of his mouth.

"You can always tell the very big, old billies," Joey said. "Their hair is yellow underneath and at the back. They get old and lazy and they pee on themselves. They don't bother to get up."

On the next pass the goat stood. It did not seem afraid or about to bolt and run but he was wary and uncertain. A breath of wind lifted the long hair on the goat and I wondered if I were far too close to the cliff if I could see that tuft of hair.

The billy twitched its ears then slowly with an air of dignity began to walk away on a narrow ledge. He traversed a ledge only about four inches wide. The old patriarch stopped once and faced the plane then proceeded to ascend the cliff face, a surface on which I could see no place for its black hooves.

Joey leaned toward me and shouted above the engine noise, "I once saw two goat meet on one of those four inch ledges. I saw one of them lift up both of its front legs, turn around, and go the other direction. I don't know how they do it."

"You would think their own bellies would push them away from the edge," I answered back.

• • •

We continued north toward the logging camp. On the next rise a large brown bear walked in full stride along the ridge. Its fur was dark brown, burnt umber, nearly black, and not blonded by summer sun. Its hair was full and long. No bare places from scratching on tree snags in summer shown on the hide. "That one just woke up," Joey said. "He sure shows up against the snow."

Although the purr of our engine was just above it and certainly loud compared to the quiet of the cave those last months, the bear never once looked up at us. Its head was set forward with purpose. His stride was long and deliberate. His front leg stretched far forward and the trailing leg stretched far to the rear. For months it had not moved in the den but now with each step it stretched as it moved. It was still mid-morning and the long blue shadow of the beast seemed also to stretch and stay alongside. At a place on the ridge where the mountain sloped to the beaches it descended, its paws placed exactly in the same footprints that had been worn into the earth for generations.

"There's something else we can try for. This is a rare thing I'm talking about and nearly no pilots have ever seen it. Fly to the other side of this ridge."

"Notice that on this side of the mountains it seems colder and there is more snow? The Japanese current from the coast warms the other side but usually doesn't warm this side as much." Joey paused to make sure I was following this. "We saw the bear on that side, but on this side any bear might be still hibernating. Fly over the edges of the snow pack where you might expect to find a cave or any place where rocks and clumps of tree snags meet the snow. If we are very lucky you might get to see what I mean."

For the next half hour I flew the snow pack on the mountain ridges. In a few places the snow dazzled in sun and my eyes watered to look at it. Other places were blue in shadow. I banked left and right and contoured a dozen peaks.

"There." Joey shouted with excitement. "There. That black rock and snag. What can you see?"

I looked carefully. I throttled back and gave us some flap to give us more time to look. "Do you see it?" he said again.

"I don't see anything, just snow and rock."

"Right where the depression in the rock is. See the steam?"

"Still can't."

"Make another pass but this time get as close to the snow as you can, like you were going to land."

I did a three sixty and flew just over the snow pack barely skimming the surface. Small gusts lifted loose snow from the hard pack and spiraled them. I glanced to where the black rock married the white and then saw what we had been looking for. Joey was pointing through the window, "There. There. There."

It was a plume of steam not much larger than a farmer's pipe smoke.

"What is it?"

He nudged me with his elbow and smiled in triumph. "A bear is hibernating there. That is steam from its breath and body heat. Congratulations. Not many people have ever seen it."

I was pleased and exhilarated. It was as if I had entered a fraternity, but in the back of my mind I wished that I had an experience the old timers did not have.

• • •

We passed over the small range of mountains on Baranoff and dropped down, crossing Peril Strait. I tipped my wings at a tugboat pulling a raft of logs and the pilot came on deck and waved back. I landed at the logging camp and we dropped off mail and supplies and took on a generator to be repaired in town. We were airborne in half an hour.

"Head back over Baranoff. I am going to show you a place where only two of us have ever landed an airplane. Another pilot and I have a little spike camp hidden in the tree line. You just have to know what you are doing to land there. I will take it when we get there and then you can do it after me."

I crossed the island at elevation passing high enough over the mountains to avoid turbulence. We passed with our town off our right wing and flew over Eastern Channel. Ahead was the pyramid mountain, a landmark from the ground.

"Take a pass over the pyramid."

I flew directly over the low mountain.

Joey pointed out landmarks as we passed. There were three peaks close together and in the center, far down the slopes was a very small lake. It was not much bigger than a pond.

Joey must have practiced his next line. "Those mountains are like the prongs of a ring holding that little jewel."

"That jewel I suppose is that little lake?"

"Right. The other pilot and I were even able to get some cutthroat trout fry and we stocked that little lake. It gets run off from the hills and there is a small stream on one end so the water is always fresh. Look on the hillside."

At least twenty or thirty deer fed like cattle on the hillside. The sun on their sides revealed them like shining copper pennies.

"You can't tell their sex now because they don't have their horns yet, but in the fall the place is filled with bucks. It's a bachelor club here." He looked at me as if he were Long John Silver telling me a secret.

"Now look at this place as if you were going to climb it. You can climb up the pyramid but it is cliff before you get to the valley. Same on the other side. It just isn't worth the hike. But you could land there easily with a helicopter," and he looked at me in gentle pride, "or in a float plane flown by a couple of idiot pilots."

I stared at the place astonished. "That lake isn't a fraction of the length you need to land and it takes more distance to take off."

Joey smiled at me like a cat with a bird in its mouth.

"Not only that," I said, "with all the hills around it you cannot make a normal approach, it would be like landing in a cup."

Joey looked at the place out of the window. "I hadn't thought of it quite that way, but that is a good way to put it."

"Oh, it has been done. Most of these hillsides are meadows but look up that slope in the trees. There where you can barely see it, is our outlaw cabin."

I stared at the site and just shook my head in unbelief.

"You ready?" he said.

I nodded.

"I'll take the wheel."

"Please," I said.

He pulled back the throttle and put on flaps. When the airspeed was at sixty he flew between the mountains and began to descend in a circle.

"I like the picture you gave about flying in a cup. We are going to circle down, down, down in it until we touch the water."

"I don't know how you are going to do it. I hope you don't mind if I stiffen out like a board. I will try to not scream."

Joey smiled and held out one finger as if he were doing a lecture when he spoke. "The misconception," he said, "is that a landing strip has to be a straight line."

We descended deep into the cup and neared the water. Joey was calm and routine in the descent. He was humming the part of the banner, "Mine eyes have seen the glory…"

"We are going to land in a circle just like we are descending in the cup. As soon as we touch we will bank left and maybe we will lift the outside pontoon. I will see how it feels."

I stiffened as we touched water. I could hear the spray from the pontoons and saw rising hills directly in front of me. He banked left in a circle with the outside pontoon in the air. We continued for a full circle and the plane settled to a stop. Joey taxied to the water's edge where a path began and we tied off on a rock and walked up the trail to his camp.

It was a comfortable cabin with double bunks, an oil stove, table and chairs. "It's rustic but comfortable," he said, "and we don't get many visitors."

"We fly in most of what we need. As you can see there isn't much wood around here but an oil stove doesn't send up smoke signals to give us away."

We walked to the ridgeline and saw snowcapped mountains lined in rows, their contours set in relief by sun and shadow. A lace of white outlined the coastline of the sea. Deep cut animal trails and deer droppings were everywhere. At a place partway up the slope I saw what I thought was a dead, white branch. I walked over and picked it up. In my hand was a very large set of bleached antlers. "I don't know if this place has ever been hunted. It's just nice to have a place," Joey said.

We looked back at the tiny lake. Here and there trout dimpled the surface as they fed on flies. "The two most important things about flying in here," Joey explained with that one pointing finger in the air, "is, first of all, maintaining a constant airspeed. Everything depends on that. You are behind the ball without that. It might surprise you," he added, "I never take reckless chances."

I nodded. That was a basic and it was interesting to know that that simple rule made or broke a landing like this.

Joey held up a second finger. "The other thing is your attitude. If these landings are like an emergency landing and you are all tense and you wonder if you will walk away from them, someday you will not.

Getting in here is just technique and that's it. We are not defying any laws of flight. In no time landing here will be routine."

"About taking off — we all know that taking off takes more strip than landing. No problem. You just go around more. Here is a trick though. Make one pass around the pond to rough up the water. When the water is smooth there is cohesion the whole length of the pontoons and it sucks you down. When you rough it up there is less water touching the pontoon." He raised his brows and nodded his head in a way that was a question, "Are you ready?"

"Let's do it."

He made a pass around the pond to rough up the water and made his take off run. It was in a circle around the pond. He accelerated around the pond twice, then lifted one pontoon from the surface and lifted off.

"Here is where you need to be patient. We descended in a circle — we need to climb out of that cup the same way."

We climbed out of Joey's secret lake and looked down and indeed it did seem to me like a jewel set in three prongs.

"Your turn," he said and I took the yoke. "I'll talk you through it if it is necessary, but I think you will do fine."

I made my approach and landing with nervousness. I was glad Joey was beside me. I knew the mechanics worked but it was not a routine thing with me. I planned to do this as often as I could in the coming days.

• • •

We got a call on the radio to pick up a passenger at a logging camp on the other side of Chatham Strait. He was a choker setter and had broken his leg when it was caught between two logs. They had splinted the leg and he was stabilized for us to bring to the hospital.

I took us down the long fjord of Silver Bay, and used its length to gain altitude to fly over the mountains to Chatham Strait. The sun was lowering and it left the snow peaks golden and the shadows in purple.

On the other side of Baranof lay Chatham, a very long strait extending from the southern tip of Baranof north to a junction of other straits, which lead to either Juneau or Glacier Bay. Chatham Strait changes its name as it continues north and terminates at Haines and Skagway. Chatham is six to twelve miles across and its waters can be terrifying to craft of all sizes. But as we approached the straits it was absolutely calm, not a ripple. At a place I could see bull kelp and a raft of sea otter bobbing among the bulbs their round heads scarcely distinguishable from the bulbs of the kelp. The sky and mountainous shoreline were reflected on the water.

"I can't remember seeing it so calm," Joey said. "I don't even see any waves breaking on the shore."

At a place I saw a red channel buoy. It stood completely upright and did not bob with wave action. A harem of sea lion lay on the buoy and sunned.

A third of the way across, I saw a "V" in the water. My first impression was that it might be a deer or bear swimming the long distance across the channel but realized the "V" was not crossing the strait but was traveling lengthwise. I dipped lower to better see. It was large, whatever it was, not a seal or sea lion. It was not a dolphin or small whale for the back fin was not horizontal. I flew just above it at about a hundred feet.

"Hey, that's a shark! Look at the size of it, Joey."

I tipped the plane to the left so he could better see it.

There was no question that it was a shark swimming on the surface with its dorsal in the air cutting the water. It swam leisurely at a patrol speed. Then I saw, spaced about a thousand yards apart and swimming shoulder to shoulder, other sharks. From one side of the strait to the other was a line of huge sharks on a patrol the full width of Chatham. "What intelligence guided them?" I wondered.

The cold menace of these predators made me shiver. Alaska has sharks of all kinds. A salmon shark took the hand off a fisherman as he was reaching over the side for a hooked fish. The sharks before me were larger than any I had heard of. These could only be great whites.

The one before me was light grey and seemed white just under the water. It was not slender like a blue shark but stocky and powerful.

Each of the sharks in the line swam on the surface with its fin slicing the water. I looked at the one before me. The large fin was tooth shaped and menacing. It was thick and pale grey and cut cleanly through the skin of the water, and bubbles trailed like boiling blood from a wound where it passed. In my mind I could hear the tiny popping bubbles hiss in the wake.

I descended lower just to the side of the nearest great white.

For the first time Joey seemed nervous. "W-What are you going to do?"

"I am going to touch that fin with my pontoon."

Joey's eyes seemed bigger. He stretched his neck to see over the nose. "Are you sure?"

"Yes."

He braced both his legs on the floorboard, one hand pressed against the ceiling.

"Are you s-sure?"

"Yes. Not the leading edge of the pontoon. I'm going to touch the fin with the part just under my window."

We were just a couple of feet above the water, the fin a dozen feet away.

Joey drew a long, long breath. I could hear it over the engine noise.

I took a quick glance at him. His lips were parted, teeth clinched together.

My airspeed was constant.

"Now, Joey."

I heard a "ker flap" as I touched and felt only the tiniest tap as the pontoon touched the great white.

I powered and lifted off. Joey exhaled. He was still pried to the floorboard when he looked back at me and grinned.

"You idiot," he laughed.

I felt like one of the guys.

• • •

We tied the airplane to the dock and I left my pickup in the parking lot. I wanted to walk. The air smelled humid as soil gave up its moisture. Scores of gulls roosted on the roof of the fish cannery. A troller that had just unloaded her catch was hosing her deck and hold. A pair of sea lions circled the boat. I didn't want the day to end just yet.

I was walking on solid ground with a sea breeze coming on my face and already the events of the day were memory. I needed to say them in my mind with words to make them indelible — "Billy goat that could climb a vertical cliff with ease, a brown bear that ignored me as not being a part of its world. Joey sharing his hideaway with me. A logger named Muck whose only comment was, 'Same leg as last time.' And that sinister shark — to tap it on the fin and say, 'you're it.'"

I decided to eat where I breakfasted.

Near the entrance, passing by, was the old man who told me about the landslides.

"Thankee," he said shuffling up to me. "It were just like you said. Them man hole covers were lifted high into the air — just the water holdin' 'em up. I never saw the like."

I looked at him closely. He had one of those noses that were puffy and red and full of veins, but he lacked those features that showed hardness and wickedness. In fact he looked for all that — kind.

"Sir, I'm sorry," I said. "This morning I did not ask your name."

There was a mild surprise in his voice when he answered.

"My name is Bill," he said with a squint in his eye and a smile that said, "thankee for making me a person."

He didn't offer his hand. Years of experience told him that people were not eager to take the hand of one whose skin would be moist and sticky, whose fingernails were the color of earth.

"My name is Hanson," and I offered my hand. "Do you read, Bill?"

"Some. I go to the library."

"I just read one by a guy named Van Der Post about the Bushmen in the Kalahari Desert. Those little pigmies are only about four feet tall. Do you know how they greet each other? They say, 'I saw you coming from afar.' I don't know why I told you that." I thought for a minute. "Ever get in trouble with the law?"

"I get stopped sometimes but not for any crimes."

"That rhymes, Bill."

He rubbed his bristled chin with his hard hand. I thought I could hear the bristle sounds in his stubble.

"It do, don't it."

"Ever eat in here, Bill?"

"Onct or twict."

"How about letting me buy you dinner and you can tell me about your life and I can tell you a story about a great white shark?"

# Siluk and the Whale

Grandmother sat in the shadows of the room as was her custom now. The early degrees of daybreak that entered the room seemed to seek out her white hair and in the dimness nested there, her hair appearing very white. Her face was as pale as the moon and with her wrinkles seemed not unlike viewing the moon through the branches of a bare willow tree. Her lips were pale purple in the dimness and she mouthed her lips over her empty gums and stared ahead.

It was at a place where the rafters met two walls across from the door that she gazed — where woven grass baskets hung, and a child's skin doll. But grandmother did not remember if it was she who had made the doll or if she had but played with it herself as a child.

"Grandmother, eat this," Siluk said. "It is what you like." He placed a plate of fish on her lap, fish that had been pounded together with dried berries. He placed one of her pale, veined hands on the fish. "You can eat this by yourself."

It was not so long before this day that Grandfather would cut seal meat into small pieces and chew them soft for her and she would eat them. Grandfather was gone now, and the rest of her teeth, but she liked the soft fish and berries and ate with satisfaction.

Siluk noticed of late, however, that Grandmother often stopped between bites and gazed at the rafters and he tried to read her thoughts in her eyes. Sometimes he saw wonder and perplexity as though she did not recognize the thing before her. Sometimes there was surprise as if she were meeting someone in the village she had not seen in a long time. Sometimes he thought he could see longing and sadness and it was then that Siluk would go to her and put his hand to her face and brush her hair.

Siluk finished his own breakfast of dried seal meat and tundra tea and stood, still holding one piece of meat in his hand. "Grandmother, I am going to hunt for the seal today. I will be among the ice flows off shore."

He looked at her face and bent low in front of her. She slowly turned toward him as if she were waking from a deep sleep but she did not answer.

"Auntie will come in to see how you do during the day." When he got no answer he continued, "You will be good without me for a while."

Siluk waited again to see if she understood. "I am going now."

Grandmother returned her gaze to the rafters and the skin doll with the ivory face and its white hair of polar bear fur. Siluk sighed and closed the door as he left.

• • •

Siluk wore his raincoat and pants made of intestine skins and carried his kayak paddle and lance with its line and float over one shoulder balancing it with one hand. His fur mittens hung from lanyards, which exited his sleeves and flopped as he walked appearing much like the motions of a seal as it moves across the snow.

At a place in the village street, ice was turning to water and children made sailboats of sticks and with youthful breaths, moved them across the large puddles.

In passing, with his hand that did not hold his tools, he messed up the black hair of a nearby child. "Watch for storms with those boats."

"We will, Uncle Siluk."

At the end of the village at the water's edge he slid his skin kayak across the snow to the shore. He quick tied his harpoon to the side of the boat where he could easily reach it and ran its lanyard to the skin float that was balanced on the bow. Everything else he placed inside the enclosure of the kayak in front of his legs. Siluk lifted the boat over the bare rocks where the tide had erased the snow, slid his boat into the water, and left his village.

He paddled west to sea with the dim shadow of morning preceding his bow, then followed the edge of the ice pack and the broken pieces of the ice and snow that had broken off with the spring. At a place he began to enter among the flows searching the edges for seal and the occasional walrus that may have hauled out on the ice.

In places he saw the flurry of sea birds that worked schools of needlefish. Here and there he saw the urine and droppings of harp seal and ribbon seal, but they had gone and he continued to paddle. Around one bend he readied his harpoon for what he thought to be a seal in the water but it was a bulb of broken bull kelp.

"If I could just get one seal the day would be good," he thought. "If I could just get oogarook that would feed us for a long time."

Once or twice he heard a splash but it was just the edge of the ice field where pieces had broken off and dropped into the sea. He stopped to listen. Here, away from the open sea, it was calm between the flows. He could hear the distant groaning of the ice pack as if it were a living thing and waking from a sleep.

Around a corner of a flow that stood twenty feet high he saw a place to the side where it sloped to the water and snow covered its edge. Siluk examined the snow from his kayak and saw the clear tracks of a seal leading upward to the top of the flow. The tracks displayed the smooth depression at the center where the seal's body pressed down the snow and on either side were the tracks of its paws and claws where it pulled itself along. Surely there was a seal out of his sight at the top.

The snow was soft and quiet and the kayak made no sound as he touched the edge. Siluk got from his boat and did what no other hunter of his village did. It was the practice of the other hunters of the village to haul out their vessels and fix them at the shore with an anchor in the snow. Siluk however, regardless of the effort, always pulled his kayak with him when he hunted inland.

He trudged up the slope following the marks left by the seal, pulling his boat with him as he went. He stopped, his head dizzy with exertion, and tried to catch his breath. He looked back at the sea and the distance he had traveled. He had not gotten far as he plodded with the drag of the load. He felt sweat inside his parka and knew the danger of being wet inside if he needed to stop at length in the frozen air. Siluk gazed at the boat he dragged along and had to remind himself why it was he did this thing.

• • •

He was a young boy when it happened, and it was told him in the village. He had been in the village school and his teacher took him to the side. "Your father has not returned from the hunt and it does not look good, Siluk. You need to go home to your mother."

He did not get the significance of it all, but he saw the concern in his teacher's face. "Go home now, Siluk."

Siluk's eyes welled up but he would not cry. He knew that he would learn more at home. Home, at that moment, was closer to his father than any other place on earth. He ran down the boardwalk clutching his coat with one hand, the sleeves flopping behind him. His footsteps were loud on the frozen boards. White puffs of steam blew from his open mouth as he ran.

At his house, many villagers had gathered at the door and boardwalk. Two men sat on the boardwalk and quietly waited. The pastor was praying with his mother, one veined hand on her shoulder.

His uncle, Mitook, met him at the door. Mitook placed his hands on both of Siluk's shoulders to stop his run. "Siluk," he said so quietly that his words were nearly unheard over Siluk's heavy breathing. "We have found your father's boat among the flows." There was a very long pause as his uncle prepared him for the next piece of information. "He was not in it. His anchor was hanging below in the water and the boat has been drifting."

"I do not understand, Uncle. Is he okay? Where is he then?"

I think your father anchored his boat to an ice flow and the edge where he was anchored broke off when he hunted ashore. Your father was probably following the spoor of oogarook on the ice. I do not think he fell from his boat. I hope he is alive but he is probably stranded on an ice flow."

When Mitook saw that his nephew assimilated the information he continued, "The ice is floating out to sea, Siluk. We will all look for your father, but there are thousands of icebergs and flows. They stretch for miles at sea, sometimes all of the way to Russia."

Siluk pressed his face to the glass of the window as the men of the village gathered outside the house. They met at the boardwalk and the headman and respected hunters stood on it just a foot above the rest so they could be heard and seen. Their speaking was solemn and calm, learned men in the ways of the ice pack arriving at a deliberate course of action. When it was clear that a course of action had been decided, the pastor raised an arm and prayed and the men said, "Amen." The circle opened and each of them proceeded to do his part.

There were a few umiaks in the village and the men manned them carrying supplies and binoculars, and each boat had a radio. Only two of the vessels had outboard motors and they proceeded to the more distant areas to search. The other umiaks paddled and took the nearby areas to search the icebergs. Their search continued for days. The Coast Guard said they would search but the weather was overcast for several days and they could find nothing on the flows. For a time the wind blew westward off the ice pack and they wondered if he floated all the way to Siberia. But then the winds and current moved southward and the ice melted as it went.

In his dreams, Siluk saw his father on the flow alone and helpless. He could see him in his dreams sitting on the ice with a small square of fur under him, his head hung hopelessly down, his spear propped in the ground beside him. Did he listen for the sounds of searching airplanes? Did he build shelter? When the flows moved inexorably southward and the ice melted from under him did he see his life melting away with it? One night he dreamed a polar bear hauled up on the flow upon which his father lay and crawled toward him with its padded feet and Siluk woke up screaming.

Siluk remembered his mother during these times. Every morning when it was light enough to see she would plod to the shore and climb the highest pressure ice and watch the open sea. She did so every day, even after the last umiak had ended its search and said, "It's no use." Sometimes Grandmother would climb beside her and bring her black seal meat and they would sit side by side in vigil and watch. Siluk decided never to be without his boat.

He remembered Grandmother telling him then — before she mouthed and stared into the shadows — when she was still wise, "All of us, Siluk, are on an ice flow all our lives and we do not know our time." But her wisdom brought no comfort then.

• • •

He caught his breath and continued to pull his load. He felt a heavy, cold, arctic breeze on his face that blew over the top and he felt safe to set his anchor. Quietly and slowly he followed the furrow in the snow and over the very next rise saw the seal. It was asleep and alone and too far from the edge to quickly get away. He retrieved his heavy club and crept to it.

He struck the sleeping seal on the crown of its head. One blow. It was instantly dead. The body shook with the blow as if it were only blubber inside. It made one shiver in death and lay there, a trickle of blood seeping from its nose staining the white snow.

He rolled the seal on to its back and made one incision from nose to tail the depth of the blubber. It was soft and white above the black meat and he cut off chunks and ate them raw.

"Grandmother could eat this," he thought. "She could mouth this soft blubber and be content."

When he had eaten enough, he placed the seal in the bottom of his boat close to where he would sit so the bow would not rise too high in the water. He let the kayak down with the anchor rope, easing it down before him until he made the water line.

He slid the slim tip of the kayak into the skin of the sea as smoothly as a sharp knife, parting the water to either side, with but a hint of wake. He took care not to bump the sides of the boat with his paddle as the slightest sound would vibrate through the great depths. He was annoyed when a few droplets of water fell from the paddle blades into the water, droplets that were as unwelcome as a whisper in a cathedral. He knew there was no help for it as one side of a kayak paddle was always leaving the surface.

At every side Siluk could see huge, tall icebergs, the size of government buildings. They were the blue-green of gigantic emeralds, transparent to a depth. They cast their color deep into the clear water becoming light green in the depths. His eyes followed the edge of the ice in the water until it disappeared into blackness untold fathoms below. Among the icebergs the water was crystal-clear.

Where he paddled near the ice, the air was cold, a cold with a bite to it. He felt the pinch of the cold on his nose and he could smell the freshness of the ice. It did not carry the salt smell of the sea or the iodine smell of a low tide.

He pulled his parka hood farther back and placed one hand behind his ear to better hear. There was a total silence and he felt absolutely alone.

A breath of air passing across the top of a nearby iceberg tossed grains of hard snow that slowly fell into the sea with a hiss. He looked around him among the dozens of bergs nearby. He could get lost among them. A shift among them could squash him between them. One of the flows could roll over and cast a wake that would bury him. All was quiet. Nothing betrayed the presence of a resting seal.

A white sea bird with black tips on its wings dipped low over him between the flows and Siluk could hear the air over its wings. The sound of its passing seemed caught between the crystal ice flows. He sat still in his boat not moving at all. From somewhere where he could not see he heard a blow, a mammal expelling the air from its lungs at the surface. It was loud, but distant and came from something very large. "Perhaps," he thought, "it comes from on the other side of this very flow beside me."

He stealthily paddled around the flow but when he arrived he heard the blow of the whale on the side he had just left. He returned and waited. Again he heard the blow. The sound was abrupt and amplified by the ice and bounced back where he sat in his small craft. The blow surprised him and he looked to the side as fast as a reflex. Electricity shot through his body. Only yards away was the huge, tall, black fin of a killer whale. The back and fin stood fully ten feet higher than his kayak.

He felt terror. His body tensed like a cornered mouse. The whale slowly passed by him as on a patrol. It did not dive but slowly sank like a submarine, its fin last to descend like a periscope. Behind the vanished whale was a ripple of wave that carried both light and shadow. It was gone and Siluk felt utterly alone and very small.

He listened and heard thumping like a diesel engine far away and realized it was his heart. His harpoon seemed an absurdity to him.

He heard the loud blow again this time on the other side of him. The powerful whale glided by him. At least six feet of fin was above the water. It exchanged air again and the steam shot into the air and the killer whale again descended into the depths. The mist of the whale's breath descended on Siluk and he felt it on his neck and face and the smell of its breath hung about the kayak.

He looked to the edges of the flows around him. Could he make it to any of them? Did any of them have slope to land so he could land and run away from the edge. But he knew that the killer whale was known to leap from the ocean onto the ice pack and break off chunks with sleeping seal on them. His mouth was dry as he thought on these things.

Then he heard the sound of parting water and looked to his front only yards away. The killer whale had extended its head out of the water. The Eskimo could see the thick, powerful mass of its body, the lethal blackness of it, and the white cheeks around its mouth. And behind the white cheeks was the whale's eye. It was far bigger than the saucer that Siluk gave to Grandmother.

He looked directly into the whale's eye and he could see that the whale was looking at him in his small kayak. He saw movement in the eye. There was intelligence in the eye. The eye said, “I see you.”

Then the whale descended into the depths. There was no splash. No urgency in the maneuver of the whale. Siluk did not move. On an impulse he looked down into the water. At the edge of the iceberg, he could see the blue and green continue down, down into the blackness of the sea and then he saw the blackness of great bulk rising upward and sliding under his boat. And last he saw the patch of whiteness of its cheek.

# The Nancy

Albert Jasper stood at the wheel of the fishing seiner "Nancy" rolling a cigar round and round in his mouth. His small eyes were porcine in his thick round face, small and dark, and focused on the sea before him. From the port side, an ocean swell crawled under the boat, lifted it high into the air and then slid out from under it on the other side and disintegrated into foam on the rocks to starboard. In passing, the swell dragged the Nancy sideways toward the rocks of the shore and Jasper instantly increased throttle and turned the wheel against the will of the wave. The bow drove deeply down into the next swell and shuddered as it very slowly climbed out of it. Seawater slammed the pilothouse and poured through the open port window. Wind moaned in the rigging of the vessel. Saltwater covered the windows like sand blast. Jasper could not see. He squinted his eyes next to the glass and willed it to clear enough so he could see what was next. He knew the passage was shallow and worried that the bow would bury into the bottom or his boat would be destroyed on the rocks.

The window cleared slightly and he took the next wave quarter on and buried deeply into it and pitched to starboard. As the bow rolled and strained to clear the wave, everything slid off the dash. Charts flew out of their tubes in the ceiling like wasps from a honeycomb. Heavy objects fell on the deck outside with muffled thuds and rolled until they were stopped by the guardrails, then rolled back again as the boat pitched in the sea. The deck hand who was inside the pilot house got on his knees to pick up the charts but the roll of the next wave threw him flat on the floor where he slid in seawater across the pilot house. He rolled to his stomach and grabbed the deck with his fingernails and tried to claw to the high side of the pilothouse.

Ahead of the next wave Jasper saw that the water was glass smooth and knew that large rocks were below the surface. He took them to the right. Here the channel was narrow but there were black treeless reefs to the seaward that muted the swell. Locals knew the passage but he did not, and he doubted that any of them would try it in bad weather.

To Jasper's left the sea broke against steep rocky reefs and exploded high in the air into white spray.

Jasper continued to lean forward with his face close to the window of the pilothouse. His legs were splayed for balance and one hairy hand was on the ship's wheel and the other on the throttle. Carefully he studied the water for signs, fast water or white splash as he navigated the shortcut.

The deck hand stood upright with a bloody nose and braced himself by pushing his hands to the ceiling. The blood ran freely from his nose to his mouth, the salt of his blood tasting the same as the salt of the sea. "D-D-Does it look bad?" he said. "Will we make it?" But Jasper did not answer.

The deck hand wiped his nose with his sleeve. "H-Have you been through here before?"

On deck outside, two crewmen in orange rain gear were chasing loose and rolling propane canisters before they could break the railing. One canister slammed a leg of one of the men against the rail. He screamed above the noise of the sea, "He will kill us all for those herring," but the spray and the wind snatched away his words.

The passageway seemed to widen and the huge waves became swells that Jasper knew they could handle barring hidden danger under the surface. He breathed easier as the seiner left the passage and entered the sound. With the fetch of the sound and fog coming from Silver Bay, the starboard shore disappeared but he knew that he was through the greater danger. The roll of the sea diminished and Jasper proceeded by azimuth toward the harbor still ever mindful of white spray in the water, which could signal hidden danger.

"I have never been through there before," he finally answered the deck hand. "We lost two days with that rudder and we had to make it up. We are already on two-day notice and the fishery can open any time. This boat will not miss it."

Off to his two o'clock was white splash and something black. "Spray on a rock," he thought. He placed his binoculars to his eyes and watched the place. There in the white splash was a sea lion.

"Get my gun!" Jasper looked to see who was nearby and he dashed for one himself. He ran from the cabin in his deck slippers careening off the door with his shoulder. "Who has a gun?"

Close by he could see a female sea lion with its huge and bulging eyes. There was fear in the eyes of the animal. It looked frantically left and right, left and right.

Then Jasper saw a fin in the water. It was huge and black and fully four feet of it was out of the water. It cut a "V" on the surface. A thin white spray trailed from its wetness. It was the straight nearly vertical fin of a bull killer whale. Standing nearly straight up, the fin sped toward the sea lion. The sea lion saw the fast approaching fin and raced for the seiner. There was terror and desperation in the sea lion. With a burst of speed the sea lion sped to the boat and just as the Nancy exited a large swell and the stern of the boat was low in the water, she exploded from the water and landed with a loud thump on the lower deck of the seiner.

"Off! Off!" Jasper shouted.

The sea lion glistened black and wet on the deck. It stared backward at the fin at the edge of the boat. Its eyes bulged in its head. Jasper grabbed the first object he found. A shovel. He ran to the animal and began to beat it. "Back! Back! Back in the water!" He screamed at it. "Get your medicine." Jasper struck at its bulging eyes. Jasper's voice shrieked at the animal.

His hands shook in anger. He continued to beat the animal but the sea lion chose rather to be beaten than face the killer whale. He tried to pry the creature off the boat with the shovel. The flat of the shovel sounded "splat, splat," on the wet flesh. "Help me shove it back in the water!" he shouted at the crew but none of them wanted a part of it. Jasper began to beat the creature with the knife-edge of the shovel. Finally, its fate sealed, the sea lion dove face first overboard. The crew watched it enter the water as the black fin sped toward the shivering animal.

The killer whale grabbed the half-ton animal by its fin. The sea lion pulled to get away but it was tossed high into the air. It flew fully thirty feet upward, spray flying into the air, then landed on the water and disappeared under. Seconds later and thirty feet away it came to the surface. The frightened animal looked for the fin and a place to escape. The sea lion swam again for the seiner but the orca struck first. Again it was thrust into the air.

Jasper began to shout and laugh and taunt the sea lion. "Eat my herring will ya? Take your medicine. Get 'em, whale!" He danced on the deck of the seiner and slapped the side of the boat with the shovel.

Jasper glanced toward the crew. "See that? That whale does my bidding. Sea lions eat my herring. Whales eat sea lions."

Then to the killer whale, "Tear 'em up, whale!"

Fascinated with the scene, the crew of the Nancy braced themselves at the guardrail against the swell and watched death unfold before them. Other fins joined the first. Some were the crescent shaped fins of females. The killer whales seemed to take turns throwing the sea lion high in the air. Even in the air the animal cast its head about desperately seeking escape. Its eyes bulged dark in its head.

More whales arrived and circled around the sea lion creating a wall preventing escape. When the sea lion dashed to escape the nearest whale would grab it in its teeth and toss it into the air to land back into the circle. A juvenile whale was herded into the circle with the dazed sea lion — school to practice the art of killing. Minutes later it was tossed again into the air, but this time in pieces.

"Atta boy," Jasper shouted. "Atta boy." He stopped for breath. The crew of the boat released their grips on the guardrail, no longer watching the attack on the sea lion but rather watching Jasper. Jasper breathed heavily. He stared at the crew, suddenly self-conscious. "This is the way it is. We are the high liner, the best boat of the fleet. Way I see it — all the herring are mine. Mine," he repeated, pointing to his chest with his thumb. "The humpback whales eat my herring but I can't go around shooting whales. I would like to but the Feds would be all over me.

"Sea lion and the other boats take herring too. My herring. But I can do things about that." With the back of one hand he wiped some splashed blood from the stubble on his face. He tossed the shovel to the deck and turned to go into the pilothouse, gesturing to the deck where the animal had been and ordered, "Clean off that blood."

• • •

The Nancy received directions from the harbormaster to transient moorage and made for the correct place. The skipper eased the boat to the spot, and tapped reverse engines to a full stop and they tossed her lines to the men on the dock to tie off.

Jasper stepped off the Nancy. Before him, as he looked up, was a lanky young man in a black watch cap and a red halibut coat. At his feet was an army duffle bag. He still held in his hand the end of a rope with which he had just tied off the Nancy to a cleat.

"What are YOU doing here?" Jasper managed to ask.

"Hi, Uncle. I just landed on the plane. M — Mom said that you would have room for me on this run." The skinny young man was nervous before his towering uncle but he stood firm. "Mom says that it is time for you to take me on and for me to make my way. So here I am. I'm going to fish with you."

He didn't ask it. He stated it. And Albert Jasper was pleased at the backbone in his nephew.

"I can't take you," Jasper stated. "You don't know anything. And look at you. You are skinny as a pole. You don't have any muscle."

"Uncle Albert, I don't quit. There's a lot about me you don't know." He paused for only a second. "And I learn fast."

Albert Jasper for the first time in years looked at him. This kid had been through it all. A drunkard father. He had been kicked around all of his life, but the kid never complained and always fought back. He worked hard at whatever he did. And he took care of his mother.

Jasper studied the thin face with brown stubble on his chin. There was yearning in his eyes, yearning to be accepted by his uncle and to do well.

"Michael, this sac roe fishery is for the best boats with the best crews. You can make half a million dollars in one set or you could lose that much. One mistake and I could lose the boat. This is a cutthroat business." Here Jasper paused, "And I am the worst of the lot. You won't like me. I won't let anything get in my way. I mow down the other boats if they get in my way. It is everyman for himself in this one."

The kid stood patiently listening, determination lined in his face.

"Teach me. I never quit." The kid looked at his uncle full in his eyes. "Mom says you will take me."

Jasper ran a fat hand over the black stubble on his face. He spoke quietly and slowly so the rest of the crew would not hear. "My ol' man, your grandfather, was a bully and a drunkard. He would slap me around for fun. When he would come home I would hide behind the couch. One night he caught me and was wailing on me with his fists and it was your mom that kept me from being busted up.

"Your Mom is the only person I care about. I am going to take you on for her." He shook a finger at the kid. "But you better not slow me up or you are outta here, understand?"

"Yes Uncle."

"There came a day that animal, my ol' man came at me and I took it no more. I whipped him with my fists, the only time I used a closed hand on 'im, and told him it was the last time he would go through that door. And it was. That story can be told by a thousand people like me. But with me that day was like a narcotic. I took that anger like a coat and I have been wearing it ever since. I don't think I will ever take it off."

Albert Jasper shouted to one of his crewmen, "Mister Merculieff!" Then he lowered his voice when he arrived, "This is my nephew, Michael. He is coming with us. He doesn't know a thing about anything. I want you to teach him everything he needs to know about the sac roe, start to finish. He needs to know exactly what to do. And I want it now. Get him a berth."

Albert Jasper placed his thick hand on his nephew's shoulder. "This man, Michael, is the most experienced fisherman I ever met. He is much older than he looks and is the only man I call mister. He can teach you all you need to know. The others cannot. You call him Mister Merculieff until he tells you differently." Jasper shuffled his bulk onto the vessel.

"My name is Yuka. I am Alutiiq." He spoke as if his jaws had been wired up, but each word was precisely pronounced before he went on to the next one. "My people came from the Aleutians and Pribilof Islands. We are half Russian and half native. My white ancestors were really from Finland. They were indentured to the Russians and chose to stay when they married our mothers."

Michael could see the truth of his words in the person before him. Yuka had the square Scandinavian features of a Finn but his hair was black with thin grey streaks. His eyes were black and shiny as polished argillite. Wrinkles crisscrossed his face and below his eyes like a fish net which seemed to hold his skin together next to his face. The grooves of the wrinkles were dark as though water never saw the deep recesses. Regardless of his age, Yuka moved smoothly with the vigor of a younger man.

"Down these stairs, Michael."

"My name, 'Yuka,' means 'morning star' in our language. When I was born my mother looked out of our sod house and saw flashes in the sky. She thought it was an omen. But I learned from my uncle that it was the beginning of the invasion by the Japanese in the Aleutians and what she saw was flares the coast watchers sent up." He smiled at Michael. "Now you know how old I am. This is your bunk, Michael.

You can put your bag there. I will show you the head and galley and the rest of the boat on the way out. I think we should walk on the dock and I will explain about herring and sac row — that is what we are fishing now. The others will not hear me explain it to you."

They walked together down the black planks of the dock toward the ramp that led to shore, their steps sounding loud and hollow above the water. On either side of them hundreds of vessels were secured in their births and seemed to breathe with the rise and fall of the harbor swell. The March wind from the sea was cold and a fine mist was falling.

"Let us make this very simple. Simple so people like us can understand." Yuka spoke softly in his clipped speech. "Everything in this ocean eats herring. The birds eat herring. The whales and seal and sea lion and the salmon and the halibut — all eat herring." They saw an eagle perched in the mast of a troller as they walked. "Even that eagle eats herring when he can get it. Without herring there is nothing for them to eat. My Aleutiiq people know this. No herring, no salmon."

"I understand."

"If we catch too many herring there is nothing for the salmon to eat and soon there is no salmon to catch. When I was a young man we would only catch herring for bait to catch the salmon and halibut. The Norwegians would catch herring too. They eat pickled herring. I never could see eating bait.

"Now we have what they call sac row fisheries. Before the herring spawn their eggs on the kelp and sea grass at the shore, the eggs are inside little sacks inside the mother. Those sacs of eggs are called roe. Well, the Japanese want them to make caviar. They would eat the caviar that every herring in the world could make. We fish for the herring to get their eggs. So there is the danger that we could fish all the herring in the world and then there would not be any salmon and other fish. So the government has to decide just how much herring we can catch and still have enough left for food for the rest of the ocean."

Michael listened without interrupting.

Yuka pulled up his collar and drew his watch cap over his ears against the wind. "The Japanese want the herring roe at just the right time, just before they spawn when the eggs have just the right amount of oil for their taste. So the government will do some test sets and the Japanese merchants will test it and say. 'Okay now it is just right.'

"So they get together and Japanese say the eggs are just right and the government will say, 'This is how many tons of herring we can catch so Yuka's village will still have salmon.' Fifty seiners have permits to catch those herring and your uncle has one of them. They will give a time to start fishing and they will weigh what each boat catches each day. If they did not catch all of the quota one day then they will say, 'You can fish two hours tomorrow at noon.'"

"I got that, Mr. Merculieff."

"Okay. Let us go up to the ramp and I will show you how we catch the herring. You can call me Yuka if you want but I like how you call me Mr. Merculieff. How did you get here, Michael?"

"It was my mother who got me here. I think that she is sick but she won't tell me. I think that she wants to make sure I can make it in the world. I think that she is thinking that I can learn all I need to know about life from my uncle."

Yuka stopped walking. "You are very wise for your age to see all of that. I have fished all over this country in many boats. You can learn much about hard work and risk and rewards. But you must be careful not to follow everything about your uncle. He is a very hard man. He does some things that are not the right things for you to do."

"My mother is a Christian lady and I think she is afraid of that too. She loves my uncle but she knows his hard ways."

"My grandmother was a shaman," Yuka said in a manner of fact way.

Michael stopped in disbelief.

"But she was a good shaman." Yuka said and emphasized the word "good." "She never did any of the bad things."

Michael in his Christian upbringing could not believe there was a difference, but he held his tongue.

"She was a dream walker. Have you ever heard of them?"

"No."

"My grandmother would travel in her spirit during the night when everyone thought she was asleep. She would go to different places in the world and come back with the news of what happened in the night.

"In the morning the people would come to her and ask her, 'Where did you go last night, Mother?' She might say, 'It was at a place called London but I would not want to live there. It was foggy and I could hear strange noises in the fog but could not see them.'

"They would ask her what happened in the night and she would tell of the news in the world. We would test her but she was never wrong. We would remember what she told us and sometime later someone would come with the news that what she had said was true, like when a president was shot but he lived. Her white hair would stick out as if the wind had blown it in her travels and she would tell us where it happened and who it was. She might say, 'I saw who shot him.' She would say, 'I saw that, I was there.'

"One time she saw an animal in her travels that she had never seen before and she said that a man told her that one would come to our village. She described it and we never heard of it before either. Then one day a bush pilot came to the village with the mail and gave my father some cigarettes. On the package was the animal that she saw. It was a camel and it did come to our village.

"Let us go up the ramp. See one of the seiners is overhauling her nets looking for tears that the herring can escape from. Their nets are set up like ours."

At the top was a huge dock with a very large shelter made of massive timbers built for the use of fishermen. Over the shelter was a roof that was covered with cedar shakes. The sides were open to facilitate working on fish gear. A seiner called the "Pride of Bristol" was moored to the dock and its net was hoisted over the dock where two men in fleece pants and wool jackets overhauled it. Loud music was playing over a speaker that was hung from a rafter.

"See, as they pull the net through the pulley how long the net is. It can be a hundred fathoms. For you, Michael, that is two football fields long. The net can be more than a hundred feet wide. See on the one-side floats are tied. That keeps that end of the net all the way to the top of the water. On the other side of the net are weights or a lead line to keep the net wide open and vertical in the water.

"Look down at the water at the end of the seiner. See that skiff attached to the stern? That skiff looks small compared to the seiner but it is about twenty feet long and built very strong. It has the same size engine as the seiner. The skiff is very powerful. When we find a school of herring in the water we try to encircle it with the net. The skiff has one end of the net and it takes off with it and drives around the school while the seiner goes the other way to complete the circle around the fish."

Yuka slowly pronounced each word as if he were a slow student reading a paper. With his lined face it appeared that Yuka himself were speaking through a net and it was too tight around his jaw to speak clearly.

"When the circle is completed the skiff attaches his end of the net to the stern. Then they pull in a line that is attached to the bottom of the net and cinch it up like a purse so the herring cannot dive out of the bottom. They pull in the net close to the seiner and wait for the tender to come alongside to suck out the herring." He paused for a moment. "Aren't you cold, Michael?"

Michael lifted the collar of his halibut coat and thrust his hands into his pockets. "I did not see a hold where we put the herring."

"We don't do that anymore. We pull the purse full of fish to the boat and the tender comes alongside and sucks out the herring. We could have a thousand tons of herring in the nets. Enough herring to sink ten boats our size. As long as the herring are swimming in the net they do not weigh anything. If every one of them decided to do the same thing we could go down like a rock. But they are a million brains just swimming around in the net."

"Hey, Chief!"

Yuka stopped and waited for the voice. He had shaggy red hair and was short, about twenty-five years old. He wore black baggy fleece pants tucked into his rubber boots and a loose fitting wool shirt. His appearance was of a Russian Cossack walking on a country road trying to get home before dark.

"Hey, Chief."

"Yuka," Merculief corrected.

"Yah, Yuka."

"This guy gonna be on the crew?" He looked at Michael as if the decision ought to be his own.

Yuka ignored the question. "Michael, this is Mister Snyder. He runs the seine skiff on the Nancy. He is the one that pulls one end of the net and tries to surround the herring schools with it. Everything that he does is fast and reckless."

Snyder thought this last was a complement and smiled. "Yah, I just got bailed out of jail on a 'reckless' so I could go on this trip." Snyder's teeth were spaced far apart and air passed through the openings as he breathed in. He smiled broadly with his lips closed and added, "And this year we will be the fastest haul in the fleet. Everyone else has the old nets with all that drag. Capt'n Jasper got the new synthetic nets — tougher, with fine mesh and almost no drag. We can scoop anyone in the fleet."

"Don't be telling that to anyone," Yuka said. "I think the captain does not want that out."

"Yah, whatever. Well I'll see you on the boat. The skipper wants to check out the area in the morning. He wanted me to tell you."

• • •

The Nancy's diesel engine warmed up at its moorage sounding like the low growl of a bear in a barrel, strong and ominous. She loosed her bowline and reversed her engine until the bow parted from the dock, then loosed the stern line and geared forward leaving the harbor for the open sea. She proceeded north of the town where it was told that the herring were schooling and looked for sign.

The biting wind of the night had abated and the sea was calm and readable. The sky was clear and promised sun to warm the bays and coves which would encourage the spawn.

Michael brought his uncle coffee in a large mug with a handle covered with string that had been tied into fishing knots.

"Did Yuka teach you everything?"

"Yes, he knows a lot."

"You know what you have to do now? Can you do it quickly

without thinking about it?"

"Yes. We went over it and over it. I dreamt about it in my sleep."

A crewman entered the pilothouse. His nose was flattened and swollen and his eyes were black with the edges turning green.

"Beautiful." Jasper said.

"I'm not your type Skipper."

"Have you met Wenberg?" Jasper asked.

"This morning at breakfast."

Outside the window one of the crew limped by and coiled line. It was clear that he could not put much weight on the leg.

Wenberg said, "That was from the propane tank rolling on the deck. Nothing broken. He'll be all right."

Nearing Starrigavin Bay the sun finally crested the mountains on the right, its yellow finger pointing across the bay to the spouts of twenty or thirty whales.

"Those humpbacks are eating my herring." Jasper growled.

They maneuvered toward the feeding whales. The steamy spray of their breaths shined molten in the sunlight. Hundreds of gulls swarmed and dipped among the whales snatching herring at the surface and those that spilled from the humpback's mouths. They steered between the whales and the shore and looked for sign of herring.

"Look at that shore!" Jasper roared, throwing his mug on the deck, shattering the ceramic mug and splattering coffee. "Look there. They're spawning already. They waited too long!"

The shallows were aqua, a pale light green of the Caribbean. White sperm foamed where sperm splashed on the rocks. The exposed sea grass was covered with a translucent yellow-white of lain eggs. Gulls stood in the shallows on orange legs and picked at the backs of exposed herring.

"What's the matter with those people?" he stormed.

Merculief said quietly and calmly, "This is the only place that I see spawn, Mister Jasper. Maybe it is not too late."

"Maybe you are right again, Mr. Merculief. We'll check around Crow Island. See what's happening there."

The Nancy motored around the rocky point of Crow and into the gravel shallows of its cove. Snyder was on the bow, his arms and legs in motion, never at a stop. "There!" he pointed. He retracted his arm and pointed his finger at a spot again as if his arm were cocked. "There," he shouted. He pointed again and looked over his shoulder at Jasper to be sure he was also looking at the spot. "There's yer sea lion, Skipper."

There thirty yards at the two o'clock was a huge bull in the water and a harem of six or eight cows. They were not alarmed; they just bobbed in the water watching the Nancy. The females bellowed and bobbed their heads and stretched their necks in the water.

"Just you hold still," Jasper muttered to the sea lions. He kicked away the shards of his coffee cup and ran to the rail with his double twelve.

Snyder grinned broadly. "Get 'em, Skipper."

He aimed the first barrel at the face of the bull and squeezed off, the pattern exploding the water around the bull. The shot hit the bull square in the face but did not penetrate the skull for a kill. Pellets of buckshot hit both sides of its mouth tearing flesh upward into a painful grin. Chunks of flesh were torn off the edges of its face and one piece of shot hit just under the right eye. Blood and a white fluid, like tears, slid down the face.

Terror struck the herd and some of the females immediately sounded while others remained on the surface not knowing how to deal with this new danger.

Jasper gave the bull the second barrel just as it sounded. The pattern hit the shoulder above the flipper. They heard the slap of the hit and saw water spray where the pattern hit wet flesh.

The bull surfaced sixty yards out with the harem around him, their heads stretching for a better look at their new adversary. The bull, seemed to manage with its wounds but looked long at the Nancy as if to indel its memory into its brain. Jasper shot one more time at the herd but the pattern was broad and spent.

"We better move away from here," Merculief quietly said. "People don't like shooting at sea lions."

Michael stared at the place, now empty of sea lion. "Why did you have to do that, Uncle Jasper?"

He leaned his shotgun against the door and looked at his nephew in disgust, and then slowly entered the wheelhouse.

The radio announced the sac roe fishery would open at noon. The seiner turned toward Sitka for the briefing and the start of the season.

• • •

The maneuvering of the seiners in the sound at the noon hour was not unlike a very large pack of jackals circling a cornered lion, ever circling, seeking an opening to the target and rushing in to strike. Sitka Sound held a huge mass of herring whose presence created vast black shadows in the water that revealed the movements of the various schools.

Some fifty seine boats shuffled for position in the sound to be over the greatest mass of herring possible before sending forth their respective skiffs to enclose them in their nets. The Nancy cut across the bow of the seiner "Katlian," whose captain slid open the side door of the pilothouse and shook his fist at Jasper.

Jasper kept a constant eye on his sonar to find the greater mass for the haul that he wanted. Sonar showed only smaller schools and he ignored them. He would take only the super haul.

Above the fleet was a frenzy in the sky as well as on the water. A dozen and a half spotter airplanes circled the fleet. It was prearranged that they all circle clockwise to lessen the chances of collision, and some of them were assigned differing levels of altitude to separate the traffic. Hundreds of gulls and bald eagles soared on columns of air among the planes and from the water, with their bellies in shadow, the birds indistinguishable from airplanes.

Ahead of the Nancy, Jasper closely watched the "Captain's Hope," one of the oldest seiners in the fleet. Her captain, Ingvar Svensen had the reputation of being a consistently top fishing boat. Her captain still had a wood seiner and used the hemp nets with the thick webbing that pulled slowly through the water. Her captain used his sonar but often deferred to his spotter plane for directions to large schools of fish. The spotter was diligent because his pay would be a share of the catch.

Jasper poked his head out his window and tried to spy out the spotter who directed Captain's Hope. In the swarm of aircraft he could not identify the plane. He checked his sonar for schools but found scratch. He studied Svensen's silhouette in the wheelhouse of Captain's Hope. Jasper was still finding only scratch in his sonar. Jasper turned his small black eyes again to the seiner he shadowed and saw the silhouette of Svensen on his radio. The captain threw his microphone to the dash and did an abrupt correction to his ten o'clock. It was clear that he was being directed by the spotter to a herring mass. Jasper would not miss this set.

"Snyder, get up high and spot for me!"

"Got it, Skipper!" he shouted back and climbed the rigging. Jasper watched with his head out of the cabin window. It was only minutes before Snyder excitedly pointed ahead of the bow of the Captain's Hope. He pointed to a spot ahead of the shadowed boat. "There!" he screamed through his shark-like teeth. "There." The words could not be heard but his shaking fingers spoke plainly.

"Get ready. Get in the skiff."

Snyder swung down like a red haired monkey and ran to the skiff at the stern.

The crew of Captain's Hope sprang to action. The operator of their seine skiff detached with its end of their net and began the pull to surround the mass of fish. The skiff operator began to pull the net clockwise but the parent seiner could not place its half of the net going the other way because the Nancy was in the way blocking it.

Svenson's set was clearly going to be a good haul. Only a third of the circle had been made but inside the loop the water was a dark shadow of fish. Above the set, hundreds of white gulls swarmed above, catching herring at the surface. The sides and scales of herring sparkled in the sun in the water. Inside the loop the water began to boil with herring even though only a part of the circle had been made.

Jasper put his boat in neutral and ran to the stern and stood before Snyder. He pointed at the opening of Svensen's net. "Snyder, I want you to scoop that net. Do you understand me? Go in there and scoop that net. Do you know exactly what I want you to do?"

Snyder nodded like a retriever dog waiting for the command to "fetch."

"I want you to take your end of our net and go inside his net along the edges and come out the same hole."

Snyder was annoyed that it all had to be explained to him. "I know what to do."

Snyder leaped to the stern of the skiff and started the engine. Blue smoke poured from the motor as he started it. He looked like a red haired Pac Man with his wide tooth grin. "Yes!" he shouted and he was off pulling the thin Kevlar net through the water. The bow raised into the air and settled. The wake of the skiff and net was white in the water.

Captain's Hope still had a third of the way to go to complete her set and enclose her catch. Snyder shot straight to the opening in the net. Men on the stern of Svensen's boat began to shout and tried to wave off Snyder, waving their arms as a deck crew of an aircraft carrier would wave off a jet. "No, no, stop!" But Snyder came on.

Snyder shot through the opening of the net, past the furious crewmen, and raced along the inside of its perimeter enclosing all of the catch that was inside Svensen's net. Snyder continued the circuit passing at the stern of Svensen's boat, her crew shouting and screaming at him. Some of the crew threw bottles and tools at him. One of the crew came on deck with a rifle but the captain turned the barrel. Snyder exited the opening of Svensen's net and brought his own end of the net to the stern of the Nancy and clipped off. He leaped from the boat to the deck and gestured to the other boat and laughed and taunted them.

With Svensen's catch enclosed in his own net, Jasper drew the ground line taught, closing the purse and called for his tender as he eased away from Captain's Hope.

"Snooze, you lose," Snyder taunted at the rail swinging his behind at the other boat.

Merculief stood beside Snyder and quietly said, "They may kill you if you keep that up."

Michael stood frozen at the rail. "My uncle stole their fish," he muttered.

It appeared that the men of Captain's Hope would chase and board the Nancy but at the last minute their captain said to his crew, "We still have time to catch some herring. We can deal with them later."

• • •

That evening three crewmen of the Nancy decided to celebrate. The closest bar was located in what had been the Indian village during the Russian days. The Russians had been gone a hundred years but the same Indian houses remained, dark grey and unpainted. The bar was at the beginning of the village on the narrow street that fronted the harbor. Across from the bar were several large buildings set on pilings and twice a day the tide would slide under them like a prowler and then would silently leave. Outside the bar on the sidewalk, a man sat with his back against the outside wall, his feet splayed straight out. He snored softly in his sleep with his right hand tightly gripping a bottle that was in a brown paper bag, which had been twisted tightly around its neck. His pants were wet at the crotch and mucus was dried around his mouth. Nearby, but apart from the drunken man, a long-haired black dog lay on the steps and waited for its master.

With the deepening dusk the lights inside the bar now illumined patrons who were unseen from the street minutes before. Patrons filled all of the booths. Fishermen hunched over the bar on the row of stools, their drinks held between both hands, their elbows on the bar. The space between the booths and the bar stools was taken by those who had to stand and some customers overflowed to the alley. From the street, the sound of clinking glasses and the din of voices and occasional shouting could be heard. The smell of spilled beer and smoke flowed from the building into the night air outside.

Red-headed Snyder was three steps ahead of the other two. He was loudly talking before he even passed through the open bar door. Wenberg followed Snyder. His broken nose was swollen and he could breathe only through his open mouth. One eye was puffed up and turning black. Samson Veck, the third man of the crew followed a distance behind on his bad leg, looking ahead at the bar door as if to say to himself, "I can make it that far."

"Make room for the Nancy!" Snyder shouted as he entered the door.

But Wenberg behind him froze at the door. Something he heard above the noise inside caused him alarm. He thought he heard an ominous voice saying, "Just let 'em all the way in, boys." Ice ran up his spine. He shivered and stopped.

At the door a huge fisherman with blond hair so light it was almost white met Snyder at the door. "Greetings, Nancy," the voice said in a tone that said, "Here is what's coming." With that the big man slammed a fist into Snyder's mouth knocking his head back. The fisherman grunted, "Aaah!" He grabbed his punching hand with his other one. His knuckles were sliced to the bone on Snyder's teeth. Blood splashed on Snyder's sweatshirt. Like magic, a marlinspike appeared in the blond fisherman's good hand. He swung it at Snyder's head but Snyder's legs went out from under him on the slippery floor and the punch missed. On the floor Snyder saw a bottle. He grabbed it by the neck, smashed off the fat end, and with both hands rammed it upward into the inner thigh of the big fisherman. The fisherman screamed and Snyder crawled hands and knees between his legs and bolted for the door. He fled with several angry fishermen in pursuit.

Wenberg, at the door, took several blows to his face and his already broken nose and one that hit him squarely between his eyes. He took a punch to the solar plexus that doubled him and he dropped to the sidewalk in a fetal position that saved him. He curled tightly into a ball with his hands over his head. The punches to his body felt farther and farther away and then he felt nothing at all.

Samson Veck, who never made it to the door, was completely missed in the fight. The frightened dog from the steps ran to his side and he stood like an observer and never took a blow.

Snyder raced toward the harbor with several men chasing him. At a place where the corner of a waterfront building blocked his pursuers' view, he dove under a building. His pursuers continued past him for a distance, then doubled back when they lost sight of him. He crawled deeper under the building and hid behind a piling and some debris. He covered himself with wet seaweed, a piece of broken board and a discarded toilet seat.

"He's under here! He has to be!" Someone shone a flashlight but Snyder's camouflage was convincing. They came under the building with flashlights. Snyder shut his eyes and hoped the kelp and seaweed hid him in their search.

"Keep looking," one of them said. The men moved their search under the next building but Snyder was not convinced there was not someone watching for movement. He held his breath.

"I will stay here until the tide drives me out or I know they have given up," he thought.

Snyder did not move in his place. He exhaled as quietly as he could and listened for movement around him. He could hear tidal creatures moving in the seaweed and clams squirting between the small rocks. Here and there he heard crab moving in the debris. The soil smelled of sewer and the iodine of the ocean. He began to shiver and hoped the movement would not give him away.

He lay there more than an hour and his shivering was uncontrollable and he knew a revisit from the men would find him. He waited.

Something tapped his boot. He thought they had found him and were mocking him in his hiding place. Slowly he looked toward his feet. Enough light came from the harbor to illumine the area around him. The tide was up to his feet and lapped the calves of his legs. His feet lost their feeling and his teeth began to chatter. He felt his body stiffen.

It seemed an hour passed and he heard shuffling in the timbers above his head. Was it one of the men moving toward his hide out? Then he saw it was a creature. A mink? A Norway rat?

He felt the stickiness of the blood on his hands and tried to wipe them clean with kelp grass.

In the far distance he could hear the noise of the bar across the street. "In a few minutes I will have to move because of the tide. I will shinny higher up with my seaweed and board. I will give it another hour if I can last and then I will move," he thought. "If I can make it to the Nancy I will be safe."

• • •

"You smell like a toilet!"

Snyder smiled broadly with his big teeth. He considered the

comment from his skipper almost as a complement. After all he had spent half of the night evading several determined pursuers. He fought off a giant of a man and marked him for good. He had lain under an old building and let crabs crawl over his belly and he kept his cool under relentless searchers. His recalled with satisfaction how he controlled his fear when two people crawled under his building and made their way toward him. But they were just drunks who polished off a bottle then passed out just yards away from him, never having seen him there.

Snyder considered his condition rather like a purple heart, like a commando's torn uniform after a harrowing mission. He did not regard his stink as a pejorative.

"I wonder why it was that two cops came to my boat looking for a red-headed man who just laced a man open," Jasper continued. "It was lucky for my boat that they could not find anyone on this vessel matching that description."

"And you, Wenberg, can you see anything through those slits you call eyes? I need crew who can see and work. Would that be you?"

Wenberg moved slowly, straightening like a new plant in the spring, slowly unfolding itself.

"The hospital cleared me. I can fish," he said.

The Nancy's engine was running. Merculief sat on the stern rail holding a line in his hand.

"We have an opening in two hours and we are leaving now. I mean right now — I don't want cops taking my crew away before the opening. And," here Jasper paused so none would miss his meaning, "I don't want anyone from the other boats coming around the Nancy. And I certainly can't trust any of you idiots."

Albert Jasper slowly looked at each of his crew in turn and their fitness for the day. His eyes stopped on his nephew. He made a decision.

"Michael, I want you to get your things and get off my boat."

Michael was stunned. He stuttered, "b-b-but why?"

"Right now."

Ten minutes later Michael was on the dock exactly as he had arrived. He wore his red halibut jacket. His black watch cap was on his head. His duffle bag was at his feet.

"I put your crew share money in your bag. You will be o.k."

"But why, Uncle?"

For a moment Albert Jasper thought of explaining his thinking, then resolve took over. He looked his nephew straight in his green eyes.

"Michael, you are not one of us."

The Nancy left the harbor wrapped in the purr of its diesel engines. The nephew could see his uncle in the wheelhouse with both of his hands on the wheel. Jasper never looked back at his nephew who stood staring after the seiner from the dock. As the seiner left the dock, he saw Yuka on the stern. Yuka raised his hand in a wave, then went inside.

• • •

They were not the first seiner to arrive at the sound set aside for the opening. Far from it, the area resembled the scores of landing craft that maneuvered and prepared for landing at Normandy. Boats criss-crossed one another and their wakes created a chop on the water. Several vessels approached the sides of the Nancy and the crews glared menacingly at them, some shaking their fists. Vessels passed directly in front of her bow to cut them off. One seine skiff approached and roughly nudged her bow and pushed her from the fleet until Samson Veck hobbled over with a bucket of slop and hurled it at the driver.

"Snyder, come up here," Jasper shouted below.

He ran to the bridge, a huge smile on his face. His upper lip was puffy now all the way to his nose where he had been struck at the bar. "They're asking for it out there ain't they?" Snyder said in observation.

Jasper ignored the comment. "They are going to do everything against us to keep us away from any good hauls today. We might even have to go to the outside edge if there are any schools to find there. You need to be ready for anything I tell you. But I don't want you to do anything illegal to get us in trouble.

"I hired a spotter from up north in Bristol Bay. He is going to work for us on shares. He just got to town and hasn't heard the bar talk. He is flying in one of those planes up there — the red Piper Super Cub."

Snyder glanced into a grey sky that swarmed with airplanes. They all looked grey and unrecognizable to him.

"We worked out some signals for the radio and we have a marker on deck so he can find us. He told me that we have 'ceiling,' whatever that means, and he should be able to see the schools plainly."

Red-headed Snyder moved briskly to his skiff, started his engine, and seemed to inhale the blue smoke with pleasure.

The radio squawked, "Ten minutes to opening."

Everywhere the Nancy tried to go another vessel cut her off. Snyder was about to explode in anger in the skiff.

"Mister Merculieff, try to settle him down."

"Five minutes to opening."

Sonar showed schools in several directions but in each case Jasper was cut off by another vessel.

Jasper's Piper called him, "Gander, this is Goose."

"Yah," Jasper said into the microphone.

"There is a huge school to your ten o'clock, a hundred yards. Really big. None of the boats are near it. I think you can have it to yourself."

Jasper turned the wheel and made for the place at speed.

"Five, four, three, two, one, the fishery is open."

For the first time the other seiners ignored the Nancy. All fishing boats were engaged in their own sets.

Ahead, Jasper could see the sign himself. The blackness of the school filled his horizon. Gulls seemed to shift from the pack and hovered over his bow. Jasper shouted, "Now," to Snyder and pointed to the place he wanted to set. The Nancy began to surround the area with the net, Snyder pulling his end of the net counter clockwise as Jasper pulled the other direction.

The catch was clearly gigantic. As far as the net reached it was full of herring. Jasper shouted into the microphone for his tender to come to him. "Come quick." The Nancy crew drew in the bottom of the net completing the purse and preventing any herring from escape out the bottom. Fifteen hundred tons of mindless floating herring were enclosed in the purse. Three million pounds of fish suspended in the water.

The surface of the water began to boil with herring. The air above them was a frenzy of gulls.

Jasper looked possessively toward the rest of the fleet but they were all busy tending their own nets. He screamed at his tender to come quickly and get a second tender too.

They began to draw the nets in with the power block until the catch was fast to the seiner. Jasper eased the Nancy into deeper water away from the fleet and any interference.

Snyder danced on the stern deck, his red hair flopping about.

Then there was a strong jolt to the vessel. Snyder's dance caught him on one foot and the jolt left him flat on the deck. Merculieff staggered but kept his balance. Wenberg banged his head on the tackle and went down. The port side and stern began to list and sink. The list became a full roll that continued without abatement. The stern was quickly below water line and began a downward descent. Seawater began to pour over the rail and poured through the doors and hatches of the boat. The Nancy was not just sinking, it was being pulled under by an inexorable force.

The whole stern half of the boat was under water and the engines sputtered and stopped. The bow of the boat began to lift high into the air like the nose of a great white at the side of a boat.

Snyder could not swim. He shrieked and ran into the bowels of the Nancy and upward into the cabin where Jasper was rising to his feet to regain the wheel.

"We're going under, Snyder!"

Then the rest of the boat was pulled under completely. A million rising bubbles rose to the surface in a hiss. In minutes the Nancy was gone from sight. Nothing of her remained on the surface.

Millions of tiny herring minds that only thought of swimming weightlessly in the water moments before, now as one mind chose to dive into the depths of the ocean at the same time.

There, to the port side of the sunken Nancy, about the right distance for a good double twelve shot, was a figure in the water. It was a very large bull sea lion with one sunken eye and patches of torn flesh not yet healed. At its mouth at the corners, its flesh was torn upward — almost like a smile.

# The Murder of Parley Smith

During the night there had been a soft rain that ended before sunrise and left its freshness in the air and its shine on the parking lot. From the trees on the other side, arctic sparrows thrust out their throats and loudly sang.

Sunrise shone brightly and its reflection in the wetness of the lot stung my eyes and made them water as I walked to the police station. I squinted and held one hand over my eyes as I went. The smell of frying bacon drifted from one of the homes nearby.

At the door I glanced back and saw the mountains above the houses. Most of the winter snow had melted but what was left was molten gold with the rays.

"How pristine and pure all of this is," is what went through my mind. Then I walked into the police station.

• • •

As I entered the hallway and the door shut behind me, I had to stop to let my eyes adjust to the comparative darkness. From the cells next to the ready room, a drunken woman was screaming and from the metallic banging I knew that she lay on her back on one of the bunks and was kicking the bunk above.

Male prisoners in the next cellblock across the hall were making bawdy comments and cursing. Another prisoner was dragging his cup back and forth across the bars of his cell — because he knew it annoyed everyone.

There was no smell of bacon here, nor that of maple syrup thinning over Aunt Jemima waffles. There was instead, the sour, stale odor of prisoners' clothing in the lockers. Many of their owners had not bathed in weeks or had been arrested in wet clothes, and their shirts and pants brought the scent of gutters and bars and trousers soiled with feces and urine. Clothing caked into armor by hardened vomit simmered in the lockers.

I made room for a brown-skinned man with long, black, greasy hair to pass me in the hall. He was being released from the drunk tank and was escorted by an officer. The look in his eyes as he glanced in my direction was of utter hatred. He was a "regular" in the police system and multiple knives were always found on him at the time of each arrest. It was said that he once staked out a live dog and skinned it.

"Come on, Williams. Time to go," said the officer.

Williams squinted at the bright morning light outside. "I left your knives at the corner of the building. You can collect them there."

• • •

As I made my way to my locker the detective entered the hallway holding some papers with both hands and motioned me to come into his office. I will call him Charles, Sergeant Charles, for he may still be alive somewhere. Charles never moved fast. Every movement and decision of life was done at a pace of someone venturing out on the ice. He was measured and sure and dogged in all that he did. He looked at me with his brown eyes and spoke quietly and slowly.

"I have a report of a murder and I want you to come with me."

He said it like I would say, "I found this rock and I want to know what you think of it."

"The report I just received stated that there was blood everywhere and it looks like he was beaten to a pulp and drowned in the toilet. No one has been to the scene yet. I want you in on this from the beginning."

It was easy to misjudge Charles. He may well have been one of the most average people I have ever met. Medium height, medium brown hair, which could only be combed the way it grew from his head. He was middle age, around forty. He was not muscular but solid, although his body tended to whisper his age. He was not a good shot, not a good driver, not athletic. He would have been the last pick in the department for the policeman poster photo.

But Charles, Sergeant Charles, had other things about him that I admired and respected.

He never gave up. He was like a bulldog on the scent. He plodded. He talked to informants. He assembled clues. He solved cases.

One spring we got a call from a lady who had been walking her dog on one of the more remote roads of our Alaska town. Her dog scented on something in a deep ditch nearby. It broke away and would not return to her when she called. Two black ravens that were busy at something in the snow were chased off by the dog. It barked continuously and circled round and around an object protruding from the snow. When she came up on her dog she discovered the decomposing body of a drug dealer in the melting snow. He had been "offed" sometime in the fall and it took the ravens, melting snow and a dog with a good nose to find his body.

Our part of the state isn't an area of extreme cold. It freezes, thaws, some snow falls, freezes, and then thaws again. The body was not conducive to great forensics. But Charles stuck to the case.

After a time he narrowed it all down to a suspect. But the family of the suspect got wind of it and proceeded to destroy the key evidence. They got the murder weapon from their son and on a family outing, walked the five-mile trail along a scenic river near the town.

They dismantled the pistol and one of them tossed a spring as far as he could across the river.

A hundred yards farther down a firing pin was tossed the other way into the muskeg. Then a barrel was tossed into an area of rapids in the river. In all, every piece was hidden over a five-mile stretch of trail. No one would ever find this pistol they thought.

Sergeant Charles learned of the family's attempt to destroy the evidence and decided that he would find and assemble the pistol. It was a daunting challenge. He got metal detectors and sniffer dogs to the area. He pulled in every off duty officer in the department, a bevy of volunteers, and the class of municipal police recruits who were training at the academy to accomplish the task. After a great deal of effort he found and retrieved every screw and spring. The assembled pistol was sent to the crime lab and it was affirmed to be the murder weapon.

Another time he found a Chevrolet in which a murder had been committed. Charles disassembled the entire car, crated and shipped it to the crime lab in Seattle where the car was reassembled and the experts proved it to be the crime scene, and they detailed just how the crime was committed. The vehicle was broken down and re-crated and shipped back to Alaska where it was assembled again. The Chevrolet was used as evidence of the crime scene and jurors could sit in the seat of the car if they chose and see where bullets had exited the window and the blood stained seat and the source of fingerprints. Charles and the DA secured a conviction in the trial.

Charles was a good and honest man. He had a family of five kids to feed so he moonlighted from his work at the department. When the bars closed at four in the morning he got out of bed and cleaned the beer and puke out of the booths and tables. He cleaned and scrubbed the sticky floors and shined the toilets. The "low-lifes" and bottom feeders would laugh that this cop had to clean up after them. But Charles took it all and put food on his family's table.

All of this worked to his success as an investigator. He was unassuming and quiet. In fact, suspects thought they were smarter than he and cleverer. They smiled at him and were talkative — until he lay out the evidence and their statements and they were caught.

He was avuncular and many criminals imagined they were in the presence of their grandfather or favorite uncle and so they talked and wanted it all off their chests. They found it easy to confess everything to him and were glad to do it.

• • •

"Let's take my car," he said. "It's already warmed up."

He put on his police jacket and I wanted to help him put it on. He put a camera in his pocket and a large notebook and pencil in the other. I could imagine him licking the lead of the pencil before he wrote. He took a clipboard and lined paper and the car keys.

"His name is Parley Smith. Know him?"

"Yes." I said. I was surprised. "I do know him. Not well, But I know him."

"Tell me, as I don't know him at all."

"He is the barber in that tiny shop on the main street."

Parley Smith's image entered my mind. I recalled him in his shop. He would sit in a chair along the sidewall and read the paper. When a customer walked in he simply walked behind the barber chair — one of those big red ones that swiveled around and you could jack it up and down.

He would hold up a large towel like a bull fighter does and without a smile or greeting say, "How do you want it?"

In the time I knew him I never saw him smile or make social conversation.

It was Ben Muhler who introduced me to him. Ben came to town out of Fallen, Nevada wearing a white cowboy hat and a short white mustache and proceeded to sober up every drunk in town. He was tall and thin and petted every dog that graced the sidewalk or bed of a pickup truck. Half the town stopped drinking including a couple of the bar owners. Ben was loved. He started treatment programs and a halfway house.

Ben was a veteran of the Normandy landing. One day he said to me, "Do you want to know what my retirement is?" Then he unfolded in clear cellophane a postage stamp. "This stamp was cancelled the day the civil war ended in eighteen sixty five. The cancellation was hand written by a postmaster somewhere. 'Richmond has fallen' was written across the stamp." He smiled broadly and with his boney old hands, gently refolded the stamp and placed it in his wallet.

Ben was a father figure to me.

One day he said to me, "There is someone I am trying to help. He is retired out of the Navy. A thirty-year Chief. He is trying to get on his feet and he is starting up a barbershop on the street."

I took the hint and told him that I would bring him some business.

One day I brought my two little boys in for haircuts. They were little and squirmy and really did not need haircuts. Half way through the first haircut one of the boys got fidgety and Parley lifted him up a foot in the air and forcefully sat him down. It was hard enough that I stood up and gasped. My boy was frightened and wanted to cry. It was right at the edge between discipline and anger so I let it go, but I knew that if he did it again that I would clobber him.

I paid and left the shop.

• • •

As Charles and I walked to the car I told him my experiences with the victim. Smith looked like an ordinary guy but didn't seem to have any social skills. It is as if nothing in life had any interest for him. I could visualize him behind a Chief's desk counting his days to thirty years retirement but then having no plans thereafter.

The Sergeant listened carefully to what I said. He nodded, tossing me the keys. "Here, you drive."

He lived on a side street that joined the main street of town. When the Russians owned Alaska the building was a prosperous shop of some kind, but recent years proved that most customers rarely ventured from the main street. The building was changed to a small apartment.

We parked directly in front of Parley's door and Charles walked slowly to the doorway.

"The person who called me said the front door was ajar and they called inside. They said they thought something was wrong and they went in and found him draped over the toilet. They said they shut the door behind them and came straight to the department. That was about a half hour ago. I will contact them later for a more complete statement."

Charles paused at the door and waited for me to catch up. As I got out of the vehicle I looked at every window and door of every building. I looked for people and what they were doing. When I was satisfied, I joined the sergeant and we went inside.

The place was a mess. Newspapers were strewn about. There were old copies of the "Navy Times" in a corner with glass rings stained on them. A coffee table was upended as was a chair. Blood and matted hair were stuck on a corner of the coffee table. I saw blood smears in several places. At the door frame leading to the next room was a long bloody smear that ended in a clearly defined handprint. Brown blood had splattered the wallpaper above the wainscot and spread into the paper and looked like dry pressed flowers.

There was only one picture on the wall, a fishing boat on the high seas, and it was canted on the wall as though the entire picture was sinking in the sea as well.

I was nervous that Charles assumed the apartment was empty and that no criminal was lurking nearby, but the sergeant seemed unconcerned so I let it ride.

The most consequent thing to me was the odor of the room. It was the smell of death. There was a smell of dereliction about the place to be sure, but the odor of death itself hung like an invisible mist in the room.

I had been a commando behind enemy lines for three tours in the war and I grew to recognize death. Not putrefaction, but fresh death. Behind the lines, it was death you dealt out or received.

I once went through three rifles in some extended fighting. The second rifle belonged to a Communist officer who I had killed. His smell clung to the rifle and as I used it in the fighting, I could smell the fear and adrenalin and I knew exactly what he felt at the time of his death. I knew that my olfactory skills were not admissible in court nor were they a matter of police science, but I felt I could often reconstruct a scene based on the smell in the room.

We went into the bathroom and found Parley Smith. He was nude, on his knees before the toilet. His hands and arms hung limply down.

A piece of white toilet paper extended from one bluish hand and the paper was very white in it.

His head hung nearly into the center of the toilet with his nose and lips pulled grotesquely to the side exposing his teeth. Parley's eyes were half open and in the opaque surface I could see the reflection of the toilet bowel and vomit, as if his last view of life was of porcelain and puke.

His arms and legs were purple in rigor mortis as were his mouth and nose. The bowl was filled with yellow and green liquid and there was a pinkness to a part of it.

Parley Smith's body was a mass of bruises. Many of them were yellow and some were green as though sustained on previous days. Others were bright blue or purple.

• • •

We took some photos of the body and then tried to move the face from the toilet to better view. The body was stiff.

"What do you know about rigor mortis, Officer?"

"At least four hours," I answered.

"I am going to do more photos and measurements. Maybe you could see if you can find anyone around here who may have seen something prior to that."

I nodded and went to the back door and retrieved a piece of paper towel to put over the doorknob as I opened the door. The handle was sticky with something and the paper stuck to the handle. The door opened to a small courtyard that could not be seen from any street. There was a narrow passage between two large buildings that led to it and there were a half dozen apartments facing the court inside.

I saw a middle aged woman on a low balcony with her hair in curlers and a thin towel wrapped around her head.

"Hello, I'm Officer Hanson. Could I talk with you a minute?"

She didn't seem surprised to see me as a policeman.

"Took you guys long enough to get here. That barber fellow has been causing problems for weeks now. Every night it sounds like a war in there. Then he comes out in his underwear," and she paused indignantly, "or nothing at all."

The woman took another puff on her cigarette and held it up like a celebrity.

"The other day he hauls off and pees in my flower garden." She pointed her cigarette at a patch of roses and pansies. "Right there." The woman on the balcony took a long puff on her cigarette. "And he just stands there and sways back and forth like hear hears music."

"Ma'am, did you see or hear anything last night? Did anyone come around his place? Was there anything out of the ordinary for him?"

"Just his regular banging around."

"Has he been in any fights? Anyone got a grudge on him?"

She took another puff and rolled up her eyes. "Nah, just the same."

• • •

I checked out the other nearby units but found no one at home and I returned to Smith's apartment.

"I called the mortician," Charles said. "That's them now."

Two of them came in with a gurney.

"It's a tight fit in here," I told them. "He is a large man and is stiff. If we can roll him to the right and two of us get his shoulders and two of us get his legs we could back out."

With effort we removed him from the bathroom and laid him on his back on the gurney. He was still in a tight ball, shaped like a fetus. His back was on the mattress but his knees were drawn up nearly to his snarling head. The only part of him that was not stiff and solid was a small mass of his hair that had been in the toilet. Balls of thick liquid dripped reluctantly from the hair to the rubber that lined the gurney.

"I think he might roll off," the mortician with white hair said. "Let's lay him on his side."

They covered Parley with the blanket, strapped him down, and placed him in the hearse.

• • •

"Let's lock the place up and put some tape on the door," Charles said.

Sergeant Charles moved slowly to the task, arms swaying, his back slightly bent. He ran his hand through his hair and the curl in the middle sprang back into its accustomed place.

Charles looked at me like an older seasoned cop trying to teach a younger one. "By every appearance this has the look of a brutal murder. We will still have to locate any witnesses there might be and wait for the lab. Do you see anything unusual, Officer Hanson?"

"Yes, the blood and bruises were not done at the same time. Some are old and some are fresh."

"Good. There is hope for you."

Charles peered at me with his tired eyes. He spoke quietly and slowly as though he were concluding a lecture.

"This is what we will find. It will take a while, but this is what we will find. We will find from the crime lab that there is no water from the toilet in Mr. Smith's lungs. I took a sample for the lab. We will find from the pathologist that his liver was shot. We will find that he was very intoxicated at the time of death. We will find from our investigation that Mr. Smith did not go to bars. He probably got his bottles every day at the liquor store and drank every night but sobered enough to go to the barbershop every day.

"The bruises are because his liver was shot. The slightest bump will bruise him. He has been stumbling around knocking over everything. He falls, bleeds, and grabs a wall for support."

Sergeant Charles sounded tired as he spoke.

"I have seen this before." There was a long pause before he spoke. "There was a killing here all right. Mr. Harley Smith killed himself. He, by decisions he made every time he woke up, drank himself to death in this lonely empty room."

# The Letter

It is said that high flying geese can detect an eye blink on the ground. Willard Barney wondered then, if they could see him shiver in the blind. But then, the blustery northern wind that penetrated his loose clothing and made him shake also shivered the brown grass about him. Perhaps then, shivering was good camouflage.

He thought on that as he slowly, very slowly, daubed the drip on the end of his nose with the back of a forefinger, then very slowly brought his hand down to his leg and wiped the finger. The wind was bitter this day and its cold fingers pinched his nose. "Here I am in my second childhood running through the woods with a runny nose."

He wondered how it was that a goose that could see so well, would be fooled by white bed sheets spaced in a grain field. They were crude forms shaped by folded cloth and propped with black sticks. "Perhaps the vision of golden grain destroyed their judgment," he thought.

His mind continued in this vein, for the geese were not now on him. "People are like that too. The collector who has paid a fortune for a fake painting will insist on its veracity. The greater his loss, the louder he protests. The cops are wrong. The experts are mistaken. He cannot admit his folly. The greatest defender of the thief is the victim." He marveled at the absurdity. "How my mind wanders when I am shaking in a hunting blind."

He blew his nose, this time woodsman style. "Sometimes sick people are like that too. They will deny the symptoms. The doctor is wrong. The lab made a mistake. Like the goose, he sees only the golden grain. He tells himself, 'I feel fine.'"

The sky was full of passing geese. Thousands of them. They flew high in long thin skeins that appeared on the parchment of sky like faint and faded handwriting. The horizon was a haze of waterfowl.

They came from the north, flock after flock, pushed by a strong and bitter wind that stung and watered the hunter's eyes and made him squint. Throughout the night he had heard them passing over his cabin and he could mark their kind by the tones of their honking. His dog would raise her head in the dimness and cock her head with their passage.

He smiled at his dog from his bed and said, "Tomorrow… tomorrow."

Once during the night he heard the whistling of passing swans and he pictured the many ponds and potholes of the distant tundra from which they came. Each pothole would have a pair of them. They nested all summer and at a signal with the change of season, the pairs and their young came together and flew south.

Willard and his dog were in the blind before daylight. They watched the near black clouds that lay in ranks give way to pale light, the color of very old letters from an attic. A few teal braced their wings and passed very low over their heads in the darkness. The air passing over their feathers whooshed like incoming rounds and Willard, who had been to the wars, ducked his head. The sky was filled with passing flocks and their calls merged together into a cacophony. They passed high and their lines were like old scars on a retina.

His blind was at the water's edge. It was a makeshift blind made of dead tree snags and brown beach grass. His dog was a smallish yellow lab and was nearly invisible in the golden grass that bent in a bow with the wind. The area around him had once been burned in a forest fire and thin wispy spruce remained like bleached bones poking from the earth. Beaver had dammed the creek upstream one year and left the area flooded and marshy and the water was ankle deep and brown with its mixture with the soil. Across the pond the dead trees stood like white whiskers and the hunter thought on this and stroked his own.

All morning, flocks passed by out of range and seemed to descend on the far side of Minto Flats far from his blind. He shivered. His back ached with the cold. "I'm feeling my age this morning," he said as he looked at his dog. She thumped her tail on the earth and put her chin on his thigh. He stroked her head and scratched her ears.

"Here come some," he said to the dog as he readied himself. The dog looked toward the oncoming flock and froze in place as she had been taught. "Snow geese," he said quietly to the dog.

Willard slowly lowered his head and rolled his shoulders forward and blew on the call, his body covering the movement of his fingertips. He looked upward lifting his head as little as possible and wrinkles lined his forehead. But the flock ignored his spread of decoys and passed too high to shoot.

His dog froze in place and waited. "Good girl, Sally," he said to his dog.

He slid deeper into his brown Filson coat and raised the collar higher on his neck. He did not let down the earflaps of his cap for he wanted to hear the approach of the flocks. He pulled a liverwurst sandwich from a cellophane wrapper and gave a chunk to his dog.

This time he heard the honking of the "snows" long before he could see them. They were low enough to see the individual geese. He watched the lead goose fall from its position at the point of the "V" and be replaced by another. He saw their white bodies with the black tips on their wings. Were they too high for his twelve? Then there was another flock, lower than the first but they were still high.

He hoped to shoot and have them crumple in the air and fall in the pond in front of him where Sally could get them with ease. He readied himself and took aim on the front goose leading it a body length. He shot twice. He could hear the pellets strike the chest of the bird, like raindrops hitting dry leaves. But the shot had no effect on the goose. Moments later he heard the dropping BBs rain down on the calm pond. His shot had lost its energy by the time it hit the bird and bounced off.

The dog looked carefully at the flock. Would one of them cascade to the earth for her to retrieve?

"Next time, Sally."

Another flock of "snows." They came head on as before and he stood and shot. Again he heard the strike of the pellets on their chests. They did not flinch in the air. Clearly the BBs were bouncing off the curved feathers.

He had an idea. Quickly, he broke the action of his double barrel, inserted two more shells, and just as the flock passed he shot at the trailing goose from behind. There was no tapping sound like raindrops on dry leaves this time. The pellets passed between the feathers from behind and penetrated the bird.

The goose did not crumble and drop to the ground as he hoped. It left the flock, no longer flapping its wings. Its wings were braced straight out like an airplane and it descended into a long glide. It was clearly wounded but the glide would take it far from the blind.

Sally never took her eyes from the descent of the wounded goose. Her world centered on one wounded snow goose. She shivered in anticipation. Her hind legs were set to spring to the chase. She waited, whimpered once, asking to go.

"Get it, Sally."

She was gone before the sentence was finished — a yellow flash. She tore through the brown grass. Brittle brown twigs snapped. Bare willow limbs struck her face.

Willard saw the huge splash of water under her feet and could hear the dry grass hiss with the dog's passage. He watched as she glanced skyward at the descent and direction of the gliding goose and ran just as a baseball fielder knows where the ball will land.

Willard held his twelve gauge in one hand and ran after his dog. He followed the course of the chase at first by the snapping twigs and the parting of the grass ahead.

He ran several dozen steps before he tripped on a grass covered log and fell face down into the mud. The black soil was soft and he felt his face skid into it. A sharp pain shot up one wrist but it was functional and whole. He checked his shotgun for mud and continued at a run.

Limbs and red willow branches slapped his face where his dog before him had passed under. He ran again, this time with his shotgun held vertically against the branches.

At a place he stopped — less to listen for the progress of his dog's chasc, but more because he gasped for breath. He wheezed. With effort he drew breath.

The hunter leaned forward, one hand on his knee and drew several full, long, deep breaths, filling his lungs completely. The first intake of breath frightened him for it produced a sound like that of a goose.

He straightened — too quickly perhaps, for he was light headed and dizzy.

When he was ready he continued to follow, this time not in a run. He walked fast and stumbled over the uneven ground.

He listened again and heard a short honk of a goose nearby at the edge of the willows. There was a snapping and rustling sound in the brush and he walked heavily toward the spot. As he neared the place Sally emerged. She was muddy and wet and had a live goose in her jaws. The dog ran to the feet of her master and presented it to him.

"Good-hugh — hugh-girl-hugh, Sally." He puffed.

The goose seemed nearly as large as the dog. Blood came from above one of the dog's eyes. Above one orbit of the eye was a pronounced swelling. From the Goose? From sticks along the chase? The dog panted and seemed proud.

Willard killed the goose and carried it by its orange legs. The white head and wrinkled neck were long and dangled on the ground.

"Let's go home and have some dinner, Sally."

The Labrador walked close beside her master, fur against flesh. Every few steps she looked up at him.

• • •

He tied a metal wire around the goose's neck and hung it from a nail on the porch. It hung there above the firewood to the right of the door and it slowly spun left and right in a light breeze.

Near the hanging snow goose was a window and on the other side of it was the small table where the hunter ate and wrote his letters and where he often read when he did not have a fire going. He laid his pistol on the far side near the lantern next to his reading glasses. Near his coffee mug he emptied his pockets of shells, his goose call, and the part of his lunch they did not eat.

He removed his muddy coat and waterproof pants and set them on the rack of firewood. When they dried he would shake them clean. The goose swayed slowly back and forth in the breeze like the pendulum of a grandfather clock.

"Let's walk down to the roadhouse and get a good dinner, Sally."

The dog shivered at the prospect of a walk. Her front legs pranced.

Willard combed his lead grey hair in the mirror. "Old man, your face sure is pale tonight." He put on his checked Mackinaw coat and closed the cabin door behind them.

The path to the settlement was wide. Horse drawn wagons used this lane to haul supplies to the mines in the old days. Now it was a pleasant path among the birch trees and alders and the blowing leaves.

He tossed a stick in the river a few times to clean the mud off his dog. Along the way she retrieved sticks.

About eighty people called this place their town. In the days of the gold rush more than five hundred people lived here, mostly miners and those who supplied the mines. It was one of the prosperous towns north of Fairbanks. One artifact that survived the gold rush was the roadhouse. It remained with a bathhouse, rooms to rent, and most of all, its kitchen. Mining memorabilia lined the paths and the interior of the dining area.

Sally sat on the deck outside of the roadhouse door and waited. As Willard opened the door the smell of fresh baked bread and a roast met him.

"'Lo, Will."

"Hey Jack."

The owner had bushy black eyebrows and thin black hair. He wore a striped shirt with the sleeves rolled up and was wiping his hands on his apron as he met him. He was one of those men who was skinny yet he looked very strong.

"Get any? I figured you would be on the flats with all of the flocks in the air."

"Just one. They were flying high for me. They must all be landing by Minto, or maybe they are passing by and going to the grain fields around Fairbanks."

They shook hands.

"Sorry my hands are wet. Just washed."

"I got it hanging by the neck with a stiff wire. What do you think about me doing the goose English style? I hear that they hang it up like that and when the head falls through the noose it is properly seasoned to cook."

"Uh huh. Be sure to invite me to dinner."

"Why do I think that you don't mean that?"

"Where do you want to sit?"

"I think I will sit by the fire. I was froze to the bone today. What smells so good?"

There were a few other people in the dining area and Jack lowered his voice. "Will, I know moose is our favorite food. But you know it is illegal to sell wild game in a restaurant. Now with moose season going on and all I don't want you to get the wrong idea. My wife has this recipe for a beef roast that makes it taste just like moose. I mean you couldn't tell the difference."

Willard rolled back in his chair and rubbed his stomach in a circle. "I guess I will have a super-size one then. Bless your wife."

Jack winked and turned to go.

"Oh," Willard said, "maybe tomorrow I might shoot a snow or Canada goose or two and you can have turkey on your menu."

The owner put the order in at the kitchen and sat at the table across from his friend.

"Hey, Jack. Now that I am thinking about it. You are about the best person I know that knows about hurt animals. Sally has a small cut above one eye but there is a nasty bump above it. She isn't favoring it but I want to be sure, you know."

"I will look at her."

A few minutes later he saw Jack walking to the front door to see his dog. On the far side of his person he held a large napkin in his hand and he knew Jack brought something from the kitchen.

• • •

"That was the best… beef roast I ever had. Thank the Missus."

Willard buttoned his mackinaw and turned toward the door.

"Oh. Almost forgot, Will. There is an envelope for you. Came in today." He extended it in his hand.

Will froze in place. His face became paper white. He stared at the envelope like it was a dead body. His body went cold. His mouth was open. He did not know what to do.

"Are you all right Will? You look pale."

Slowly with a shaking hand he took the letter. It could not have been held more gently if the letter had been printed on the fragile ashes from an old fire.

"Will?"

"I — I'm okay."

He held the letter in both hands never taking his eyes from it. He carried the letter like a child carries a tray of glasses that are filled to the brim, and shuffled to the door. Jack watched him as he trudged down the path to his cabin. He watched until he was out of sight.

• • •

Willard leaned the unopened envelope against the windowsill and it reflected double against the glass. He lowered himself like an old man into his chair, his coat still on, and gazed at the whiteness. For a time it was the only thing in the world. Geese flew very low over the cabin but he did not hear them. The wire around the gander's neck on the porch squeaked as the wind worried it against the peg. But it was the summons of the black letters that he heard. It was meant for no one else. "Willard Mason, Manley Road House."

He sighed aloud. His dog whined for she knew his distress.

He slowly stood and removed his coat.

A drink.

He searched his cupboard. Somewhere in the clutter was a bottle, had to be. There. He reached for it and broke the seal and poured some in a clear glass. Several fingers of it.

He drank several swallows and winced at the taste. He returned to his seat and the correspondence on the desk. Perhaps he could just not read it.

He looked out his window and saw the goose swaying left and right in the wind — just like a hand waving an envelope back and forth before his eyes.

The glass was empty. He did not recall drinking it. He returned to the cupboard and poured several fingers more into the glass. A preacher once quoted a verse in his hearing, "Look not thou upon the wine when it is red, when it giveth his colour in the cup, when it moveth itself aright," and had the contents of this bottle been red he might have remembered and taken its admonition, but this had no color to remind Will of the verse. The liquid in this bottle was clear when he poured and he could not know that as he raised it to his lips it caught the hue of the lantern light and left it the color of venom. He drank it.

Sally barked one time. It was loud in the small space. It was the first time she had ever barked in the cabin. She looked at her master and whined.

"I'm okay, Sally."

He poured again and sat down at the desk. Sally whimpered at her man.

"Go away," he said loudly.

Outside, the wind blustered and turned the goose around and lifted her feathers from the back like the shot entering her body this morning. The wind moaned through the porch.

Willard took a deep breath and with deliberation reached for the envelope. He ran his thumb through a corner and ran it under the seal — just as one pulls the entrails from the smelt fish. The tear was jagged like teeth. He pulled the contents from the casing.

As King Hezekiah spread the Assyrian letter out before the Lord in the Old Testament, Will spread his out on the table, pressing it flat with both of his hands.

Sally barked and leaped to his side placing both her paws on his thighs.

"Go!" he shouted.

He stared at the pages but his eyes did not focus on them. His dog again whined and jumped to his side placing both her paws on him. He shouted, louder than he had ever done to his dog. "Git, dog," and he thrust her away with a sweep of his arm.

He affixed his reading glasses and slowly read.

A moan from deep inside his body left his lips — like an answer from a dry well. He removed his glasses and looked at his reflection in the window.

Sally sensed the anguish of her master and barked again and leaped to his side. He shrieked, "I said git… git," and a sound he had never heard before left his mouth and he threw her across the room. Before he even knew it was there the pistol was in his hand. He would not remember afterward pulling the trigger. There was a bang, the report of the shot and he heard his dog yelp in pain.

Sally yelped four more times in pain and bit one time at the entry wound in her body as if an unseen animal had attacked her there. Her cries of pain changed to a howl and she dragged her paralyzed hindquarters across the floor

The pistol disappeared from his hand and Will dropped to his knees. He placed both hands over his ears and screamed, "Aaggh, Aaggh! What have I done? What have I done?"

Sally was still dragging her body on the floor leaving a swath of bright red blood.

"I'm sorry. I'm sorry," he said over and over and he swayed back and forth with his hands on his knees and wept. "I'm sorry, Sally. I'm sorry." Then he felt a wetness on his hand. Sally had crawled over to him and was kissing his hand.

"Aaugh, Sally, I'll get help. Jack knows what to do."

Will ran to the door, "I'll come back," and he slammed the door behind as he ran down the path, the gravel crunching under his running feet.

• • •

The shot had entered ahead of the hindquarters and lower than the back bone. The paralysis was temporary until the shock of the impact faded, but the wound was serious and bleeding.

She dragged herself to the door — she would follow him but the solid door bared the way.

Her blood trail led next to her bed. Here she paused and the blood pooled there. She wanted to lie down but not in her own bed. It was here too that she stood on her four legs. She was wobbly and weak. She was restless and quickly losing her strength with her blood loss. She wanted her master.

The blood trail next led to Willard's bed. It pooled there most of all, for she tried to leap to the top where she slept as a puppy, where she smelled her master most of all. Several times she tried to leap to the top but her hindquarters always gave out. Then her front legs got purchase and in pulling with them and a final help from her back legs, she got to the mattress.

She sought out the depression in the bed where Will slept each night and she made for the place. It was there that she found the place she desired, centered in the contour of her master's body near where his heart would be. It was here where she last lay down and it was here where it was that she died.

# The Empty Boat

"Snoo?"

I about jumped out of my skin. I gasped aloud as I spun around, dropping the oar that I held in one hand. The neurons in my body tumbled over each other in their circuits and failed to tell my body what to do. As I spun, I saw that my rifle was propped barrel up and useless in the bow of my skiff several feet away.

When I came through the entrance of this cove and its calm water just minutes before, I saw only empty sand beach on the shore where I hoped to pitch my tent. As far as I could see down the shore, where colors turned grey and the land was devoured by fog, nothing living could be seen. There was thin beach grass poking through small rocks. Higher up on the shore and here and there a few grey pieces of driftwood, but nothing living could be seen. Rain pelted the leaves and the wind moaned in the trees like Eastern women mourn for lost ones and I thought that I was completely alone on the rim of this huddled cove. I was standing in boot deep water on the shore holding only the bowline of the boat between me and the source of "Snoo."

In front of me was a huge, tall Indian at least six four or five. His shoulders extended straight out at his neck like a scarecrow's does with a horizontal stick as its shoulders, but unlike scarecrows, the Indian was meaty and strong. He stood there erect and unmoving with his arms hanging limply down. His large hands were closed like claws, his hands and wrists extending far below his sleeves. He wore a wool halibut coat the color of mist, canvas pants and boots. His eyes were small and intense like a hawk's. His features were down-south Indian, brown and square, not the more rounded ones of the locals. Down one cheek a deep furrow of a scar parted the flesh into two halves like the halves of a bun, and the scar was smooth and pale and white like cheese.

"Snoo," he repeated.

I caught my breath, a deep pull of air that felt in my chest like the sobs a child makes when it cries itself to sleep.

"Nuttin' snoo," I said. "Nothing's new. I just came in here in my skiff. The waves are really kicking up out there," I said, pointing with my thumb toward the open ocean. "Too much for this little boat anyway."

"Why were you out there? What did you see?" he asked quietly with a low voice that I strained to hear.

I assumed that he was talking about the search that was going on and wondered why I had risked the weather. "I was in my skiff looking for Peterson from that boat called the 'Kitty.' He is a friend."

He looked at me without expression, his mouth a straight line.

"They found her adrift outside here with no one aboard. The Kitty is a little troller, only about twenty-eight feet. It's mostly a day troller but he stays out sometimes. When the bite is on he sometimes takes someone to crew with him."

The Indian just stared at me without expression and I spoke just to fill the awkward silence.

"It had a fo'c'sle with 'V' berth and galley so he could stay out in weather if he wanted. Anyway, they found her floating with no one aboard. It is anyone's guess what happened. The weather is bad so he could have been tossed overboard, especially if he was leaning over the side pulling up his gear or fish."

The Indian did not even grunt to indicate that he was listening to me.

"Most of the time when someone goes over like that and they don't find him for a couple of days, his zipper will be down — like he is doing business over the side and falls over. That usually happens at night when the rest of the crew are asleep and they don't even miss him until daylight when they wake up. By then they do not know where he went over."

The Indian's dark brown eyes seemed to pierce mine with an intensity of an eagle when it sees its prey. "Not what happen," he said so quietly the wind in the trees nearly stole his words away.

I wondered how he could know that and I paused to see what he would add to the statement. He did not speak but continued to stand where he was on the wet, grey sand. Rainwater ran down his forehead but the stranger seemed not to notice.

I did a temporary tie to a rock with my bowline and faced my visitor.

"I don't have any food here to share with you. I was not planning to overnight so I didn't take any meals."

"Not hungry."

"Did you know Peterson or the boat?"

He seemed irritated when I said Peterson's name but did not answer me.

"I know of a couple of instances when people got gas spilled in a boat and the boat caught fire and the people had to jump overboard. They never did find the bodies. They just found the hulls of the boats, black, like burnt marshmallows but no people."

"Not what happened," he said.

I pulled my tent and dry bags from the skiff and tossed them down on the beach. I tied the anchor to the bow cleat for the depth I wanted and placed the anchor on the bow and pushed the skiff hard as I could to deeper water. I played out the line as it left the shore and when it seemed to be at the end of the thrust I pulled the bowline and let the anchor fall into the water. I tied off my lose end to an alder bush and looked it my companion.

"My name is Joe," I said.

He did not answer me. I saw a rush of rainwater that had accumulated on the top of his baseball cap roll off and slide along one cheek.

"Where is your boat?" I asked, realizing at last there were none anywhere in the cove.

"Other side."

"The other side of this point of land, at the next cove?"

"Yes."

"You walked all of the way across to here? Why?"

"Wanted to come here. Water is rough for me too."

"That is a long way to go. It is rough walking in this weather too."

The Indian did not answer. I watched as rainwater flowed in a steady stream down the groove of the scar on his cheek.

I continued the possibilities of my missing friend. "People will often get tangled in gear on the boat and pulled overboard. A longliner friend of mine got a halibut hook in his hand and it yanked him overboard. He cut the webbing off his hand with his knife to keep from going all the way down. As it was he has problems from being down so far. All the serious fishermen I know carry a knife to cut themselves free."

The Indian spoke slowly and patiently as if he were educating a fool. "Sometimes an anchor line gets wrapped around their legs and they go to the bottom." He looked at me with satisfaction in his features. "You won't find him, Joe."

Suddenly I felt cold. Shivers went up my back. At that instant I knew what a mouse feels when the barn snake coils itself before it.

"I was hoping I might find him alive on the shore somewhere, just waving to me — 'come get me, Joe,' or at least I hoped to find his body to bring home." I looked down at my boots and thought out loud, "I guess there are many things that might have happened."

The Indian looked at me with those black eyes, this time with a flash of anger mixed with satisfaction. "Sometimes," and he looked at me directly to make sure I was listening to him. "Sometimes a man messes with another man's woman and that kills him."

I thought he would pounce on me.

"You are very wet. Did you fall in?" I asked.

Water was pouring from him. He walked a couple of steps toward my boat. His boots were full of water and they sloshed when he moved. His clothing could not have held more water.

"Raining," he said.

But I knew that no rain could fill someone's boots. He was soaked inside out more than any rain could do. An image appeared in my mind of the man before me doing his business and slipping out of the boat and swimming to shore, leaving the troller to drift in the current.

He looked at my boat. It was a decent boat and reliable but I certainly had no business in the sea outside the cove.

"Run good?"

"First pull," I bragged. And I was angry with myself for blurting that out. "My tent is small, or you could stay here. Are you walking across to your boat?"

"Yes."

As he said that he turned and walked toward the cove where he said he left his skiff. He walked slowly, his arms hanging to his sides without swinging. Even in the distance in the fog I could see those large hands dangling out of the sleeves and felt their menace.

I did not believe there was a boat on the other side. If he intended to walk the whole way in to town it would take days, weeks. He would have to walk completely around three fjords and some smaller inlets. He would need to go over some lesser mountains. Somehow he would need to get possession of a boat. I felt exposed and vulnerable on the empty, bare sandbar.

• • •

I set my tent up high on the beach where the sand meets the grass and above the line of debris the high tides bring in. I did not place it into the line of alder trees because I wanted to be able to see the full expanse of the cove and its tree line.

Truth was, I did not believe that there was a boat in the next bay, nor did I believe that the Indian would cross the point of land this late in the day, so close to the coming darkness. There was certitude in my mind that that giant in the water-filled boots would visit my site this night.

As I set up my tent I faced my body toward the line of trees the stranger had gone. I considered as I worked that he walked like Sasquatch. I looked carefully for any anomaly, or hint of movement in the underbrush. I tossed my dry bags inside the tent and unrolled my sleeping bag and knew that I would not dare to close my eyes inside its comfort.

I sat inside the doorway scanning the horizon. The rain was diminishing somewhat but it was still miserable to be in it. I pulled out a candy bar and ate it and realized that I was ravenous. I felt guilty that I said that I did not have meals to share. I had only the sandwich I made for the day. I pulled out the buttered egg bagel and its slices of hard salami and ate hungrily.

I dried off my rifle and wished that with the heavy rain that it had open sights. The scope was fogged and rain soaked.

Finishing off my bagel, I lay back against my rucksack and scanned the cove again. Shades of evening rapidly diminished my view. I could no longer see into the tree line with the darkness and shadow under the tree boughs. Even my own sand beach blended its grey to the grey of the dimming mist.

I pondered the course of my evening. I determined that I would not stay in the tent this night regardless how unpleasant it would be outside in the storm. But I would be sure to leave the impression that I was inside it throughout the night.

I considered that he would want my boat. I also considered that he might conclude that he said too much to me. Perhaps on the morrow it would be my boat they would find floating without me in it.

With the overcast and the rain, the night fell quickly. I lit my Coleman lantern and left it at the tent door. The area around the light appeared very dark which was what I wanted.

I waited for a rainsquall to proceed with my plan. As I waited I saw the intense blackness of a squall moving toward me with a gust of wind. I heard the hiss of the first rain on the water and slipped out of the tent and made for my boat. I knew that I could not pull the skiff in to the shore and then replace it to its present place without the anchor chain dragging on the bow and sounding over the entire bay. I removed my boots and coat and bending low, duck walked toward my boat. The stones were sharp and the water was as cold as needles on my feet. I breast stroked to the boat.

The stern, with the weight of the motor, was lowest in the water and I placed my hands on it and swung up and into the boat. For once this day I was glad for a heavy squall of rain. I was confident that I made no sound getting into the boat. I removed the cowling from the motor and with the tool that I had taped to the stern removed the spark plug and put it in my pocket. This boat would not move without me.

I glanced over the railing before sliding over the side. Not twenty feet away in the water was a dark shadow. There was perceptible movement in the shape. Something was moving toward my boat. I felt dread and near panic. I slid a leg over the side and without making a splash, entered the water and side stroked to shore.

• • •

I crawled on my belly so I would not be in silhouette against the dim sky. I was so cold my fingers would not obey me. My whole body shivered. I retrieved my boots and coat and rifle and low crawled toward the tree line.

Where the gravel met the line of debris of high tide, broken clamshells sliced my pant legs at the knees and drew blood as I crawled over them. I rolled to my back and pulled on my boots and jacket. Because my skiff was jellco white I could just make out its form in the darkness. I saw a tipping of its form as though a weight were entering it.

"Just try starting it," I laughed to myself.

I rolled back to my stomach and crawled into the trees and sought for a place of elevation where my campsite would be in view.

The rain hissed in the grass and leaves and erased the sound of my progress. I was soaked through but the exertion of my progress warmed me as I moved. I found a place behind a large tree and rested my back against it and faced my campsite. I could see the glow of the lantern but then quickly looked away to not lose my night vision.

I was satisfied with my location. My back was covered and I could rest as I faced the danger. Rain pelted my legs and brought its icy cold to my core. Carefully I reached to my side for vegetation and clawed it with my fingernails, and finding moss, covered my legs. Then, against my will, I fell asleep.

I became wide awake.

I did not know how long I slept. The rain had stopped. It was the occasional dripping in the leaves that wakened me. A very slight passing of night air chilled me like a cold breath.

I kept still. I heard a drop to my side. And again. Another in the same direction. Was it raindrops or movement of something breaking twigs?

I listened intently. I did not notice that I had not breathed as I listened. My mouth was open as I listened.

More drops. Or twigs.

Adrenalin filled me as I attempted to decipher what I heard. I wished for rain to end the terror of the drips but willed myself to listen.

Another squall passed through. I became very cold exposed to the rain. Slowly with my hands I pulled more moss over my legs.

The rain fell heavier and again I fell asleep.

This time I dreamed.

I dreamed someone behind my tree threw a noose that coiled around my neck and pulled me tight and I heard a voice that said over and over, "You won't find him, Joe. You won't find him Joe. You won't find him, Joe."

I started awake again.

This time it was a brightness in my eyes.

The pale fingers of the moon had parted a few black clouds and it peered down at me. I was conscious that my hands were very white in the light and I guessed that my face would be seen clearly from the water. Moving as little as possible, I put muddy soil on the back of my hands and raised them to my face and soiled my features with dirt.

The rain had stopped. I only heard an occasional drip far away. I listened without breathing for any sounds of movement.

When I came to this tree it was a comfort to my back but now my mind imagined a giant of a man creeping up on me from behind and I could neither see nor hear him. I held still.

I began to make out a shade of lightness that marked the surrounding hills and knew that dawn was coming. I did not know if that would expose me or give me release and opportunity to leave the cove.

The wind diminished in the trees and I knew that the seas outside would be less formidable.

I heard a songbird in the distance.

• • •

I remained in place as still as a scarecrow, moving only my eyes. I studied every leaf and bush. I listened. Only the occasional bird. I watched the far side of the cove. Nothing moved.

The day became cloudless and bright with sunlight.

I remained there at least an hour. A small bird with black and grey wings and a rust colored throat like a wound flew to a limb nearby and inspected me. I heard no other sound other than the flutter of its wings as it flew away.

Then there was a new sound. At first it was a distant hum of a boat motor, then like the cavalry, it burst into my cove. A modest sized speed boat with just a windshield entered full speed and veered immediately at the sight of my tent.

I knew the driver. His entry into the cove reminded me of Toad driving his roadster in "The Wind in the Willows," only his skin wasn't green, it was pink — pudgy pink with brown freckles. His eyes were big and round at the discovery of my tent.

I left my station behind the tree and walked stiffly over to the campsite and his boat.

The boat's wake slammed against the hull — it had made a circle in the water — and the wake splashed against my boots. I washed my hands in the wake without stooping and I cleaned them and washed the mud off my face.

Jeremy leaned over the bow of the boat, his blue baseball cap with the name of his father's business tipped backward so it did not blow off in the wind of the boat.

"Oh, it's you," he said.

"Sorry to disappoint you. You were thinking I was Peterson from the empty boat, weren't you?"

"Yah, you look awful."

"Snew," I asked.

"Nuttin snew. I came in and saw your tent and thought, 'maybe…'"

"You aren't at work," I observed.

"Yah, the company gave us all the day off so we could look for that missing guy."

"Peterson," I supplied.

"Yah, him."

Two other boats entered the bay.

"They couldn't keep up with me," Jeremy laughed.

"I take it that you haven't seen anything, then."

One of the other boats pulled alongside my pudgy friend and shut off his engine to better hear. "We have been in every cove and bay and checked every island and the shore from town to here — nothing."

"Are you bagging it or are you going to look some more?"

"We will look a little more up the coast. It sure beats working, being here. The Coast Guard said they will give it one more day. They are sure they have looked at all the coast line and haven't found anything floating."

I looked at one of the guys. "Could you stand by a minute until I make sure that my boat starts?"

It took only a few minutes to bag the tent and toss my dry bags into the boat.

"Hey, it sure looks tore up around your tent."

That certainly did not escape my notice either. All around my tent in the torn up soil, soil assuredly torn up to display a track, were several human tracks. They circled my tent and approached the entrance. They were huge and at the place where my door was, there was a pair of huge footprints as though the person had been standing there rocking back and forth.

In the boat I cleaned off the spark plug and blew it dry before wrenching it into the hole. I pumped the fuel ball hard and pulled the starter cord. The sound was sweet salvation.

I smiled at the guys and thanked them.

Then I bragged, "First pull, every time."

# The Great Catch

In those days before the war, when Alaska was still a territory, many of the local fishermen on the coast had no boats with motors, or if they had them could not afford the fuel to run them. The big boys, the halibut schooners, came out of Seattle with large diesel engines and full crews, and in the fog one could hear the muffled thumping of their engines an hour before they could be seen. The strokes of the engines were the rhythm of a heartbeat and to the Norwegian captains and crew, fishing was life itself.

The Scandinavian locals often built their own fishing boats, usually the same design they had used in the old country — rowboats — and in them, bravely went to sea. Some trolled for salmon by rowing. Others jigged for halibut. Some fished for halibut and cod with long lines and the many hooks that are attached to them. At the end of each haul they rowed with their catch to the buyers and just got by.

• • •

Peder Toveson had been rowing the last eleven hours continuously. A very light rain, the kind that hissed when it fell on calm water, fell on him and glistened his rain gear and Sou'wester, then collected into drops before rolling down his back. Although he was dry in his rain gear, the coldness of the water made him shiver. His bare hands that gripped the oars ached from the chill of the rain but he resisted blowing on them lest he break the hypnotic rhythm he had chosen. At times, because it was necessary, he would interrupt the pull of rowing and turn himself about to confirm his landmarks, for a fisherman rows a boat with his back to the direction he is going. He would point his boat at a landmark, turn around, and row, keeping his wake in a straight line.

He scooped a few cans of water from the bottom of the boat, stretched his back, and then returned to the monotony of rowing. Nearby a pod of humpback whales blew a ring of bubbles around a mass of krill and came up from underneath with their gigantic mouths wide open. Torrents of water poured out between the rows of baleen in their mouths leaving the catch inside. Their breaths smelled of iodine and their steam ascended in tall plumes, mixed with the mist of the rain and descended wet on his face. Drops of the splash fell like rain on his leg.

He knew he would need to row through the night to reach his fishing grounds by the dawn. It was a goal he set for himself, and he needed the light of the day to tie off his gear. At times when he had to row against the current or when the wind was contrary it seemed he was making little progress. His father once told him that his people used to row all the way from Norway to Iceland to reach the fishing grounds.

"This is no problem for you, Peder," he said to himself. "You are of that same stock."

Around Point Barunoff and its rocky coast, which he had to pass, two seas met and the waves stacked in anger. Swells that came from the great depths of the open ocean came shoreward and on entering Barunoff's shallower bottom, piled up and fractured on the rocks.

"There are old fishermen and there are bold fishermen," he said to himself, "but there are no old, bold fishermen."

And Peder turned his fishing boat to the open sea and rowed farther and farther out where the sea plunged to great depths. The chop was not present there but the swells were formidable and tall and the troughs deep. He rowed with all his strength to reach the top of each billow then at the top of each wave took care the slide down would not drive him inside the next wave. With his oars he steered so he would not broadside and tip into the sea.

From the deep water outside of Barunoff, he rowed south, parallel to the coast with the swells coming from the starboard. He quartered the waves with his oars. When he was sure that the perils of Barunoff were behind, he rowed toward that shore and its sheltered passes.

There were a few shallow passages strewn with submerged rocks where he faced forward in the boat and skulled or picked his way with the oars. The water was calmer here and he continued to row through the passages, stroke after stroke after stroke.

In his weariness, his thoughts went to the dock he left at the first light of this morning.

• • •

He had just finished coiling a long line skate into a tub, looked about to see if there was anything he had forgotten, and was about to cast off when he looked up and saw her standing on the dock. Her face seemed pale in the light and the morning breeze that came with tide change lifted the thin hair from her brow.

He re-tied the bowline to the painter and stepped to the dock.

"You did not bid me goodbye," she said.

"You were asleep. You looked so peaceful. I didn't want to wake you."

"I wanted to wish you a safe voyage."

"There is a chill. You should not have come. Look at your arms. You have bumps."

She looked at him with eyes that were as grey as the fog. "I worry for you, Peder. I would rather have you here than let you go."

"You know that I have to go, Kari. We need to make this catch."

She handed him a sack with one thin hand, a hand that was the color of white bread. "You did not take any food."

"I left it for you."

"I can get by without this. Maybe I can get credit at the store. We always buy from them." Then she smiled. "The store is always open at low tide." With deliberateness she stepped to the boat and gently tossed the bag on the seat. Her eyes opened wide and she turned quickly to her husband. "The boat is so small. I thought it would be much bigger than this."

He realized that she had never seen it since he built it. "It is small. I had to make it small so I could row it alone. But it is sea worthy. I had to make it narrow so it would row easy but not so narrow that it would be tippy."

She stood there shivering with her arms folded in front of her. "Will you be safe in a storm?"

"I will lay up somewhere if the weather is bad." He tried to change the subject by showing her the construction of the boat. "As long as I keep the bow into the swell I will live to catch fish. I made the sides a little lower than I would like so it would not catch the wind and make it hard to control. It can still hold a good catch."

She was skeptical and took his arm. "I worry so, Peder."

"I will come home to you. This boat is watertight and when the wood gets wet it will swell and it will be even more so."

Kari laid her head on his shoulder.

He thought he could feel her weep so he continued to talk to her. "I have ice in the keel under the tarp to keep the fish. All that I need to catch halibut is in the boat." He paused. "I have to go now, Kari. I have a long way to go."

Peder was Norse and did not openly display his emotions. He started to step into his fishing boat but turned toward his wife. He took her hand to shake it in goodbye but held it longer than he intended. Her hand was soft in his. His was rough, with hard, broken skin. He looked into her eyes and wanted to say what he could not.

"There is plenty of wood cut until I return," he said.

She looked thin in her dress. "I will pray you home."

Peder's eyes said, "You are all that is important to me," but his mouth could not say it.

He got into his skiff and began to row away from the harbor. He wished that he was not rowing as he faced the dock the entire way as he crossed the sound.

Every time he looked toward his village he could see her at the shore receding in the distance. He knew that she shivered and did not know that she was cold. She became smaller and smaller as he rowed away and once or twice he could see her thin hand waving to him. The wave was side to side like a breeze that catches a single stock of pale beach grass and moves it back and forth.

• • •

Thirty hours later he left the narrows and rowed into the sound. The difference of the action of the sea there was profound. There had been current in the narrows, but little wave action. In the sound, the wind from the passes between the mountains blew steadily toward the ocean and met the swells of the open sea and churned in angry conflict. Only forty yards away fin whales surfaced between the waves and blew and he could see the steam, and once or twice could see a fin but for the most part, the waves were taller than the backs of the whales.

As far as he could see, the waves were in shadow and ran deep blue to black and sinister. At the opening of the bay where the open ocean lay, the tops of the waves were white and the wind ripped them off and tossed them as spray, a spray that appeared the same as the breaths of whales.

Peder turned himself around in his boat to study the sea. His hands were reluctant to let go of the oars. They were cramped in place and the open blisters of his hands stuck to the wood. His back was stiff and ached when he turned.

The fishing grounds he sought were along the rocky shore of the open ocean outside of this bay. On his side of the bay was the lee and he followed its relative calm toward the mouth and tied off on some alder branches on the shore.

Kari had given him smoked salmon and rye bread and butter

wrapped in wax paper and he ate it slowly and studied the water. He felt guilty eating, not knowing what Kari had to eat.

He finished the bread and with his wet finger touched some crumbs that had fallen on his leg and ate them.

It appeared that the wind from the passes was diminishing and the tops of the waves no longer blew away. He sensed the tide was nearly slack and decided he would soon venture to the grounds.

While he waited, he baited the hooks of a hundred gangions and left the six-foot lengths of fishing line in a neat stack within reach. He tied a large float to one end of the long line, called a skate. When he played out the line he would tie a gangion to the long line every ten feet.

He rowed to the mouth through the still pitching sea and made his way to the open ocean. The bow of the boat pitched like a child's rocking horse as he rowed to the open sea.

• • •

He rowed far enough out of the bay to be in the swells but close enough to fish the rocky shore of the coast. As he rowed parallel to the coast he tossed overboard the end of the long line with the large float. More than a hundred feet farther along the line he attached an anchor, which kept the long line on the bottom of the sea. Every ten feet thereafter he tied on a baited gangion. When all the hooks were placed he tied on a second anchor then another buoy to the other end of the skate.

He rowed to where he could keep an eye on one of the floats and set a sea anchor. It was like a parachute dragging behind the boat and would keep the boat in place.

Peder's skiff lined up bow-first into the ocean swells and he lay on his back in the bow of the boat. He would sense in his sleep any changes in the boat's movement. He would be able to hear the waves slapping if he were to drift toward the shore.

He pulled his Sou'wester over his face and went to sleep.

• • •

He dreamed he was in the bow of a rowboat, fast asleep. Light rain wet his face and he pulled his seaman's cap over him and could hear the patter of the drops. But he was not in Alaska. He was a young boy with his father and they were rowing to the Lofoten Islands in Northern Norway.

"Will you sleep all day, then," his father said, and he threw a mackerel fish on his chest. "I will need you to row for a bit."

They had been using a very small sail when the wind was just right. There was a small receptacle for a mast but the sail was gaff rigged and needed wind on her stern. Further, they had little ballast and really no keel to speak of, so they rowed in the main.

They had rowed for ten days from their farm on one of the fjords that lined the west coast of Norway. From time to time they could go ashore and provision and rest, but to get to the grounds they would have to row.

Every year as long as anyone could remember the cod would migrate from the Barents Sea to spawn in the Lofotens. Some fishermen rowed for weeks to get to the grounds. They set their nets and fished every day for the months of the run. Some of the catch would be sold and the rest would be processed and taken home to be eaten on the farm the rest of the year.

Peder's father fished the Outer Coast of the Lofotens. Those waters faced the Norwegian Sea and were exposed to the fierce raging storms. Fog, wind and rain were a norm, but the hardship made this area less fished. It was the most hardy who plied those waters.

In his sleep Peder could smell the waters and hear the slap of the waves on the boat. He relived pulling loads of cod from the nets, and rowing with the catch to the canneries and sanctuary.

• • •

He woke with a start. How long had he slept? "Not so long," he thought. He studied the sky and water. "Four hours, anyway. I don't think six. I had better pull the gear."

He pulled in the float and began to retrieve the line. He could not feel the dead weight of fish coming up as he had hoped. He looked into the water as he pulled hand over hand.

Soon he saw the first hook. Even the bait was gone. There was not even a shred of torn flesh left on the hook to suggest a fish had taken it.

Another hook. Empty. And another.

Then there was something of bulk. As it cleared the water he could see that it was a halibut but only the skull and lips were on the front of it and on the other end was an intact tail. Between these pieces were was the full skeleton, backbones and ribs and stripped of all flesh.

Sand fleas!

Each hook that he pulled was either completely eaten away or reduced to a skeleton with pieces of flesh.

With the last hook in his hand he collapsed into the boat. He wanted to weep.

"Lord, help me."

• • •

He reset his gear a few hundred yards further down the coast. His hands ached with the coldness of the water. His stiff fingers could barely hold the bait and hooks. The crusts of the blisters he received in rowing cracked and bleed.

"I will wait only three hours before I pull the gear this time. It could be the sand fleas will not have time to work."

He set the sea anchor and lay back in the bow with a tarp over him. A light rain fizzed on the water around him.

He heard the loud blow of air. "Not a whale," he thought. "The blowing is too short."

Then he heard two or three blows together.

"No!" he thought. "Sea lions."

They will often take salmon from a hook even while you are pulling it in.

But it seemed that they only checked him out in the boat and finding no interest in him, swam away.

When it was time, he leaned over the side of the boat and placed both hands on the long line and rocked his whole body backward the hundreds of times it takes to pull in a skate. This time there were no sand fleas. The first two hooks held large rockfish. He would save them to eat himself. The next three were empty of fish but the bait was still on. Then the next two held ratfish with their rat shaped head and eyes. It was said the oil from their livers was the best oil in the world. Only one small halibut was on the skate.

He iced the halibut and put it under the tarp and lay on his back in the stern. He wanted to close his eyes but knew that he would be instantly asleep. The small catch sapped his energy as surely as a thumb and finger can quench a candle.

A small wave broke over the bow and the spray splashed his face and filled his eyes. He wiped his eyes with the back of one hand, blinked and squinted. He saw the rockfish, dead on its side, its eye was large, open and peering. He gazed at the glassy roundness and the large black pupil that seemed to accuse him.

"You must move, Peder," he said to himself.

He let out a long breath which was nearly a moan, and pushed himself upright, for he had stiffened in those minutes.

He rowed nearby to an area where there was some surge and rocks and set his gear. He rowed farther off shore and set his sea anchor and lay back in the bow of the boat to wait. He did not cover his face lest he sleep too soundly and not hear or feel the area around him. He wanted to hear the distant sound of the water breaking on the rocks to gage his distance from shore.

He dozed.

• • •

In his dream he could see that day in church as clearly as if it unfolded before him in his skiff. He and Kari sat in metal folding chairs as they sang and heard the Good Book read.

Church was held in a rented teamster union hall with wooden floors that echoed the footsteps of the people as they entered for Sunday services. There was a fire in a wood stove and a small kettle of water steamed on it to keep the air moist. The union hall had no closet space for coats or boots and so snow melted into pools before each chair.

The pastor's wife played the piano and the people sang the old hymns from used worn hymnals that had been sent to them from a church in Wisconsin. They sang more with volume than accuracy and some of the old folk wiped away tears when they sang, "The Old Rugged Cross."

A white haired lady next to the stove fanned herself with a bulletin printed on a mimeograph machine. The pastor stood behind the pulpit, skinny as a needlefish and held up the Bible with both hands and all knew that it was precious to him. He had black hair, wetted back, glossy and smooth. His pant legs were too short and his white socks showed above his black shoes.

Kari sat back expectantly and turned to the place in the Bible indicated by the pastor.

He began, "The crowds which came to hear Jesus preach that day were so large the people couldn't see or hear him well, and that is the occasion of the text this morning." He read, "'And he saw two ships standing by the lake: but the fishermen were gone out of them, and were washing their nets. And he entered into one of the ships, which was Simon's and prayed him that he would thrust out a little from the land. And he sat down, and taught the people out of the ship.'"

Here the preacher slowly removed his glasses and gazed upon his people. "Where before, fish scales littered the deck of that fishing boat," and here he raised his index finger upward as if to say, 'Get this,' "now stands the Son of God giving eternal truths."

He paused to let this sink in.

"Think of that. God took the deck of a common fishing boat and changed it into a pulpit where God stood."

He replaced his glasses and continued to read.

"Now when he had left speaking, he said unto Simon, 'Launch out into the deep, and let down your nets for a draught.' And Simon answering said unto him, 'Master, we have toiled all the night, and have taken nothing: nevertheless at thy word I will let down the net.' And when they had this done, they enclosed a great multitude of fishes: and their net brake. And they beckoned unto their partners, which were in the other ship, that they should come and help them. And they came, and filled both the ships, so that they began to sink."

The preacher set his glasses on the pulpit and stepped around it to be nearer his people.

"Just as with Peter here, God can take your ordinary and make it extraordinary."

A voice among the listeners said, "Amen," and Mrs. Yatchminoff in her white hair who sat beside the stove and fanned herself, ceased fanning and thought on this.

"One more thing," the pastor said as he returned to his place and retrieved his glasses, "He told fishermen how to fish and as far as I can tell he never cast a hook a day in his life." He paused and gazed upon the eyes of each person in the room. "But then I suppose that the person who created the fish would certainly know how to catch one."

"Amen," said several in the room.

"One last thing." He lifted the bible up with both of his hands. "God sometimes gives fishermen something better than fish." And he read, "For he was astonished, and all that were with him, at the draught of the fishes which they had taken: And so also James, and John, the sons of Zebedee, which were partners with Simon. And Jesus said unto Simon, Fear not: from henceforth thou shalt catch men."

Peder, in his boat thought on these things as he nodded. "Lord, this Peder needs fish too."

He retrieved the float and began to haul in the skate. He reached far down to the waterline and grabbed with both hands and pulled. He could feel the weight of the anchor as he raised it to the surface and almost immediately felt the pull of a great heaviness attached to the rest of the line. Hundreds of feet of line coiled into the tub when he could feel the great resistance of great fish.

He peered deep into the water and saw a white spot no bigger than the bait he used, then realized that that white spot was a hundred feet below him.

Heave after heave, he pulled the skate another forty feet and looked over the side. He could see the halibut as it swayed side to side. It seemed very large even then. He continued to haul the line and when it was ten feet below he could tell that the fish on the first hook was wider than his boat.

He readied himself for the last pull and just as the halibut's head broke the surface, struck it on the head with the weighted side of the gaff hook. He flipped the hook around and gaffed the fish in the head and, pulling with his whole body, dragged it over the side. The boat canted nearly to the water line in the effort.

Quickly he struck it several more times to stun it and it lay on the bottom of the boat and shivered. Peder ran a shark hook through its mouth and created a loop to tie around the halibut's tail to draw the great fish into a bow so it could not flop.

The halibut, which weighed two hundred pounds awoke and began to slap its tail. Peder knew that a fish that size could break his legs or break the boards out of the side of the boat. He struck it again with the weighted end of the gaff hook and it quivered in the boat. He ran the loop over the tail and bowed it drawing the tail to the mouth of the great fish. Quickly he ran his knife through the gills to kill it and returned to the skate.

There were halibut on the next three hooks also. A twenty, and two forty-pounders. He pulled all of them forward to bring the weight off the stern.

The next two hooks were empty but there was a hundred pounder on the next. He gaffed and gilled it and dragged it forward in the boat.

As he leaned over the side to pull the last fish into the boat, the freeboard met the water's edge and the fisherman would have not dared another fish. In all there were three hundred-pounders and a two-hundred-pounder. There were very many between ten and forty pounds and when the line was pulled and coiled, the boat was full and the fisherman was exhausted.

Peder had pulled the line for over an hour. Fish were heaped and he began to arrange them low in the boat for stability.

He lay in his back on a tarp and looked about. The weight of the catch set the boat low in the water. There was little free board left. An errant wave over the side could swamp the boat. Extreme care would be needed not to test the water on the way back.

• • •

He rowed into the bay at the slack tide. Wind that often blew off the glaciers and through the passes into this bay abated and there was only the ocean swell behind. There was a following sea but the bow did not bury into the swell ahead and he made good time.

He rowed four hours after leaving the exposed water and rowed through passes that he chose for calmer conditions. Dozens of white gulls followed the little boat and swarmed overhead, hoping for something of his catch. Their cries brought ravens and a pair of eagles that passed low overhead and perched in limbs of nearby trees. They followed the boat from tree to tree along the way.

He found the last of the smoked fish and bread and ate it feeling some guilt as he did not know the situation at his home.

• • •

At an opening to a small fjord to his right he saw smoke. White fog and mist were common but there was a quality of blackness to this and as he wondered at the scene he began to smell the smoke. It was far more than a campfire or a chimney. It was black and ascended up through the trees along the shore. In his mind he remembered there was a homestead in that cove.

Peder rowed toward the smoke and rounding a promontory saw the place. Most of the house was already gone and what he saw was the sullen, hungry flames that lapped up the very last crumbs of the homestead. No wild flames, only coals and the crackle of them reminded him of the sounds of a wolf pack cracking the bones of a prey.

It was the boy who saw him first. He called, "Momma," and when she did not respond, as she was staring into the blackened remains of all that they owned, tugged at her hand and said again, louder this time, "Momma."

She slowly turned, surprised as she did not hear an engine, only the soft dipping of his oars as he drew near. There were three of them at the blackened cabin. The mother stood in the middle, her hair disheveled, and black soot on her face and arms. A little girl with golden hair ran to her and wrapped her arms around her leg, her face buried into her hip.

Near her, to her right, stood her son. He had brown hair and overalls and stood straight, the man of the house. He was the older child, about eight or ten, and when he saw how distraught his mother was, became the man.

Peter rowed to speaking distance. "What happened?" he asked.

She paused a long time before she answered, as if to answer was to admit reality into a world that had been merely a nightmare before. "Fire." She said the word like a verdict.

"What happened?"

"I don't know. We were just lucky to get out."

She looked about her. "We lost everything. There is nothing left. We got out some blankets and a few other things. We still have the wood shed."

"I have my doll," said the little girl. "She is really scared."

Peder looked at the child. "I would be too," he said to her.

"Where is your husband?"

"Gone. Just gone. Left us one day."

The mother looked to the ground and shook her head. "I do not know what to do."

Peder sighed. Sadly, very sadly, he looked at her. "You know there is nothing for you here now. At least for now. You have no shelter or food or way to live."

He let it sink in. "Will your husband be back?"

She tried not to weep before her children. "Don't know."

"We need to get you to town, you know that." He said making a conclusion for her so she would not have to.

Peder looked at the boy. "Maybe you could gather up what you need, what is valuable to you."

Slowly, with utter sorrow, Peder began to row into the bay.

The woman looked up in horror as Peder began to row away. Her jaw dropped open. There was terror and abandonment in her eyes.

The little girl looked up at her mother, "Is he leaving us, Momma?"

She could not answer. It was a final abandonment and perhaps death.

Peder rowed to deep water just off the home site. His body wept as he stood up and slowly took his gaff hook and drove it into the cheek of his prize halibut. He pulled with all of his might and drew it to the side of the boat and slowly dropped it over the side.

He watched it descend to the bottom. It went down slowly, slowly, almost reluctantly, drifting left and right, getting smaller and smaller until it stopped on the bottom.

And he reached for another and did the same. Then he pulled the other large fish over the side and watched them descend to the bottom.

"What's he doing, Mama?" The little girl asked.

The mother cried. Her chest heaved in large sobs. She wept loudly and could not speak.

After a time she looked to her little girl. "He's making room in his boat for us, Lolly."

"Does he know us, Momma?"

"No."

"Why is he doing it then?"

"She looked down at her daughter. "Maybe it's because he is a giant."

"He doesn't look like a giant."

"Giants come in different sizes, honey."

Peder rowed to the small dock at the homestead and tied off. The boy held the boat steady as he did so. He looked at the boy who stood straight and tried to be brave through it all.

"You are a brave young man," he said to him.

Lolly saw wetness around Peder's eyes. "Do giants cry, Momma?"

She looked up. "Maybe this one does."

"Let's gather your things. We have a long way to paddle."

• • •

The three of them lay side by side across the stern of the boat. There were a few blankets they had saved which they placed over themselves, and Peder covered them with his tarp, for rain was not out of the question. The mother was asleep between her children and had an arm around each of them. She was exhausted but at peace. Lolly lay at her side with her doll between them. Her boy was at her right side trying not to fall asleep.

"What is your name, son?"

"Ben — after my grandpa."

"That's a good name son. It's ok for you to sleep some. I get tired too. I might need you to help me. I might need the help of a strong man at the oars."

The boy smiled, satisfied. He snuggled next to his mother and went to sleep.

# About the Author

Dale Hanson is an accomplished sculptor who has led a life of adventure and enjoyed numerous accomplishments. He is a black belt martial artist, an author, a pilot of fixed wing and glider airplanes, has flown aerobatics and is a Special Forces underwater diver. He is a disabled veteran and a member of MENSA.

During the Vietnam War, Dale was a highly decorated Green Beret who served three years as a commando in the famous SOG program, whose mission involved extremely dangerous raids far behind enemy lines. This unit received more decorations and suffered higher rates of casualties than any American unit since the American Civil War. On one of these raids, Dale earned the first of several purple hearts as his right hand was mangled by a burst of machine gun fire. It is ironic that he became a sculptor, a field in which one's hands are so critical.

The artistic fruit of those hands today can be found in collections of thousands of people throughout the world. Signature to his work is a strong emphasis on artistic composition, grace, and flowing lines, combined with attention to detail.

In haiku, Dale has expressed his artistic talent in perhaps the most disciplined of written forms. With great economy of words, the writer of haiku is challenged to express concepts and insight as seen in everyday observations. In his work, Dale skillfully points out from the commonplace that which one may have missed and then makes application to life.

# Other Titles by Dale Hanson

*Haiku: Flowers in the Grass (poems)*

*The Last White Seal Hunter*

CPSIA information can be obtained
at www.ICGtesting.com
Printed in the USA
BVHW082013020720
582408BV00005B/15/J

9 780998 135342